One-Two *Punch*

KATIE ALLEN

ELLORA'S CAVE
ROMANTICA PUBLISHING

An Ellora's Cave Romantica Publication

www.ellorascave.com

One-Two Punch

ISBN 9781419960468
ALL RIGHTS RESERVED.
One-Two Punch Copyright © 2008 Katie Allen
Edited by Kelli Kwiatkowski.
Photography and cover art by Les Byerley.

This book printed in the U.S.A. by Jasmine–Jade Enterprises, LLC.

Electronic book publication September 2008
Trade paperback publication January 2010

ONE-TWO PUNCH

જી

Trademarks Acknowledgement

ဆ

The author acknowledges the trademarked status and trademark owners of the following wordmarks mentioned in this work of fiction:

Barbie: Mattel, Inc. Corporation

Cruella De Vil: Disney Enterprises, Inc.

Denver Broncos: PDB Sports Ltd.

DU: Colorado Seminary Nonprofit Corporation

Fritos: Frito-Lay North America, Inc.

Girl Scouts: Girls Scouts of the United States of America Corporation

Jughead: Archie Comic Publications, Inc.

Legos: Interlego A.G. Corporation

Little Orphan Annie: Tribune Media Services, Inc.

Rainbow Brite: Hallmark Licensing, Inc.

Samoas: Murray Bakery Products, Inc.

Twinkies: Continental Baking Company Corporation

Twister: Milton Bradley Company

Velcro: Velco Industries B.V. Ltd. Liab. Co.

Chapter One

ഇ

Beth Kennedy recognized him immediately—after all, she saw him twice a day. Okay, so maybe *saw* was the wrong word, Beth acknowledged wryly. Ogled. Drooled over. Lusted after.

She hadn't wanted to go out for martinis after work. It was a weeknight and evenings out with Sheri and Melissa had a tendency to get a little wild. Beth was now glad that she had given in. Just the opportunity to ogle Mr. Lovely-Ass was worth the hung-over and sleep-deprived misery of tomorrow.

Beth remembered the first time she had noticed him, that initial sighting almost a month ago. She had been hurrying to her Denver bus stop, worried that she was going to miss her bus and be late for work again. Only when she'd been a half block away and could see the small crowd of people still waiting at her stop had Beth slowed her rushing steps.

She'd let out a relieved breath. The last thing she'd needed was to be written up *again*, she'd figured, grimacing as she glanced idly through the glass door of a gym—the same gym she passed every day to and from the bus stop. Beth had never paid much attention to it before. It was one of those intimidating, masculine places—all free weights and punching bags and even a boxing ring—terrifying to someone who had a hard time not falling off the treadmill during one of her rare trips to the office exercise room.

Beth's fleeting gaze had skipped past the equipment, blurred the people sweating through their early morning workouts and caught on a tall man standing at the front desk. He'd snapped into focus and Beth's lungs had stopped working. Although his back had been to the door, her steps had stalled at the sight of him, so big and hard and…just beautiful. She'd halted completely and stared, the 7:10 bus and work and late write-ups forgotten.

As if he'd sensed her gaze, he had turned his head and she had caught a glimpse of light blue eyes, so striking below the dark of his closely cropped hair. His glance had jolted Beth out of her reverie. Snapping her mouth shut, she'd whipped her head around and pretended that she hadn't been staring like an idiot. Her bus had pulled up and Beth dashed toward it, the gym man's image imbedded in her brain and her heart pounding in her ears.

Since that day, Beth couldn't help but look through that glass door each morning and evening as she passed. On days that *he* wasn't there, her heart dropped in disappointment. If she had any guts, she would actually go in and talk to the guy, but just the thought of walking into the gym and starting a conversation with him made her sick with nerves. If she did manage to walk through that door, she figured she would be so nervous about the actual talking part that she would probably just vomit on his shoes.

Disgusted as she was at her chicken-heartedness, Beth continued to walk past the gym twice a day, never going inside. Now her heartbeat sped up as she watched her gym god guide his date through the happy-hour crowd.

Of course he likes them tall and skinny and well groomed, Beth thought mournfully, eyeing the brunette with him while taking a swig of her caramel apple-tini. She had been enjoying the sweet drink but now it made her stomach churn bitterly.

His date sat down on the chair he pulled out for her, smoothing the skirt of her elegant cream dress beneath her lean thighs. Beth glanced down at her own green blouse, complete with a dark-blue ink stain above her right breast. *When did that happen?* she wondered, scowling at the mark.

Sighing, she gave the blotch a few futile swipes with a cocktail napkin before giving up with a frustrated huff of breath. She had accepted a long time ago that she was a stain-magnet. Her business alone had probably put her dry cleaner's oldest daughter through college. Shoulders drooping, Beth stirred her drink absently, her attention focused again on the striking couple across the bar.

"Wow, he's hot." Sheri had followed her morose gaze. "Do you know him? 'Cause if so, lucky you."

Beth shook her head and then shoved a curl out of her eyes. "I've seen him at the gym by my bus stop—I think he works there."

"Huh." Sheri eyed the pair. "Pretty expensive-looking accessory he has there, for a gym grunt. Do you think she's his sugar momma?" She grinned at the thought.

"No. Look—he's paying for the drinks." Everything in Beth rebelled at the thought of her dream man leeching off some rich woman.

"Maybe she left some money on the nightstand last night." Sheri turned back to Beth. "Tequila shot?"

Beth stared at her. "It's Tuesday."

"So?"

"So tomorrow's Wednesday," she clarified but Sheri still looked blank.

"Remember the last time we did tequila shots?" Beth asked.

"Not really—it's kind of a blur," Sheri admitted.

"Exactly. I really, really don't want to go into work tomorrow after only two hours of sleep and with an I'd-rather-be-dead hangover."

"Pbbttt." Sheri dismissed her concern with a raspberry as Melissa returned to the table with three golden-brown shots and lime slices. Beth eyed the drinks with resignation.

"It's just one little shot," Sheri coaxed, handing her the glass.

·

9

Four rounds later, Sheri gave Beth a shove that almost knocked her out of her chair.

"Look!" she commanded, pointing a wavering finger across the bar.

"Ow," Beth complained, rubbing her sore arm and squinting blearily in the direction Sheri was pointing. Ah, the lovely, lovely man and his disgustingly thin and beautiful date.

"They're fighting," Sheri crowed gleefully, thumping her shot glass on the table for emphasis.

"Who's fighting?" Melissa asked, swiveling around in her chair.

"Don't stare, Missy—you have to be *subtle*," Sheri said in a very loud, not-at-all-subtle voice. "It's the guy Beth is lusting after."

Melissa reached across the table to smack Beth on her other arm. "You're lusting after someone and didn't tell me?" she asked in a drunkenly wounded tone.

"Ow!" Beth yelped. "Stop it, you guys—I'm going to have bruises. And I'm not lusting after him. I just admire his asic—athtetic—" She scowled and took a breath. Her tongue wasn't working for some reason. "*Aesthetically* pleasing appearance."

Sheri and Melissa exchanged looks and then burst into hoots of laughter. Beth frowned at the two of them, trying to maintain her superior and disdainful expression, but finally broke down into giggles.

"Okay, okay," she admitted, still grinning. "So maybe I lust after him just a *tiny*," she held her forefinger and thumb just a squish apart, "wee, little, itty-bitty bit."

Melissa craned her neck, trying to see him. "Which one is he—ooh, is he *that* one?" she asked, pointing. Beth lurched up to pull Missy's hand down.

"Yes," she hissed, "but don't *point* at him, for God's sake."

10

"You guys, you guys," Sheri interrupted. "We're missing the fight."

It was actually a mostly one-sided argument. The woman, flushed and narrow-eyed, was yelling at the stone-faced gym god. Beth leaned closer, as did Missy and Sheri, but the painfully bad jazz band was deafening and there were many, many loud people between the unhappy couple and the wannabe eavesdroppers.

"I wish I could lip-read," Missy threw over her shoulder, her eyes still fixed on the muted argument. She had turned all the way around in her chair, casually straddling the back so she could watch the fight. "Do you think he cheated on her?"

"Probably," agreed Sheri, never taking her eyes off the action. "Don't they all? Bastard."

The woman was gesturing angrily now, every sweep of her hands threatening to knock her martini glass across the room. Her mouth finally snapped into a tight line and she stood up abruptly, snatching her small purse off the table. As she straightened, the woman grabbed her glass and tossed the contents right into the man's face.

The three watchers squealed.

"Oh no she didn't!" crowed Sheri. The woman was striding angrily through the bar to the exit and blew right by their table, her furious gaze skimming over them. Missy whirled around in her chair and all three sipped their drinks, pretending nonchalance. After the brunette passed them and slammed her way out of the bar, the three women's eyes met and they dissolved into giggles. Beth glanced back toward the man, who swiped an ineffectual cocktail napkin across his face as he stood up to leave.

"Well." Missy sat back in her chair and blew a strand of hair out of eyes still wet from laughter. "Looks like the field's wide open for you now, Bethy. 'Nother shot, anyone?"

"Whoa, you actually broke up with Cruella De Vil?" Dominic stared at Harry with wide eyes. "And she didn't kill you?"

Harry grimaced. "Nope. She did throw a drink in my face though."

"No way." Dominic shook his head, still amazed. "Well congratulations, man. Or am I supposed to say sorry?"

"Congratulations are fine," Harry said with a short laugh. As nasty as the scene had been, he felt immensely lighter after breaking up with Candice. He should have done it a long time ago, he realized.

Dominic glanced around Harry toward the door. "Looks like someone's lost. Or she's trying to sell Girl Scout cookies or something."

Twisting around, Harry saw a little blonde hovering just inside the doorway. Charlie, who worked the desk part-time, hadn't shown up yet, so the front desk was unattended. The blonde was peering around helplessly. She did look lost, Harry mentally agreed with Dominic. She was much too soft and sweet-looking for this place.

As Harry walked toward her, he realized that this was no little girl. She had definite adult curves and an X-rated mouth—a mouth that instantly made him start to sweat. She was all eyes and lips and tousled blonde curls and Harry was suddenly very, very glad that he had broken up with Candice.

Beth watched him approach. He just grew more and more beautiful, the closer he got to her. His hair was short and almost black and she could see an end-of-the-day shadow on his jaw and cheeks. Her heart thudded, echoing in her ears.

It had taken all the guts she could dredge up to actually walk in and finally meet this man. She had hovered outside for almost fifteen minutes, pushing herself toward the entrance and then scampering away out of sight like the chicken she was. The hotdog vendor across the street had watched in fascination as Beth bounced back and forth—to the door and away, back to the door and away again. She had finally charged through, not giving herself a chance to stop until she had shoved the door open and walked into the gym.

Unfortunately, once she was in, she didn't know what to do next.

The place was full with the after-work crowd and a few people glanced curiously at her immobile form. *What are you doing here?* her brain screamed. Beth had seen this guy's type and it sure wasn't a short, chubby, disheveled, baby-faced blonde.

"Hi," he rumbled, rough and deep, making the skin vibrate over her spine. She tried to force out a greeting but her voice had frozen and all she could do was stare at him.

His gaze turned quizzical. "Can I help you with something?"

"Yes." Thank God, a word. It had come out half-squeaky and half-throaty but at least her vocal paralysis had lifted.

He raised an eyebrow.

Right—one word probably wasn't enough. Okay, what was her plan again? Beth cleared her throat and opened her mouth to desperately shove out something, anything, but before she could make a sound, her dream man was shoved aside by a shorter man with a shaved head, a barrel chest and arms roped with muscles and veins.

"Move over, Harry—important business here. Are you selling Girl Scout cookies?" the shiny-headed man asked. "If you are, I want some of those coconut ones."

"Samoas?" Beth asked, startled.

He grinned. "Yes! Do you have them with you or do I have to wait?"

"What? No." She shook her head, feeling a little like she had been dropped down a rabbit hole. "Sorry, I don't have any cookies."

13

"Oh." The bald man's face fell. "Can you bring them by tomorrow?"

"Dominic!" Harry shouldered the shorter man over. "She's not a Girl Scout. Come on, she's at least—what?" He looked at Beth inquiringly. "Twenty?"

"Twenty-four," she answered, dazed. This first visit to the gym was not going as she'd expected. "I turned twenty-four last week."

Harry grinned at her. "Happy birthday."

"Thanks," she responded weakly.

Dominic was looking deeply disappointed. "So no cookies?"

"Enough with the cookies!" Harry bellowed, giving him a shove, and Dominic shuffled back to a weight bench with a final heavy sigh and accusing glance at Beth.

"Why do I feel guilty that I don't have any cookies?" she murmured to Harry, her eyes on Dominic's dejected slump on the bench.

Harry shook his head. "Don't worry about him. He's been hit in the head a few too many times. What did you need?"

Now there's a leading question, Beth thought, her stomach flipping from nerves and excitement. At least she hadn't thrown up on his shoes. Yet. "I was thinking about joining the gym."

"*This* gym?" he asked, his tone skeptical.

Is he on to me? Beth wondered frantically. Did women come in all the time trying to pick him up this way? Of course they did—how could they not want this gorgeous man? Oh God, she was probably the fiftieth woman today to just "drop in".

"We don't have yoga," he said in a gentle voice, as if she were a little slow.

"Actually," Beth continued desperately—even if she wasn't original, she could at least be tenacious, "I was thinking more of boxing?"

He looked startled. "Really?"

"Sure. Just technique and stuff though. If someone really hit me, I'd probably cry and that would be embarrassing..." Her voice trailed off and, feeling silly, she did a weak shadowboxing imitation. "You know, pow, pow?"

Pressing back a grin, Harry gently circled his hands over hers to straighten her wrists and pull her fists up close to her face. "There."

Watching his amused expression, Beth sighed. "Am I hopeless?" she asked him. The clasp of his broad hands over hers put a quaver in her words.

"'Course not. We'll get you whipped into shape."

The image that his own words conjured up made Harry bite back a groan as he glanced down at the curvy blonde. She was looking up at him with those huge brown eyes, her sinful lips parted just a little, and he could see the white edges of her teeth. A surge of lust hit him as the image of dragging her to his office, bending her over his desk and thrusting into her flashed across his mind. Sweat broke out along his hairline and he abruptly dropped her hands.

"We'll set something up," he rasped, his voice thick and tight. *For Christ's sake, get a grip on yourself*, Harry thought desperately. He had never had such an intense reaction to a woman before, this instant, brain-scrambling lust. "Can you come by tomorrow about this time?"

"Okay," the blonde agreed tentatively. "Do I need to get a membership or something?"

Harry nodded toward the front desk, where a floppy-haired teenager had casually planted himself. "Charlie'll get you squared away. You probably want to just start with a month to see how you like it."

15

"Okay," she said again. "Thank you for your help. I'm Beth Kennedy, by the way." She held out her hand.

Harry folded it in his own. "Harry Morris." He held her hand for too long, staring at her like a dumbass, he was sure, until she tugged it gently away.

"Nice to meet you, Harry—I'll see you tomorrow," she said and headed toward the desk, her round ass swaying gently from side to side as she walked away.

Harry stared at the luscious movement, frozen. He heard a snicker behind him.

"Hot for the Girl Scout?" Dominic asked, giving him a playful shove with his shoulder.

Harry scowled at him, unsuccessfully trying to squelch Dominic's knowing smirk. "'Course not. She's a new client."

"Uh-huh. *Client*. Sure, buddy." With a roll of his eyes, Dominic wandered off to the uppercut bag.

"I'm in some deep shit," Harry muttered, trying to force himself to turn away from the view of Beth's backside. She bent over a little and cocked a hip as she filled out the membership forms Charlie had spread out on the desk for her. Harry's breath caught.

"Deep, deep shit."

"Will this day ever end?" Beth grumbled under her breath. Work had stretched into horribly long and boring hours, the time creeping by with agonizing slowness. The second the clock hit five, she was out of her chair and heading for the door.

"How's it going, Ed?" she greeted her bus driver cheerily as she swung into a seat close to the front.

"Can't complain, can't complain," he said, the same response he gave her every day.

The bus seemed to crawl and Beth thought she would jump out of her skin with impatience. Finally it lurched to a halt with a hissing squeal of brakes at her stop and she flew toward the door, waving a hasty goodbye to Ed. She tripped as she stepped down on the curb, catching the railing before she tumbled face-first onto the sidewalk.

"Careful," Ed called out after her. "Don't want you falling again. What's the hurry — hot date tonight?"

Recovering her balance, Beth grinned.

"Almost," she told Ed with another wave. Maybe not a date, but Harry was definitely hot. She rushed home, detouring around the gym so that Harry wouldn't see her in her current sweaty and disheveled state.

She took the stairs to her third-floor apartment two at a time, trying to decide what to wear. It had to be something she could work out in but that looked good too — no ratty sweats and t-shirt today.

Digging in her purse for her keys, Beth did a mental inventory of her closet. She did have those yoga pants that she never wore for yoga since they were a bit snug — and also because she never did yoga. *Snug could be good with Harry watching*, she thought with a wicked smile, finally seizing her keys and triumphantly yanking them out of her bag.

She fiddled with the stubborn lock until the door suddenly swung open, nearly dumping her on the floor. Catching her balance, she made a beeline for the bathroom, tossing her purse on the nearest chair as she stepped over a white envelope on the floor. Normally she paused to read the love notes that her mystery admirer had been sliding under her door for the past month but tonight she had a real, flesh-and-blood man waiting for her. Even if it was a workout session instead of a date, spending time with Harry definitely trumped a flowery greeting card.

She yanked her top off over her head, the fabric catching on her ears, covering her eyes and blinding her for a few seconds. She bounced off the bathroom doorframe before she managed to tug the shirt free and toss it aside. After unzipping

17

her skirt, she let it drop to the floor and kicked it away before wrestling her nylons down to her ankles, hopping on one foot to pull them free. She knew it was silly to shower before working out but turned on the spray anyway. It was bad enough that she was going to have to sweat in front of beautiful Harry—she was going to do her best not to smell like a monkey in the process.

Although she was tempted, she didn't put any makeup on after her shower—she knew it would melt off in minutes. Pulling her hair back into a cheery ponytail, she made a face at her reflection in the mirror. With a scrubbed face and her hair pulled back, she looked about twelve years old. *Nothing I can do about that*, she thought, resigned, making her way to her closet.

A sports bra was a must, Beth knew, although it was tempting to wear one of her sexy push-ups. She found a fitted t-shirt cropped short enough that it showed glimpses of her bellybutton above the hip-hugging yoga pants. The shirt was pink and Beth remembered reading somewhere that wearing pink made other people act nicer. *Although Harry had been plenty nice even without the pink*, she thought, an irrepressible smile creeping back over her face.

Harry was watching for her like a third grader with a crush. Dominic had noticed his distraction and was snickering between sets. Although Harry tried to glare the other man into silence, his eyes would eventually wander toward the front door again and that just made Dominic laugh harder.

When she walked into the gym, Harry forgot all about the other man's amusement. He had been thinking all day that she couldn't be as hot as he remembered, that he was exaggerating her beauty in his mind, but looking at her now almost knocked Harry back on his ass. She saw him and smiled and he suddenly couldn't breathe, couldn't move, couldn't do anything but gawk at her like a crazy person.

Harry was staring at her, his face intent and serious, and Beth felt her own smile falter and fall away. At her questioning look, he strode toward her, stopping just a few inches away. Tilting her head back so that she could see his face, Beth was reminded of how tall he was — how big. He made her feel tiny and vulnerable but, at the same time, protected and safe. She caught herself unconsciously swaying toward him and pulled away with a flustered smile.

"Ready?" Harry asked, the graveled edge of his voice shivering her skin.

Beth nodded, her voice stolen by his nearness. *Will I ever be able to talk normally around this man?* she wondered in exasperation.

"Come over here then," he told her, grabbing her hand and pulling her over to the far wall where shelves of gloves and weights climbed the brick. "I'll show you how to wrap your hands."

He pulled what looked like black bandages out of a box on one of the shelves.

"Hold out your hand," he commanded. As Beth obeyed, he hooked the first long strip of fabric over her thumb and began expertly wrapping her wrist and hand.

"God, your hand is tiny," he commented as he ran the wrap between her fingers. "Like a little starfish."

Beth looked doubtfully down at the appendage in question, unsure if that was a compliment. Didn't two-year-olds have hands like starfish? Harry fastened the Velcro on the first wrap and reached for her other hand.

"Now you tell me how to start," he said, throwing Beth into a panic. She hadn't really been paying attention to what he was doing. Her brain had been too busy repeating, *Oh my God, he's touching me! Dream man is touching me!* As Harry waited with an expectant expression, she frantically tried to recall the first step.

"Loop around my thumb," she remembered in relief and Harry nodded, slipping the wrap in place.

"Next?" he asked.

Okay, think! Beth forced her lust-addled brain into action. "Around my wrist?" she guessed hopefully.

"Good," he responded and Beth blew out a relieved breath. "Next?"

"Sorry, that's all I remember," she admitted. Harry smiled reassuringly and her breath caught at the way his grin narrowed his eyes and dented his cheeks. *Could this man be any more gorgeous?* she wondered.

"Don't worry—you'll get it. Now watch," he ordered and Beth made herself concentrate on the progress of the wrapping, despite the distracting feel of his fingers brushing against hers. When he finished, she held up her hands and admired the neat wraps covering her hands from knuckles to wrists.

"I look so...professional," she breathed with a grin, making Harry laugh.

"Yeah, just wait until you can actually throw a punch," he teased. "Okay, go grab a jump rope."

Forty-five minutes later, Harry's hotness had retreated to the back of Beth's mind. *Beautiful or not, he's a sadist,* she thought sourly, turning her forehead against her short pink sleeve before the sweat could run into her eye.

"Come on now—one-two," he commanded, holding up his hands, which were protected by punching mitts. "Step forward with the jab, plant your feet for the straight."

Beth obeyed, the gloves on her hands pulling at her arm muscles as if they weighed fifty pounds instead of just one.

"Knees bent."

Her leg muscles screamed for mercy.

"Stay on the balls of your feet!"

Beth popped up, wobbled and caught her balance. *There's no gliding like a butterfly going on with me,* she thought, grimly amused. *It's more like shuffling like Igor.* She snickered at her own mental joke.

"Concentrate!" Harry the Dictator barked and Beth stepped forward on her left foot as she threw the punch, her glove meeting Harry's mitt with a satisfying smack.

"You're popping your elbow," Harry barked. "Elbows in!"

Why did I ever think he was nice? Beth wondered, tucking her elbows and slamming her fist into the center of his left mitt.

"Nice," he told her. Beth gave a weak smile, panting.

"That's enough technique for today," Harry said. Before relief could even register in Beth's tired brain, he finished, "Time for strength work. Take off your gloves and go grab those ten-pound weights."

As Beth dragged herself over to the rack of weights, she wondered why she had thought that joining the gym was a good idea.

Is Harry worth all this? she asked herself, glancing back at him. He was watching her and when she met his eyes, he grinned, his cheeks creasing and his blue eyes light and happy.

Yeah, she sighed to herself, yanking off her gloves. *He's worth it.*

Harry didn't know if he could take much more of this. Every time Beth pushed the weights over her head in a military press, her tiny pink shirt rose to show a sliver of skin. Every squat thrust her ass, outlined by the tight black pants, toward him.

He was so hard he ached with it, his self-control shredding with each little sound that escaped her as her arms extended toward the ceiling. *Even her grunts are sexy,* he thought and then caught himself.

21

Focus, he commanded his brain. *This is a client. This is work.*

Her arms wobbled as she struggled to push the weights up and Harry steadied her elbows with a light touch.

This wasn't going to work, Harry realized, feeling her slick skin under his fingers, stiffening at the overwhelming urge to touch more of her, to slide his fingers beneath her shirt and up her wet back. Biting back a groan, he shifted his weight and felt his bad knee bobble under him. Catching his balance, he briefly closed his eyes against the shot of pain that zigzagged across the side of his leg. Harry opened his eyes to find Beth watching him, the weights dangling by her sides.

"Are you okay?" she asked.

"Fine." Embarrassed, he brushed off her concern and took the weights from her hands. "Bad knee. That's enough for today. Go grab a mat and stretch it out."

With a relieved nod, she moved across the gym away from him. Harry carefully kept his eyes averted from the easy sway of her walk. There was only so much temptation a guy could take.

Chapter Two

❧

"What's wrong?"

Beth looked up from her contemplation of the six steps that led from the front door of the Anchor Paper building down to the sidewalk. Sheri was watching her with a baffled half-smile.

Making a face, Beth looked down at the steps again. "Stairs hurt."

"How'd you hurt yourself this time — did you trip on the bus steps again?" Sheri asked.

Beth scowled. "No. And that wasn't my fault. The top step was wet."

"Uh-huh. Did you run into another glass door?"

"Okay, that door was really clean and hard to see. Anyway, I didn't hurt myself this time — I worked out yesterday," Beth said smugly.

Sheri looked at her skeptically. "You? Worked out? Did you fall off the treadmill again?"

"Of course not," Beth protested, offended. "I'm not *that* uncoordinated."

Sheri snorted. Beth chose to ignore the skeptical sound.

"I boxed."

"Ohhh." Sheri drew out the sound, comprehension settling in. "You actually met the gym bunny?"

"He's my trainer." Blinking innocently, Beth couldn't suppress a tiny grin. "My *boxing* trainer."

"Congratulations!" Sheri crowed. "You are *such* a rock star. I can't believe you actually walked in there—usually you're such a chicken with men."

"Hey!" Beth objected.

Sheri just waved away the indignant protest. "Oh please—you wouldn't know a penis if one hit you in the head."

"How would a penis—" Beth began, brow wrinkled, but Sheri cut her off.

"Whatever—I'm just so proud of you. Here's to you having lots of fabulous sex with that hot, hot man in the very near future." Sheri held up a high-five hand.

Beth looked at the hand mournfully. "Don't mean to leave you hanging but my arm doesn't go up anymore," she sighed.

Sheri shrugged and let her hand drop. "Never mind." She threw an arm around Beth's shoulders. "No pain, no gaining a super-hot guy in your bed, or something like that. When do you see him again?"

The mention of her next training session with Harry made Beth forget her sore muscles for a moment. "Monday," she said, her face glowing.

"Uh-oh," Sheri muttered. "You're already falling for him, aren't you?"

Flushing, Beth shook her head a little too emphatically. "What? Of course not. I don't even really know him. He's not…I'm not…I mean…" She trailed off.

"Of course not," Sheri said, obviously not believing a word of it. "Come on, gimpy—let's get you down these steps. You're going to miss your bus."

She made it to her stop on time, but just barely, running toward her waiting bus in an awkward, stiff-legged hobble.

"What's wrong?" Ed asked as she climbed on, wincing as the steps pulled at her quads.

"Oof," she grunted as she plopped into a seat. "I worked out yesterday and I'm a little sore." *Just a little*, she thought, rolling her eyes at her understatement.

Ed shook his head. "Why are you doing that? You have a perfectly nice..." He trailed off, the red of his blush showing easily through his pale skin, and focused a little too hard on his side mirror as he pulled back into traffic.

Beth grinned, amazed that the painfully shy driver had almost given her an actual compliment. Between that, Harry and her secret admirer, men were just raining down on her lately. With an amused snort, she pulled out the small sketchbook she always kept tucked in her purse.

She liked to draw to pass the time. It made her feel like she was accomplishing something during her bus rides. Also, with an excruciatingly boring job and no place to paint in her tiny, dark apartment, Beth felt like her sketches were the last link to her dream of being an artist. Everything around her served as her drawing subjects — the other riders, the old stone church they passed every day, a man and his dog walking along the path bordering the golf course.

Today it was the bus driver. As she roughed out an outline, her mind drifted to Harry. Although she had denied Sheri's assertion that she was already falling for him, Beth knew her friend was right. But how much of her crush was merely based on her fantasies of a gorgeous stranger glimpsed through a window? Could the reality of him really measure up?

Her pencil paused and she smiled into space, remembering the heat and smell of him, the way his cheeks creased into near-dimples when he smiled, the feel of his hands as he wrapped her wrists. Yes, she decided. Her daydreams couldn't even come close to the fabulousness of Harry in live and living color, smart and friendly and funny and so sexy that he melted her knees.

The bus hit a bump, knocking her back to reality with a jagged pencil line across the paper.

"Shoot," she grumbled, scrubbing at the mark with her eraser. The sketch had been a good one too. She considered the oblique profile she had roughed out, liking how she had captured the gawky, vulnerable length of Ed's neck and the way his ears protruded from his closely clipped blond hair. Even his large-knuckled hands gripping the wheel were spot on. *Oh well*, she shrugged, flipping the sketchbook closed and tucking it into her purse. Her stop was coming up anyway.

Beth's eyes immediately searched for Harry as she walked into the gym for her second training session on Monday. When she didn't see him, disappointment dropped her shoulders. The intense emotion scared her a little. *Sheri's right again*, Beth admitted to herself. She was in way over her head.

She saw Dominic doing crunches across the gym and brightened a little. Digging in her duffel, she maneuvered around the heavy bags toward him. He grinned when she walked up.

"Hey there, jail bait!" he called out. "Here to torture Harry some more?"

Blushing and smiling, she protested, "Jail bait? I'm twenty-four—that's totally legal."

"Yeah, but I'm sure Harry can think of some illegal things he wants to do to you." Dominic smirked at her as he pushed off the mat and climbed to his feet.

Beth pulled out two boxes of cookies and held them out to him. "Here. Some Girl Scouts were selling these outside the Super-Mart."

"The coconut ones?" Dominic asked, his voice hushed, as if the cookies were sacred. As she nodded, Beth found herself crushed in a huge bear hug, her feet dangling off the floor. "You're an angel! A cookie angel!"

"Hands off, Dominic," rumbled a voice behind Beth.

With her head smashed sideways against Dominic's barrel chest, Beth could only move one eye to see a pissed-off-

26

looking Harry glaring at them. Despite the death stare directed his way, Dominic's arms didn't loosen.

"But Harry, she brought me cookies!" he exclaimed, his arms tightening around Beth until the air squeezed out of her with an "oof".

"So you're smothering her as a thank you?" Harry's jealous glower had mellowed a little, probably because of her obvious lack of enjoyment of the hug. The corners of his mouth were even twitching.

If he laughs, I'm going to have to hurt him, Beth decided, rolling a desperate eye at him and wiggling her hands, the only body part that wasn't immobilized by Dominic's bear-like grip.

"Okay, enough," Harry told him, moving to pry Beth loose. "Let her go, Dom — I don't think she can breathe in there."

"Oops." Dominic released her and Beth dropped back to the floor. She stumbled on landing and Harry caught her against him, supporting her as she found her balance. Beth immediately relaxed against him, instinctively molding her back to his front. Security and comfort radiated from him, filling a space in Beth that she didn't even know was empty.

"Sorry, Beth," Dominic apologized. "It's just...you brought me *cookies*."

Is he tearing up? Beth wondered, horrified. "If you cry, I'm taking them back," she threatened.

"I'm not crying." Offended, Dominic snatched up his towel and rubbed his eyes. "That was sweat."

Beth felt Harry shake with silent laughter. His solid arm had wrapped around her rib cage when she had fallen against him and Beth realized that each breath she took brushed the undersides of her breasts against his forearm. He must have realized it too, because Beth felt a thickening bulge press against her lower back. Her breathing quickened, moving her breasts even more rapidly against his tightening arm.

27

Harry squeezed her against him, hard, for just a second — not nearly long enough — and released her. Her body wanted to follow his but he set her away. Beth heard him inhale, a hard rasp of sound.

"Jump rope," he ordered harshly, his voice rough. Beth moved dazedly toward the hooks holding the ropes.

"She brought me cookies, Harry," she heard Dominic repeat in awestruck tones as she walked away. Despite the desire roaring through her body, she had to smile.

Wow, Dominic was easy, she thought.

Harry hadn't slept much during the past five days. Ever since Beth had walked into the gym for the first time, in fact. She was attacking the uppercut bag and each twist of her body made her breasts jiggle, even in the tight confines of her sports bra.

When she had fallen against him after Dominic dropped her, his head had almost exploded — not to mention his erection. He could still feel the warm length of her body pressing along his, her round, soft ass nestled against his thighs, the brush of her breasts against his arm.

"Bend your knees," he ordered, forcing himself to focus. "Put the strength of your legs behind your punch."

Beth nodded without speaking. She was breathing hard and sweat streaked her flushed cheeks but she didn't pause, renewing her assault on the bag with grim determination.

"Okay," he said. "Take a break — get some water."

"Yay," she cheered weakly, using her teeth to pull the Velcro strap around her wrist free, tugging her glove off so she could pick up her water bottle.

Harry watched her tip her head back, her throat working as she swallowed. *Great*, he thought. Now *he* was sweating too.

"You know," he told her, "you're awfully tough for a soft little girly girl."

She lowered her water bottle to grin at him. "Who are you calling soft?"

"Just in the very best way," he reassured her, his eyes slipping down to her breasts, still heaving as she caught her breath. "So...can you beat up your boyfriend yet?" Harry mentally smacked himself on the forehead. *Smooth, man, really smooth. Can you make it any more obvious that you're interested?*

Beth just shook her head, not seeming to notice his bumbling information-gathering tactics. "No boyfriend," she said, and Harry's heart sped up. "Not unless you count my secret admirer."

"What?" he asked, confused. For a second, he thought she was talking about him.

She shrugged, taking another drink of water. "Just some guy—at least I assume it's a guy—who leaves little love notes under my door. I was just joking about him being my boyfriend—I don't even know who it is."

Harry felt an uneasy prickling between his shoulder blades. "Some strange guy goes to your house?" he asked. "Has he done anything besides leave the notes?"

"No, of course not," she said hastily. "It's just a silly crush, I'm sure. Forget I said anything."

"Uh-huh." He looked at her, his eyes narrowed. He knew it was none of his business but the idea of someone hanging around where she lived bothered him—a lot.

"Ready to torture me again?" she asked, her breath and her smile back.

After a short pause, Harry nodded. There was nothing he could do about her so-called admirer at the moment—except to teach her to fight. "Grab a mat—time for pushups and abs."

She groaned but obeyed. Harry joined her for pushups, firing out two for each one of hers, continuing even after she collapsed on the mat and rolled over on her side to watch him.

"Wow," she commented with a teasing grin. "I think you just hit a thousand. Working out some pent-up aggression?"

He paused a few inches off the floor and met her eyes. *Something's pent up but it's not aggression*, he thought, helpless with the knowledge that even another thousand pushups wouldn't help get his sanity back.

"You ask her out yet?"

Harry looked up from the paperwork scattered across the front desk and scowled at a grinning Dominic. "Who?"

Dom snorted. "Oh I don't know—maybe a cookie-bearing, curvy little person you've been drooling over since she walked in here a week ago?"

"Beth?" Harry asked in mock surprise. "Of course I haven't. She's a client."

"Idiot." Dominic leaned in, propping his elbows on the tall desk. "If you're not going to, mind if I take a shot?"

The flash of rage took Harry by surprise. He caught himself halfway into a lunge toward the other man. Taking a deliberate step back, Harry forced his fists to unclench. "You do and you're dead," he growled.

Unfazed by the jealous glare leveled at him, Dominic laughed. "Yeah. You aren't interested in her at all. Sure, man."

"As if that's not a disaster waiting to happen," Harry scoffed. "She's a member here now. Say I ask her out and she says yes—what happens when we break up? The gym's not that big—how could I avoid her when she comes to work out?"

"Dude." Dominic shook his head. "Why are you being so negative? Isn't it possible that you wouldn't break up?"

Harry just shrugged, staring blindly at some forms piled on the desk.

His face serious, Dominic asked, "Do you like her?"

Blowing out a frustrated breath, Harry turned to face Dom. "Yes, okay? I think about her all the fucking time. She's hot and pretty and smart and funny—"

"And she has a great rack," Dominic said, nodding solemnly despite a twitch at the corner of his mouth.

"Don't talk about her that way," Harry barked and then had to grin. "God, I'm a sad case, aren't I?"

"Hell yeah, you are," Dom agreed. Harry smacked him on his meaty arm.

"Hey," Dom protested indignantly, rubbing at the spot with an injured expression. "Careful with the merchandise. You said it first. Besides, just look at yourself, man. You only date girls you don't like. I mean, there was Cruella and before her that redhead — what was her name?"

"Anne."

"Right." Dominic rolled his eyes in mock terror.

"I liked them," Harry protested, although his words sounded insincere even to his own ears.

"Okay, so maybe it was me who couldn't stand them," Dominic conceded and then shook himself. "Whatever. The fact is they were scary bitches and you knew that you wouldn't give a shit when they walked away. Not much risk but not much fun either. You're what? Forty?"

"Thirty-one, asshole," Harry corrected.

Dominic waved off the indignant comment. "Whatever. The point is that you're old enough to have an actual adult relationship — maybe even with someone you *like*."

Harry stared at the other man. "When did you get all deep on me?" he asked, a smile creeping across his face despite his best efforts at holding on to his scowl. "Are we going to braid each other's hair and have a pillow fight next?"

"You can mock me," Dominic told him, poking his finger into Harry's chest, "but you know I'm right, so just ask her out already."

Eyeing the other man thoughtfully, Harry said, "You never were interested in Beth, were you? You were just trying to get me going."

Dominic shrugged and grinned. "Nah, I'd love to take her out if I wasn't sure you'd rip my head off and use it as a speed bag. She's crazy hot and when a woman brings you cookies, you know she's going to be great in bed." He dodged Harry's threatening fist and hurried away, calling back over his shoulder, "You better not chicken out now, man."

Harry turned back to the new membership forms he had been entering into the computer before Dom's interruption. *Who knew that the meathead could give good advice?* he mused, grinning to himself.

I'll do it, he decided. He'd ask Beth out. Immediately, his spirits and cock rose at the thought, excitement and nerves vying for position in his stomach. It might be an absolute disaster but, what the hell, it was worth a shot.

Sheri treated Beth to lunch—a "congratulations on your hot trainer who might somehow, someday end up in your bed" lunch. They both agreed that it needed a shorter name. The two women ducked back into the office several minutes late and hurried to their desks, hoping that no one had noticed.

Beth's heart jumped when she saw the bouquet of flowers crowded between her computer keyboard and her inbox. They must have been delivered while she was out. She smiled, touching the edge of a lily with a gentle finger.

Maybe they're from Harry, the silly, idealistic part of her brain guessed but then common sense stepped in. There was no way he had sent the flowers. She was just a client to him, she acknowledged with a depressed sigh, pulling the card from the plastic stand. Besides, she hadn't told him where she worked so he couldn't have sent them, even if he'd wanted to.

Flowers are nothing in the face of your beauty, the card read and Beth frowned. What did that even mean? If flowers were nothing, then why send them? There was no signature. She dropped the card in the trash and eyed the bouquet uneasily.

Her card-delivering admirer had stepped up to flowers—delivered to her *work*, no less. This secret crush suddenly felt less harmless. The bouquet seemed almost…menacing. Although she shook her head at her silly fears, Beth hurried to move the flowers, placing them on the floor in front of her desk.

She sat down in her chair, oddly relieved that the flowers were out of sight and still a little disappointed that they weren't from Harry. Sure, he was just her coach but there had been moments during their last session when Harry had given her a look, an intense, sexy stare that had been more than a client-trainer look. There had been something there—she was sure of it.

Chapter Three

ೞ

Fifteen minutes into their next training session, Harry snapped at her to stop.

"Take the gloves off," he ordered abruptly.

Beth stared at him, eyes huge, mouth slightly open in surprise. "Is everything okay?" she asked.

"No," Harry snapped out. "I need to talk with you in my office." With that, he stalked away.

As she trailed behind him, Beth's stomach churned with nerves. *Why is he so angry?* she wondered. She desperately tried to think of what she had done to irritate him so much. Was it the way she had snuggled against him the other day — was she about to hear a lecture about the importance of personal space in a trainer-client relationship? Was her crush on him so obvious, despite her best efforts to hide how she felt?

Harry was holding the door of his small office open, his normally cheery face drawn tight. Biting her lower lip, Beth followed him into the small room and he shut the door firmly behind her.

As nervous as she was, she realized that she had never been in his office before. A quick glance around gave Beth a blurred impression of a small, cluttered closet of a room, the wooden desk and filing cabinet taking up most of the space and stacks of paper covering everything, leaning in drunkenly precarious piles. Her attention quickly snapped back to Harry.

"What's wrong?" she asked, her voice small.

He didn't answer. Her heart pounding in her ears, Beth watched him lean in, his hard-cut mouth coming closer and closer, his blue eyes bright with heat. Catching her under the arms, Harry lifted her and sat her on the desk as if she was just a little girl.

The piles of papers tilted and slid beneath her, forcing Beth to grab his arms for balance. His biceps flexed beneath her hands and she was shocked by the heat radiating off him, almost burning her palms. While she was distracted by the feel of his thick arms, Harry bent his head and captured her mouth.

His kiss was hard, his tongue invading almost immediately. There was no soft asking, just a hard demand, a claiming of her mouth. Beth yielded to it, her body accepting his, her lips opening at the pressure.

Groaning at her soft surrender, Harry pushed her legs apart and moved between them, never breaking the kiss. He thrust his tongue into her mouth, withdrew and thrust again, muffling her heated moan. Pulling back, Harry nipped at her lips and then soothed the tiny pain with his tongue. Beth clutched the back of his head, trying to pull him back into a kiss, but he resisted her efforts with a wicked curl of his mouth and a tug of his teeth on her full bottom lip.

"Don't tease," she whimpered, fisting her hands against his skull. Harry froze and his eyes blazed, hot and radiant blue, like light through water. His mouth took hers again, fierce and rough, almost hurting but Beth didn't care. With a choked gasp of relief, she opened her mouth to his, wanting him with a desire so intense that it would have scared her if she had been thinking.

The room spun as Harry pressed her back against the desk. His earlier teasing finesse gone, he yanked her shorts down her legs. They caught on her athletic shoes but he pulled the fabric free and flung them away. His hands returned immediately to pull her panties off, tearing them in his urgent haste. Their mouths clashed together, teeth and tongues and lips meshing frantically. He yanked his sweatpants and boxer briefs down just far enough to free his straining cock, the tip leaking with need. Reaching behind Beth, he grabbed something from the desk, pulling his mouth away from hers in order to rip the condom wrapper open with his teeth.

Puzzled despite the haze of passion fogging her brain, Beth turned her head to see where he had gotten the small packet.

"You keep condoms in your pen holder?" she asked incredulously. Her desire cooled a little as she wondered how many women he had pulled into his office before her. Why else would he have protection within such easy reach?

He had been focused on rolling the condom over his erection but he looked up at her question, a small grin pulling up the corners of his mouth.

"Dominic," he explained, his voice still rough with need despite his amusement. "They keep popping up all over the gym. There's even lube in the top drawer of the membership desk."

Her first reaction was relief that it hadn't been Harry's stockpile. Her second was bafflement. "Um, why?"

He appeared almost embarrassed as he answered, "He's matchmaking. I guess he wanted us to be…prepared…wherever it happened."

"Oh." Beth felt blood rush to her face but she held his gaze. "Remind me to bring Dominic more cookies."

His smile fell away as his eyes flared with heat. "You're killing me," he gritted as he wrapped his hand around the back of her neck and yanked her in for another kiss.

Beth felt the piles of paper give beneath her as he pulled her to the edge of the desk, holding her hips in a hard grip as he bent his knees and thrust into her. His thick cock parted her tight, hot passage and a deep moan vibrated in Harry's chest.

He felt so good, so right. His fingers dug into the soft give of her hips and he slammed into her, wild thrusts hard enough to shake the desk. Beth climaxed instantly, wave after wave of ecstasy breaking over her, leaving her only vaguely aware of

Harry's shudders as he exploded, following her into mindless pleasure.

Beth gradually came back to reality. As she felt the lumpy mounds of paper beneath her and Harry still inside her, insecurities began slipping in. Was this it? Had this been his goal and now that he'd had it—or had *her*, rather—would he escort her to the door for the "thank you, ma'am" part that followed the "wham, bam"?

And what a wham bam it was, she thought, trying to hold back a fatuous grin. Her one previous lover—another art student in college—had not prepared her for the crackling attraction between her and Harry, the irresistible, frantic need that had overwhelmed her reservations and any trace of common sense.

Still panting a little, Harry raised his head from where it had been resting next to hers. Their eyes met and Beth was stricken with awkward shyness. She had never been in this situation before. *What should I say?* she wondered, self-conscious under his intent gaze.

"Well, shit." Harry was the one who broke the silence and his pithy summation made Beth laugh and relax. He pulled out of her and her laughter faded, replaced by a sense of loss.

Don't be silly, she told herself sternly. *It's not like he can stay inside you all the time—think how awkward work would be.* That thought made her smile again, and Harry grinned back at her as he straightened and tossed the condom into a trashcan next to the desk before adjusting his pants.

Feeling exposed, Beth pushed herself off the desk, reaching for the floor with her feet. A pile of paper slid under her hand and she almost fell. Harry's hard hands grabbed her around the waist and gently lowered her to the ground. Her torn panties circled one ankle and she hurriedly stepped out of them and grabbed them up. Embarrassed again, she blushed hotly as she scanned the room for her abandoned shorts, her wadded-up underwear clutched in one hand.

"Sorry about those," Harry said, nodding toward her fist, his eyes heating again.

"Huh," Beth retorted a little skeptically, holding back a grin. "You don't look sorry—you look pretty proud of yourself." Her eyes seized on the gray puddle of her shorts and she hurried to pull them on over her shoes, nearly falling over in the process.

"Easy there." He steadied her, eyes alight with laughter. "Just so you know, that wasn't my best performance. I'm not really a two-minute man, you know."

Beth lifted a teasing eyebrow.

"Honestly!" he insisted, moving closer to her. "In fact, I was wondering if you would mind if we skipped the rest of your training session—"

Beth's heart plopped into her stomach. *This is it*, she realized. Here comes the brush-off. *Stupid, stupid, stupid*, her brain raged at her. Now she couldn't even come back to the gym—and she was really starting to like boxing! Bracing herself, Beth plastered on what she hoped was an unconcerned, breezy, I-do-this-sort-of-thing-all-the-time expression. *At least I got to experience sex with my dream man once*, she thought gloomily.

"And just go up to my place," he continued. "I live above the gym, and we could order in or something if you're hungry," he went on, and Beth's heart leapt at the realization that he wasn't dumping her after all.

Geez Louise, she thought. The way her emotions were jumping around, it would be a miracle if she didn't fall over from a heart attack before the night was over.

Harry was watching her expression, a little anxious when she didn't answer.

"Or we can finish your session," he offered. "I just don't know if I can trust myself in public with you. I probably wouldn't even be able to make it five minutes before you were facedown across a weight bench and I was fucking you. Dominic would never let me live that down."

Blushing and sputtering with laughter, Beth could feel her pussy reawakening, beginning to pulse at the image of her stretched helpless over a bench, Harry driving his cock into her as the gym patrons stared.

"Actually, he would probably enjoy the show—and the view," she added, bravely running her fingers across the taut roundness of one of his ass cheeks. She could feel the muscle clench even through the two layers of fabric that covered it.

His face tightened and Beth heard the hiss of a sucked-in breath. Taking the halfstep needed to close the small distance between them, Harry pressed one large hand against the bottom curve of her ass, lifting her roughly against him so she could feel his re-emerging hardness against her belly.

She immediately yielded to him, softening around the hard press of his body, molding her curves against him. His head lowered and Beth closed her eyes, waiting impatiently for the demanding invasion of his kiss, but he stopped instead, so close that she could feel the heat of his breath on her swollen, needy lips.

When he paused, unmoving, Beth's eyes opened. Harry was staring at her mouth, his eyes so hungry that her breath caught.

"Upstairs," he gritted, the roughness of his voice making her skin prickle with goose bumps. "Now."

"Okay," she whimpered, not moving. Beth didn't even know if her legs would support her if she tried to walk right now.

Harry pressed his face into the curve of her neck for a moment, took a deep breath and abruptly set her away from him. He took a step toward the door but turned back to the desk, fishing a handful of condoms out of the pen holder and stuffing them into his pocket. He grinned at Beth.

"Let's go," he said, grabbing her hand and swinging the door open. The noise from the gym rushed in, the rumble of voices and clang of metal against metal merging with the rock music playing over the sound system. In a panic, Beth glanced down to find that she was rumpled but at least nothing was exposed.

As Harry towed her through the gym, cutting a determined path through equipment and people, she couldn't stop the blood from flushing her cheeks. A few of the guys were watching their progress, smirking, as if it had been obvious what she and Harry had been doing in his tiny office with the door shut. If they hadn't guessed, her mussed clothes and deep blush would have tipped them off. That and Harry's intent look as he hauled her behind him to the metal stairs against the far wall of the gym.

Beth tried to hide her hand holding the remains of her panties against her leg. *Where is a pocket when you need it?* she wailed mentally. When they reached the base of the stairs, Harry tugged Beth in front of him and urged her up. She could feel his heat along her back and one of his hands curved around her hip.

When they reached the landing at the top of the stairs, he reached around her to open the door and rush her through. As the door swung shut, Harry fumbled for the lock, barely waiting until he heard the click of the deadbolt before shoving Beth against the wall. She squeaked at the speed of the movement but didn't resist the force of his body.

Her obedient softness almost blinded Harry with a red haze of lust. He had wanted to go slow, to make this one last, to show Beth that he could be careful and gentle, but his body was relentless, his cock urgent.

He hadn't meant to drag her into his office but watching her round ass in those tiny shorts, the bounce of her breasts and the shadowy glimpses of cleavage had driven him insane with desire. He had pulled her into his office to ask her out, thinking that, if he had that out of the way, he could get a shred of self-control back. Instead, once the office door had closed and they had been alone together, he had to have her. Right then, right there.

Now he couldn't think of anything except getting inside her again. His mouth slammed down on hers, demanding entry. Beth moaned and her lips parted for his marauding tongue. He thrust in and out of her mouth, mimicking how his cock had plunged into her grasping pussy just a few minutes before. Parting her legs with his knee, he pressed hard against the juncture of her thighs, drawing a whimper from her as she pushed back, as if seeking more — more pressure, more hardness, more of him.

Beth sucked at his tongue. Ignoring her insistent hold, he withdrew and nibbled her mouth with small kisses. She nipped his bottom lip with her teeth in retaliation.

Harry growled and kissed her hard, pulling back just long enough to yank up her tank top. He heard a seam tear as he hauled it relentlessly over her head. *The way I'm ripping her clothes off her, I'm going to have to buy her a whole new wardrobe,* Harry thought absently, but then his conscious mind blurred again.

Harry broke off the kiss and Beth followed his mouth with hers, making a small, disappointed sound at the loss of contact. He was breathing hard, staring at her breasts. The black sports bra made her skin look creamy white and her harsh pants pressed the flesh of her full breasts up over the gripping fabric. Harry's eyes fixed on the movement.

Breaking his paralysis, Harry ran a gentle finger along the line where black spandex met the smooth line of her skin. Abruptly, he tugged her bra up to expose her breasts. Although Beth gasped at the sudden movement, she raised her arms obediently, allowing him to pull the bra completely off.

As her breasts were released from their restraints, the pink-tipped orbs bounced free, drawing a guttural groan from Harry. He dropped to his knees, cupping her breasts in both hands and pressing the white mounds together. Pulling a tight, erect nipple between his lips, Harry sucked it deep into his mouth, drawing hard before allowing it to slip out until just the edge of the nub was between his teeth. He raised his head

41

a little and let the weight of her breast tug at her nipple still captive in his mouth. Mewing, Beth tipped her head back against the wall and her hips twisted toward Harry.

Turning to her other breast, Harry teased the stiff tip with his tongue. Beth's hands worked in his hair, tugging on the short strands and then easing to massage his scalp. He nipped lightly at the straining bud of her nipple, which made her tighten her grip on his head, and then he sucked strongly, using the flat of his tongue to press the tip of her breast against the roof of his mouth. Pulling back, he let his teeth scrape against the edge of the swollen nub, wringing a wanting cry from Beth.

Harry trailed wet, sucking kisses down her belly to the edge of her shorts. He hooked his thumbs over the waistband and eased them over her hips, letting them fall to puddle over her shoes as his tongue circled the rim of her bellybutton. Switching his focus to her feet, he untied her shoes and pulled them off. Beth held on to his bulging shoulder to keep her balance as she stood on one leg and then the other. His thumb traced the arch of each foot as he slid her socks off.

She stood in front of him completely naked. His breath coming in quick pants, Harry stared at the triangle of hair at the top of her thighs, the damp blonde hair curling shyly over her folds. As he let his fingers trace through the silky strands, he tugged a little at her curls, fascinated by the wetness decorating her inner thighs.

Shouldering her thighs farther apart, he used two fingers to open her pussy lips and expose the gleaming, deep-pink flesh to him. He pressed his face between her thighs, scratching the delicate skin with his stubbly cheeks. She wobbled and Harry grabbed her hand, tugging her down to the floor.

Beth went to her knees willingly, happy that her shaky legs didn't have to support her weight anymore. Harry kissed her, pressing her back until she lay on the floor, her head spinning from the hard, urgent pressure of his mouth. The tile was cold against her back and bottom, a shocking contrast to the fire of her skin.

He pushed her legs up and apart and fixed her with a stern glare. "Hold," he commanded and Beth obediently brought her hands beneath her knees, keeping them folded up on either side of her chest, spreading herself for his possessive gaze.

Grunting in satisfaction, Harry lowered his head to her exposed pussy. She tensed, waiting for his mouth to touch her, but he paused, teasing her with his breath. Beth trembled with the urge to shove her hips toward his mouth, make him lick her, suck her, but she remained still, waiting.

"What a good girl," he murmured, tracing her inner folds with two gentle fingers. He lightly pinched her clit, making her jump, and then soothed the nubbin with the tip of his tongue. Everything Beth was feeling was centered in her pussy—she was not aware of anything except for the amazing sensations his fingers and breath and tongue were drawing from her.

Harry licked her folds with broad strokes of his tongue, pressing up into her and then lightening the pressure, flicking her clit with the gentlest of touches before deeply licking her pussy again. Beth pulled her knees higher, resisting the need to grab his head and press him against her wet flesh.

His tongue ventured downward, lapping at the sensitive skin beneath her pussy. Her bottom clenched as he licked lower, tracing the puckered hole below. No one had ever had her there, not even with a finger, but his tongue felt incredible as it probed her virgin opening, awakening nerve endings she didn't even know she had. The dark, tempting thought of Harry pushing his cock into her ass made her pussy gush with moisture.

As if sensing her arousal, he thrust his tongue deeper and she clenched around him, holding him captive. The pressure made him jerk his head back and Beth felt a shuddering breath against her damp skin.

She raised her head from the floor. "Wasn't that…okay?" she asked anxiously.

Another puff of air hit her inner thigh, a breathless laugh this time. "Hell yeah," Harry groaned. "So 'okay' I almost came."

"Oh." A tiny smile touched her mouth as she let her head sink back to the tile.

Without any warning, he dipped his head and took her clit between his lips, sucking at it gently. Beth's hips twisted against his mouth. He tugged the swollen nub between his teeth and she came, her head tucking back as she cried out.

Harry suckled her gently as she recovered, tasting her liquid release. When her breathing had slowed just slightly, his mouth grew more demanding, his tongue lashing her pussy. Beth's fingers dug into the backs of her knees as she keened, his mouth driving her even higher than before. He replaced his tongue with a thick finger and then two, plunging into her hot depths while he flicked her clit with his tongue, teasing it until her back bowed off the floor.

His fingers left her pussy and his tongue returned in a wide, bottom-to-top stroke. The tip of one wet finger was tracing the cleft of her ass, probing gently at her anus.

"Would you let me fuck you here?" he asked, his voice rough and uneven as he pressed steadily against the tight hole until it accepted his finger to the first knuckle.

Beth's stomach jumped but then her lower belly melted and moisture trickled out of her pussy. Raising her head, she stared at Harry, her eyes dazed with passion, tiny curls sticking to her damp temples and forehead.

"You can fuck me anywhere," she gasped, her head falling back as he thrust his entire finger into her, forcing her over the edge into another startling climax.

Harry pulled his hand away and knelt between her thighs, yanking his pants down and letting his erection spring free. Digging a condom out of his pocket, he tore it open and

44

rolled it on as Beth watched him hazily, still floating on the last ripples of pleasure from her most recent orgasm. Harry covered her hands with his and forced her legs even higher, even farther apart.

Despite her brave words, she felt a twinge of apprehension. He must have felt her hesitation because he paused, meeting her eyes with an uneven laugh.

"I'd love to, but your sweet ass will have to wait until I have a little more control," he admitted hoarsely and drove his cock into her slippery, wet pussy. Beth clenched around him and Harry groaned. The muscles of his jaw bunched as he clenched his teeth. He pulled out slowly, slowly, until just the head of his cock remained inside her, and then pushed back in, more slowly still. Beth felt every inch of his cock as it slid against her pulsing inner walls, still vibrating from her last climax.

With her legs pressed up, Harry felt huge. Beth almost laughed—Harry was huge! She could feel the slow friction as he filled her completely, bumping her cervix with the head of his cock, and the heat began to build again in her pussy. Raising her hips to meet his thrusts, Beth was suddenly impatient—she needed more.

"Faster!" she demanded, ignoring a small, hazy part of her brain that was amazed at her bossy tone. "Go faster!"

Growling, Harry obeyed, slamming his hips against her in hard strokes, sliding Beth across the slick floor with the force of his thrusts. His cock disappeared inside her with every plunge and he angled their hips so that he rubbed against her already swollen clit on each downbeat.

Her body tightened again, preparing for release, while her mind protested. *Not again surely? It's too much*, she thought blurrily but toppled over the edge of climax anyway, screaming Harry's name as she came. Her muscles clamped down on his pistoning cock, yanking him over into his own orgasm, his hips jerking, his hard, muscled arms quivering as they braced against the floor on either side of her head.

With a final groan, Harry collapsed, catching himself at the last second before his heavy body crushed Beth against the hard floor. He tipped his dripping head forward into the curve where her shoulder met her neck and kissed her softly, tasting the salt of her sweat. Boneless and exhausted, Harry felt himself drifting off, almost falling asleep before he realized that they were still on the floor. Of his hallway. His uncomfortable, *tiled* hallway.

Sighing, he pushed himself to his knees, leaning most of his weight onto his undamaged leg. Beth had wrapped her legs and arms around him sometime after that final climax so she followed him up, clinging like a baby monkey. Harry grinned and pushed a lock of hair out of her face. She smiled back sleepily and rested her cheek against his chest.

Glancing down, Harry rolled his eyes. Christ, he hadn't even bothered to take his shirt off.

"Up you go," he told Beth, helping her to her feet after she reluctantly released him. She offered her hand but he brushed it off with masculine bravado as he stood—and almost tripped. Obviously, his sweatpants hadn't come off completely either. He glared at the fabric that had slid down around his ankles.

Harry shoved his boxer briefs the rest of the way down and kicked his shoes and the whole mess of fabric off his feet. Getting his socks off took some hopping around but he managed, although Beth was giggling at him the whole time. He stripped his shirt off over his head and tossed it away. Her laughter was cut off with a surprised squeak when he hauled her against his chest, holding her up with her feet dangling off the ground. Leaving his discarded clothes where they fell, he headed for his bedroom with Beth in his arms.

Shoving the door open, Harry headed straight for the bed, tumbling them both onto the comforter and landing on top of a laughing Beth.

Chapter Four

ହେ

The summer light was just fading from the room, turning the walls pink with the sunset. Beth couldn't help smiling as she looked up at Harry, who met her eyes with a happy grin of his own.

"Are you hungry?" he asked hopefully.

"Again? Don't you need a break?" Beth teased, tangling one of her legs around his.

"For *food*," he clarified, shaking his head. "Such a sweet face with such a dirty mind."

Beth smacked him with a pillow. "My mind is the dirty one? Whose finger was in whose ass? Wait...that wasn't very grammatical, was it?"

His eyes darkened. "Were you serious? About wanting to...do that?" he asked, all teasing gone. She felt his cock stir against her leg.

Blushing, she glanced away from his intent gaze. "I never have before and I know this whole thing is brand new, but I..." She trailed off, the color in her cheeks deepening. Taking a deep breath, she bravely met his eyes. "I want to do everything with you."

Harry jolted at her words, definitely erect now. "Fuck. I mean, me too. I've never been so turned on by a woman before and I'm not just saying that because I want to get in your ass."

"Well, obviously you don't have to." She grinned, still blushing. He laughed and started tickling her neck with tiny butterfly kisses.

"Wait, you promised me food!"

47

"Don't want to eat anymore," he muttered sulkily and nipped her earlobe.

"Fine," she sighed, pretending that her heart wasn't racing out of control from that little bite. Well, the bite and the way Harry's full lower lip stuck out when he pouted. "But it's my turn," she insisted, pushing at his shoulder.

Harry allowed her to roll him to his back, tugging her with him so she was sprawled over his chest. "Okay," he said, mimicking her resigned sigh. "Have your way with me."

"Yay!" Beth straddled his chest, contemplating the fine specimen beneath her. *Where to start, where to start,* she thought, almost rubbing her hands together in glee. She had been dying to touch him ever since she'd first glimpsed his beautiful ass through the gym door. Combing her fingers through his furred chest, she flicked his small nipples with her nails and watched his reaction, noticing how his cheekbones darkened and his jaw got tight. *Sensitive,* she thought. *Good.*

She leaned over, her hair falling to brush his chest with a silky tickle, and caught one of the brown nipples lightly in her teeth, holding it captive as she flicked it with her tongue. Beth felt his rumble of pleasure more than she heard the sound as it vibrated his chest beneath her open thighs.

Using her teeth, tongue and lips, she worked her way down to his ridged stomach, tasted his sweat, felt the jerk of his muscles as she licked and nipped at his skin. As she slid lower, she could feel the prod of his wet-tipped erection on her ass. Her belly jumped and warmed.

Beth lifted up and sank down again, trapping his cock beneath her body. It felt like a hot iron bar along her pussy and her moisture seeped out to coat it. Harry's hips jerked involuntarily and his cock slid easily against her wet flesh, the tip rubbing against her clit.

As his body surged beneath her again, trying to shift to a position where he could push inside her, Beth played, dipping her fingertip into his bellybutton, tugging the hair tracing down to his groin and scratching her nails lightly against his skin.

"Please, Beth?" he groaned, his hands tight on her hips.

"Not yet," she reproved him teasingly, sliding farther down his body until she knelt between his legs. "I haven't even gotten to the good part yet." Beth slid her fingers down the length of his cock before giving him a firm squeeze.

"Jesus," he swore, his hips bucking under her touch. "You're going to kill me."

Beth nuzzled the skin where his leg met his groin and traced the vulnerable crease with her tongue. Cradling his balls in one hand, she closed her other around his shaft and pumped, moving the soft skin with her grip. Harry hissed out a breath and liquid beaded on the tip of his cock, drawing Beth's curious tongue. She licked at the moisture, spreading it around the head. Harry fisted his hands in her hair.

"Do it, Beth," he gritted, his eyes glittering. "Now."

She obeyed, swallowing the length of his cock, concentrating on relaxing her throat and letting him slide even deeper. Her cheeks worked, suctioning him wetly, and her head followed the command of his hands, moving up and down on his slick erection.

Harry's fingers tightened and he pulled her harder to him at the same time that his hips rose to meet her mouth. Her lips were stretched around him and he filled her almost painfully with his girth but Beth loved the feeling of him taking control, fucking her mouth, butting the back of her throat with the head of his massive cock.

Her hand was wrapped around the base of his erection, fingers wet from following her mouth up his shaft. She slid her hand away and Beth felt him push her even farther down on his rigid cock, driving the head into her throat. She swallowed him as she slipped her fingers beneath his balls, burrowing into the crease between his ass cheeks, finding the small hole hidden in the dark crevice.

Circling the puckered entrance as Harry had done to her, Beth nudged her fingertip into the ring of tight muscle, pushing in gently but relentlessly until her finger was buried in the clenching heat of him. He stiffened momentarily and then his hips began thrusting in short, fast surges, pulling almost off her finger as his cock slid into her mouth and plunging back onto the invading digit as he lowered his hips.

On one upthrust, Beth tucked the tip of a second finger in with the first and Harry slammed down on them with a guttural cry. His muscles clamped onto her fingers as his hands shoved her head down, forcing her to take his cock as deeply into her mouth as she could. He came, shouting his release as his semen jetted down Beth's willing throat.

Gently sucking on him as he recovered, Beth slid her fingers from his ass. She had never tried that before but she was greatly pleased by the success of her experiment. As she pulled her mouth from his softening cock, Beth glanced a little tentatively at his face. It was all well and good to do all sorts of things in the heat of the moment but afterward might be a little awkward, she worried.

Chest still heaving, Harry's eyes were closed. He opened them when she glanced at him, as if he felt her gaze. His lips curled at the corners when he saw her anxious expression. He reached for her and hauled her up so that she was lying on his chest, feeling the rise and fall of his rib cage. He kissed her gently.

"That was…really, really good," he said, pressing his lips to hers again, this time a little harder. "Intense. Amazing. Where did you learn that? Wait—don't answer that. I don't want to know about any of your former boyfriends. I'd just want to kill them all."

"I learned it from you, silly." She rolled her eyes. "You just did it to me."

"Huh. I'm a pretty good teacher then." He grinned at her proudly and Beth laughed and smacked his shoulder.

"Enough gloating, caveman," she told him, trying to roll off his chest, but his arms tightened, holding her there. "You promised me food *hours* ago." Narrowing her eyes at him, Beth gave him her best stern glare. "You better not have the man's version of a stocked kitchen, either."

"What?"

"You know—some spoiled milk, a half-empty jar of peanut butter and fifty zillion protein bars." She poked him in the chest for emphasis.

Harry looked offended. "Of course not. I'll have you know that my jar of peanut butter is half *full*."

With that, he rolled them both out of bed, Beth laughing and clinging to him as he stood up, swinging her with him. She twisted her legs around his waist and locked her hands behind his neck. "Is your knee okay with this?"

"My knee's fine," he responded with enough masculine bravado that Beth knew he wouldn't ever tell her it was a problem, even if his leg fell off. "Shower first?" he queried.

"I *suppose*," Beth agreed in tones of dramatic resignation, although a shower actually sounded wonderful. He hauled her into the bathroom and directly into the small shower stall. She shrieked as the water hit her back, cold and sudden, stealing her breath.

Smacking his shoulder, she gasped, "You rat! You used me as a shield."

Harry just blinked at her, all innocence. "How could you say something like that?" he asked, wounded. "All I care about is your comfort. See, it's getting nice and warm." With those words, he rotated so that his back caught the stream and Beth was left with a bare mist deflected off his wide shoulders.

"Okay, that's it," she growled, stifling her laughter. "Put me down, you shower hog." Wiggling until he relinquished his hold, she slid to her feet and squeezed around him into the spray. "Just wait until I actually know how to box," she threatened and Harry cringed in mock fear.

"Where's the body wash?" Beth asked, looking around.

"You mean the soap?" Harry handed her a bar.

Looking at the white rectangle ruefully, she ventured, "So, I'm guessing there's no point in asking if you have a pouf."

"A what? Did you just insult me?" he asked, a grin tugging at the corners of his mouth.

"That's what I thought," she sighed, soaping her hands. "You probably don't have conditioner either. Men are such barbarians."

Harry growled, "I'll show you a barbarian." He snatched Beth off her feet, pressing her against the shower wall so he could kiss her.

She turned her face away. "You promised food!" she shrieked, giggling as he bit at her neck, her laughter quickly transformed to sighs as his searing tongue licked at the trails of water trickling down her throat.

"Fine," he sighed, allowing her feet to find the floor again. "If you prefer food…"

"I didn't realize it was an either-or kind of thing," Beth said, arching an eyebrow.

"Food *and* sex?" He sounded so much like an excited little boy that she had to smile. "I can have both? It's like heaven."

She laughed, soaping his chest. "Food, sex and showers. It's like a spa in heaven. Or at least a locker room in heaven."

"Let me get in on that," he ordered, commandeering the soap. "I want to wash your front."

They washed each other, hands slipping into soapy crevices until they were both panting with need and laughter.

"Food time," Harry decided, although his voice was rough and growly. Turning off the water, he snagged a towel and started to dry Beth off, rubbing her head briskly.

"I can manage, thanks," she told him, pulling the towel free. "Keep doing that and I'm going to have BoJo the Clown hair."

Harry grinned and grabbed another towel for himself, watching as Beth finished drying off.

"Can I borrow your comb?" she asked.

"You could if I had one." He ran a palm over his head. "Don't really need it—this is the longest my hair's been in years."

Beth finger-combed her damp curls, making a mental note to bring a few necessities from her apartment the next time she came over to Harry's place. She glanced at him uncertainly—there was going to be a next time, wasn't there?

"What?" he asked.

"Nothing," she mumbled, hiding behind the fall of her hair.

"Sure?"

She nodded.

"Want to eat?"

She nodded again.

"Good." He grabbed her hand and hauled her out of the bathroom.

"Let me wear your t-shirt," she ordered, grabbing at the doorframe to redirect them back toward the bedroom.

"No. I like you naked." Harry ran a hand over her hip in emphasis, raising goose bumps across her skin.

"Not while cooking—it just isn't sanitary," she objected. "Besides, what if there's grease spatter? That could be painful."

He paused at her last statement. "I should probably put something on." Reversing back into the bedroom, he yanked on a pair of shorts. Pulling a clean t-shirt out of a drawer, he tossed it to her.

Beth pulled the shirt over her head. It enveloped her, falling to mid-thigh. Harry watched with a cranky expression.

"I like you better naked," he muttered, swinging her up into his arms.

"My legs are going to atrophy into useless lumps if you keep carrying me around like this," she told him, although she didn't make any move to get down.

"I like carrying you around. You're wrapped around me like a little spider monkey." Wrapping an arm under her hips, he headed for the door.

"A monkey?" she repeated, offended.

"Pipe down, woman. I'm busy hunting our dinner." He smacked her lightly on her ass cheek, making her shiver.

"Like that, do you?" Harry looked down at her, eyes alight. "That's interesting. We'll have to...experiment with that later." His hand ran under his t-shirt and across the sensitized skin where he had just spanked and Beth quivered again.

His eyes went hot. "Or maybe..." he began, the raspy edge back in his voice. But then he shook himself, a full-body movement like a dog after a bath. Beth squealed and clung to him so she wouldn't be shaken loose.

"No more sex until after food," he told her, or maybe himself, firmly. "Otherwise, in a few weeks, they'll just find the empty husks of our bodies in that bed."

"We would be *smiling* husks though."

Harry laughed. "Definitely smiling," he agreed, striding into his kitchen and plopping her down on the marble-topped island with a kiss on the nose. Reluctantly, Beth untwined her arms and legs from around him and watched him rummage in the fridge.

"Italian, Chinese or Greek?" he asked.

"Irish, actually. Well, half. The other half is Swedish and Spanish and even some Luxembourgian."

Eyebrow raised, he smiled at her over his shoulder. "Good to know, but I was talking about food. You're rather a mutt, you know."

"Melting pot, that's me. Oh, and Chinese would be fabulous. Well, depending on how old it is—you seem to have a whole world of leftovers." She peered around him doubtfully, trying to see into the refrigerator.

"Fresh from…yesterday?" His voice was a little unsure and it was Beth's turn to raise an eyebrow at him. "No more than the day before, I'm positive."

"Uh-huh," she said skeptically. "Do you always have this much takeout or is this just part of your break-up recovery?" Immediately after the words left her mouth, she wanted to suck them back in. *Oops.*

Harry paused, white food cartons dwarfed in his hands. "How did you know that I just broke up with someone?" he asked curiously.

Beth blushed a little, pretending great fascination in his kitchen tile. "Oh, well…hmmm. So, I sort of saw you…" Her voice trailed off. Setting the cartons on the island, Harry bracketed her lap with his arms and leaned toward her, his mouth stern but his eyes were twinkling.

"Are you stalking me, little girl?" he mock-growled, moving even closer. Beth's heart sped up in a mixture of arousal, excitement and adrenaline, with a touch of embarrassment thrown in.

"No," she said a little sulkily. "I was there first."

Harry nipped at her pouting lower lip. "Where?" he asked, although he sounded distracted now, his stare fixed on her mouth.

"Tony's," she admitted breathlessly.

It took a moment for her answer to sink in but when it did, Harry jerked back. "Tony's?" he repeated, startled. "So you saw…" Breaking off, he rubbed a hand over his head and glanced at her ruefully. "You saw the whole drink-in-the-face thing?"

Beth nodded, a smile twitching at the corners of her mouth.

Groaning, Harry let his head fall back for a moment and then looked at her. "Yeah. That was one of the less smooth break-ups I've ever participated in."

"We were wondering—" Beth stopped, afraid that it would sound tacky.

"What?" he asked, his voice resigned.

"Well, what instigated the whole..." She mimed the drink toss.

Sighing, Harry turned and boosted himself onto the island next to her. "She said that she had put too much effort into arranging our future for me just to break it off," he told her, glancing at Beth from the corner of his eye. "Just for the record, I usually don't spend the first date talking about my ex."

"Sure you don't," she teased, then laughed when he gave her a wounded look. "No, it's okay—I'm interested. Were you guys engaged or something? What do you mean, 'arranging our future'?"

Spreading his hands palms up in a baffled gesture, Harry shrugged. "I have no idea. We were definitely not engaged. We had just been dating for two months—less, actually. I wouldn't have kept it going for that long but..." He looked a little sheepish. "It was easy—no, I don't mean *she* was easy," he clarified when Beth gave him a sharp look. "She's my sister's friend, so everyone in my family was happy with it and her family was happy and so...I just let it drift on. My mistake. I didn't realize until I got that unexpected martini shower that she was thinking long-term."

Beth looked thoughtful. "Oh. The consensus at our table was that you had cheated on her," she told him, startling a bark of laughter from Harry.

"Christ, we really entertained the bar that night, didn't we?" His cheekbones were flushed and he scrubbed his hand over his severely cut hair again. "Nope, no cheating—unless *she* had something on the side. I doubt it though—she didn't really seem too excited about sex." Reddening even more, he glanced sideways at Beth. "In fact, just tonight, we've—"

Breaking off abruptly, Harry jumped down from his seat on the island. "Enough talk about Candice—there's something wrong about talking so much about an ex with the new girlfriend. Let's eat Chinese."

Pleased, Beth couldn't hold back a grin. The new girlfriend. Well, that definitely sounded like an extension on the one-night stand.

Harry eyed her suspiciously. "Why are you smiling at me like that?"

Shrugging, Beth just grinned. "No reason. Now hurry up with that Chinese."

He snapped a salute and popped the cartons into the microwave.

"That looked professional," she commented, throwing a salute back at him when Harry glanced at her, a questioning eyebrow raised. "Military?"

Nodding absently, he dug in a drawer and triumphantly pulled out two pairs of chopsticks. "Army. Up until a couple years ago, actually."

"Really?" As she thought about it, Beth wasn't too surprised. He did have that...commanding presence about him. "Were you in Iraq?"

"Afghanistan." His short tone did not encourage any further questions, so Beth decided to change the subject.

"What should I call you?" she asked instead, drawing another puzzled look from him. "Sergeant Harry? Lieutenant Harry? Special Agent Harry? Oh wait—that last one is for the FBI, isn't it?"

He laughed. "Captain."

"Cap'n Harry. Oh, that's even better. Can I say 'Aye, aye, Captain'? Or 'Captain, Captain, O my Captain'?" Beth squealed as he wrapped a quick arm around her waist and pulled her off the island with a growl. Wrapping her legs around his ridged waist, she was reminded vividly that they were both still half-naked.

Harry buried his face in the curve of her neck, rubbing his rough cheeks against her delicate skin and making her giggle. He pushed the oversized crew neck of the t-shirt to the side and nipped her newly bared shoulder and Beth's laughter turned to a sigh as her skin heated next to his. Her legs tightened and moisture began to dampen her pussy, open against his hard belly. She knew that Harry felt the wetness of her desire because his stomach rippled beneath her and he groaned.

Beth could feel his skin heating, his heart accelerating, his breathing shorten and catch. His need for her fueled her own lust and she pressed her body against his, wanting to be closer still. She would have climbed inside him if she could have.

Harry kissed and licked his way up her neck, sparking shivers of arousal down Beth's spine. He ran the point of his tongue along her jawline and tugged her earlobe with his teeth. Beth shook and melted, all rational thought driven away by the rush of sensation shooting across her skin as his tongue traced a circling path into her ear.

His calloused palms slid down her back and under her shirt to cup her ass, curling around the round cheeks to let his rough-tipped fingers explore the furrow between. Dipping lower and lower, he teased her with delicate touches, dancing around her tight rear entrance before moving around to her swollen, hungry flesh. Beth held her breath as he barely brushed the lips of her pussy with a fingertip, wanting to grab his hand and force his fingers into her, assuage this wild ache building in her dripping folds.

She groaned in disappointment when his hands slipped away, easing along her thighs to her knees and calves. Harry unhooked her legs, gently pulling them from around his waist and easing her down until her feet touched the floor. He pulled her shirt off over her head and kissed her hard, a short, deep kiss, before flipping her around to face away from him. Beth didn't have a chance to recover from that quick movement before he was lifting her again.

She was facedown across the island before she realized what was happening. Her hips balanced on the edge of the cool marble and she couldn't reach the floor with her feet, leaving her legs to dangle helplessly. The cold countertop pressed against her nipples, the contrast between the hot, hard, prickling tips and the chill of the unyielding stone intense, bordering on painful. Beth jerked away, pulling her breasts from the cool surface. Contrarily, she missed the searing sensation and pressed back against the marble, harder this time.

Harry's hands were tracing the muscles running parallel to her spine, gliding past her shoulder blades, moving along her waist and dipping into the dimples at the base of her back. Beth's pussy clenched as his hands brushed her ass and her flesh quivered beneath his fingers. His grip grew firmer, squeezing, massaging, separating and pressing the cheeks back together. She jumped when she felt his teeth—not biting, but threatening, nipping the sensitive globes and then soothing them with the flat of his tongue.

Harry kissed the very base of her spine, a wet, open-mouthed kiss, and Beth felt a flush of sweat break from her skin despite the cool surface of the marble. As Harry licked downward, Beth's ass cheeks clenched beneath his palms and he kneaded her flesh reassuringly. She felt the tip of his tongue circle her anus and she shook as the nerve endings awoke again, pleading for more. Harry plunged the tip into the tight hole, working his way in, thrusting against the resistance of the ring of muscle.

Beth's breath sobbed in and out and her juices coated her thighs as he licked at her opening. She scrabbled for purchase with her feet but there was just air. Harry stilled her flailing with a firm grip on her thighs. He pushed her legs apart, opening her to the cool air and his invading tongue, which had moved to lap the wetness smeared across her thighs.

Suddenly, Harry pulled his face away and stood behind her. Beth sobbed at the loss, needed his thrusting tongue and scratching cheeks between her thighs.

"Patience," he scolded and a hard hand smacked against her ass, the sound echoing in the kitchen. His hand fell again, this time on the other cheek, hard enough to shove her forward, her pelvic bone bumping the edge of the island, sending a flash of heat across her lower belly.

Beth held her breath, hoping for more as moisture trickled from her inflamed pussy. Ever since she had first noticed Harry, especially after she had seen him up close and saw his hard, square hands, Beth had wanted this. It was especially sweet to be spanked as she was sprawled helpless across the island, at the mercy of his calloused hands. When he paused after the second smack, Beth couldn't resist wriggling and tilting her hips up toward him.

"Like that, do you?" Harry's voice had gone as rough as his hands. "I know it turns me on like crazy to see that beautiful ass jiggle and turn pink when I spank you."

She moaned at his words, twisting her hips desperately against the cold stone countertop. Laughing shortly, he complied with her wordless pleas and swung his hand against her bottom again. "Greedy girl," he rasped, sliding two hard fingers into her slippery pussy with a suddenness that made her gasp and then groan again.

He continued to spank her with one hand while fucking her with the other. Each time his hand smacked against her flesh, she tightened around his fingers. Harry's breathing grew erratic as her wet, sucking pussy pulled at the thrusting digits and he pulled his hand from her as abruptly as he had entered.

Shocked by the withdrawal, she turned her head and saw him pull a condom from a drawer next to the sink.

"Dominic stocked your kitchen too?" she managed to croak.

Harry gave more of a groan than a laugh. "No. That was me."

"Really?" Beth's voice was steadier. When Harry wasn't touching her, she could actually speak somewhat coherently. "Most people...um, *eat* in their kitchens."

"It's my junk drawer," he explained, his voice still rough as he rolled on the condom. "I have everything in there." As she opened her mouth to respond, his hands found her ass again and Beth instantly forgot what she was going to say.

Drawing her hips toward him, Harry plunged into her, filling her completely with a single thrust. Beth pressed her forehead against the hard surface of the island, panting, feeling her body adjust to his invasion and stretch around his cock. *It's amazing,* she thought dazedly, *how he seems to fit me perfectly.*

Harry began to stroke in and out, and all thoughts left her mind, shoved out by rushing sensation as he pounded against her, his hard thrusts moving her body against the smooth stone of the island. His roughness drove Beth higher and her vulnerable position, stretched across the marble, feet unable to touch the floor, excited her even more.

He gripped his fingers deep into the flesh of her hips, pulling her against him with each plunge, and her ass burned pleasurably with the heat of his spanking. She came hard, screaming his name, muscles squeezing brutally around his cock. His thrusts came faster, rougher, more erratically as he lost control and exploded into orgasm, his release jerking from him in endless shudders.

Beth felt Harry's hand rest against her back briefly before he groaned and pulled out. Feeling empty without his hard cock filling her, Beth sighed soundlessly, her cheek resting against the marble and her breath fogging the glossy surface.

Wrapping his hands around her lower ribs, he gently pulled her away from the island and set her carefully on her feet, keeping his hands against her until he was sure she was steady.

He dropped a kiss on her shoulder and Beth turned to look at him, smiling at him a little shakily. *This man could be dangerous to my peace of mind*, she thought, and her smile faltered. Watching her seriously, Harry leaned over to kiss her so softly, so gently, that it almost made her cry.

"I'll be fine. I just live a few blocks from here," she explained for the fiftieth time. She wasn't sure if she should be charmed or exasperated by the stubborn set of Harry's mouth.

"I'll walk you. Charlie opened the gym this morning, so I'm free."

Beth shrugged, giving in. When she thought about it, she was happy that their night together didn't have to end quite yet. Glancing down at herself, she made a face. She wasn't quite as excited about her outfit. She had pieced together the remains of her workout clothes and topped them off with an enormous hoodie borrowed from Harry to block the morning chill.

"I look like I don't have any shorts on," she commented, tucking the sweatshirt around her hips, only to have it slide toward her knees again. With a sigh, she let it go.

"You'll have to bring some clothes over next time," Harry told her. Beth gave him a sideways look, her heart leaping at the "next time". *I'm such a dork*, she thought. Shouldn't a twenty-four-year-old have enough experience to know a one-night stand from a…what? Longer stand?

"That was too fast, wasn't it?" Harry's words yanked her out of her contemplations. She tilted her head at him curiously and he continued. "I know we've just been out once—actually, we haven't been out at all—" He shook his head. "Whatever. I shouldn't have mentioned you bringing stuff over, should I?"

Beth blushed. "No, I...umm...it was..." *Nice,* she thought in exasperation. *Way to be coherent.*

Scowling, Harry crossed his arms over his chest. "I'm supposed to wait a couple days and then call you—I know that. And then I ask you out for next weekend or whenever and you tell me you're busy so I don't think you like me too much and then we end up going out *two* weekends from now—well, fuck that."

Dropping his arms, he stalked toward her, backing a wide-eyed Beth into the wall by his front door. "I want to see you tonight," he growled, bracing his hands against the wall and trapping her in the cage of his arms. "I already want you again and if you make me wait two *fucking* weeks before I can be inside you, I'm going to go insane." He dropped his head and kissed her hard.

When he finally pulled his head back, Beth sucked in a shaky breath. "Okay."

"Okay what?" he asked, the blue heat of his eyes burning into hers.

She swallowed. "I'll bring clothes with me the next time I come over."

"Tonight?" It was more of an order than a question but Beth didn't mind.

"Tonight," she agreed.

With a pacified grunt, Harry kissed her again and stepped back. He opened the door for Beth and she stepped out into the gym on shaky legs. *God, he's hot when he's bossy,* she thought. She gave a slow smile, starting down the stairs as Harry locked the door. Hot, bossy and very eager to see her again, she mused, her grin growing.

Harry caught up with her, tossing his arm around her shoulders as they weaved their way through the equipment and the early morning crowd.

"Morning, Charlie," Harry greeted him. "Everything okay?"

Charlie looked at the two of them, surprised, and then grinned. "Everything's great, boss. Hey, Beth. How're things?"

Blushing, Beth gave him an awkward wave. "Umm...fine?" she muttered and Harry laughed. She elbowed him in the stomach.

"Oof," he grunted, although he didn't lose his smirk. "Remind me to quit teaching you how to fight."

"You'll still be my coach, right?" Beth asked, his teasing reminding her of her concern. She would never have guessed it but she liked boxing—the training part of it, at least. It wasn't just a means to an end—or a means to a Harry— anymore.

His arm tightened around her in a hug. "Of course. You can't pay me though. I'll feel like a boxing ho if you do."

"If I don't pay you," she argued as they walked out into the early morning sunshine, "doesn't that make *me* the boxing ho?"

"Ah, the old 'boxing ho' conundrum." Harry nodded sagely. "Only one way to settle this."

"What's that?" Beth asked.

"In the ring."

She snorted. "Okay. I'll win."

Raising his eyebrows, Harry said, "Think so, do you?"

"Well, duh. You can't hit a girl." She grinned at him triumphantly.

"Right." Harry thought for a second. "Then there's only one *other* way to settle this."

"Yeah, I know where this is—"

"In bed."

"You'll win there," she told him.

He looked pleased. "You think so?"

"Of course." Beth blushed but pressed on. "Even after one night, we both know you have the upper...hand."

Harry's eyes blazed at that. With a twist of his body, he had her pressed against the brick wall of an old house and was kissing her. Arousal was instant, shocking her with its intensity. Beth wrapped her hands around the back of his skull and kissed him back—hard.

With a groan, he raised his head, panting. "Fuck," he gritted out. "Any more of that and we'll be giving the kiddies walking to school an x-rated show."

Beth just stared at him, dazed by the desire that still ran hot beneath her skin. It was as if her body was a stranger's, with powerful, unfamiliar emotions and needs.

"You okay?" Harry asked, peering at her closely.

She gave herself a shake. "Sure," she said, pasting on a casual smile. "Come on, if I don't get home to change I'll never make my bus."

"I'll drive you to work," he offered but Beth shook her head.

"I can still make it. As long as you don't...distract me," she told him with a teasing smile. "See?" She pointed. "There's my building."

Harry followed Beth up the three flights of stairs to her apartment. Although he was preoccupied by the sway of her shapely ass as she climbed the steps in front of him, he still noticed details about her building, none of which made him happy.

"Half of the light bulbs are out," he grumbled, eyeing the dim corners of the hallway. He turned to see Beth struggling to turn her key in the lock. "Here," he told her, shouldering her aside. "Let me do that.

"The door to the building was wide open," he complained, fiddling with the key until he heard the lock click. "Anyone can come in."

"Thanks," she told him when he held the door open for her. "Yeah, the landlord isn't very good about getting things fixed and it's an older building, so everything is always breaking. The rent's cheap though." She stepped over a white envelope on the floor as she walked into the apartment. "Come on in."

Harry closed the door and turned the deadbolt. Her apartment was…interesting, he decided, glancing around. He was used to the exposed ductwork and open spaces of his loft. Her place had small rooms painted funky colors, battered wood floors and a general feeling of tattered corners and lopsidedness, as if everything had settled unevenly over time. It seemed cozy and comfortable enough but the security sucked.

Bending over to pick the card off the floor, he glanced at the front of the envelope. It just said "BETH" in printed, block letters.

"You have a letter," he called out. She had disappeared while he was checking out her apartment.

"It's just a card from the mystery man. I get one every day," she yelled back. Harry followed the sound of her voice to the bathroom, which was as small and ancient as the rest of the place. She was adjusting the spray on the shower in her shorts and torn tank top, which was almost enough to distract him from the card he held. Almost.

"Mind if I open it?" Harry asked, turning the envelope over.

She shrugged. "Sure. It's always the same thing though, so don't expect anything too exciting."

He ran his thumb beneath the flap, tearing the envelope as he opened it. It was a greeting card with a photo of two lovers walking on the beach. Harry made a face.

"I know—my secret admirer has really bad taste, doesn't he? Although the flowers were pretty enough, I guess," she admitted.

"Flowers?" Harry looked up from the card.

"Yeah—they were delivered to me at work." She glanced over her shoulder at him. "It's not a big deal—I don't even know who this guy is. It's not like I'm ever going to date him or anything."

On the inside of the card was a printed verse, syrupy and rhyming. Underneath, in the same block letters as those on the envelope, was written, "WE WERE MEANT TO BE TOGETHER." There was no signature.

"I don't like this." Harry tossed the card next to the sink. "Have you reported this guy to the police?"

Beth looked at him quizzically. "Why? He sends me cards. That's not illegal."

Crossing his arms over his chest, Harry corrected, "No, he *brings* you cards. To your extremely unsecure apartment, where you live alone."

"Cap'n," she soothed. "It's fine. He's just a lonely, shy guy with a crush." She pulled her tank top over her head and tossed it away. "Now, are you going to wash my back or not?"

Although unconvinced, Harry was distracted as Beth stripped off the rest of her clothes and stepped into the shower with a come-hither look over her shoulder.

"I'd rather wash your front," he told her, his voice suddenly raspy.

"Well, get in here then," she ordered and he was quick to obey. He'd do something about this secret admirer of hers after their shower, he decided, yanking his shirt over his head.

Chapter Five

ဆာ

Sheri made a beeline to Beth's desk as soon as she arrived at Anchor Paper, blurry-eyed but glowing.

"My God," Sheri sighed. "I can tell you had a disgusting amount of fabulous sex just by looking at you."

"Why don't you say that just a little louder — I don't think everyone in the warehouse heard." Beth tried to look stern but ruined it with a huge, sappy grin. "And it was tons of very, very, very fabulous sex."

Sheri rolled her eyes but leaned in closer, eager for details.

"I'm not going to give you the play-by-play," Beth scolded. "Let's just say it was amazing and leave it at that."

"Mmm-hmmm." Sheri looked skeptical. "And how do *you*, Miss I've-Only-Had-One-Other-Lover-In-My-Entire-Life, know what amazing sex is?"

"Well, there were the multiple orgasms and the have-to-have-it-now sex in the kitchen and then in the shower — Hey!" Beth cut her defensive rant short when she saw Sheri's smug expression. "You're trying to get the details out of me through insults, you sneaky weasel!"

Sheri grinned and shrugged. "It was worth a try. Kitchen and shower in one night, huh?"

"Well," Beth tried unsuccessfully to force down a blush, "it was *all* night. And this morning."

"You stayed the night?" Sheri hooted. "Our sweet little almost-virgin has fallen with a vengeance!"

Since she definitely knew she had fallen, and dangerously fast, Beth could only shrug.

"What's he like—besides the sex, I mean? Or did that even come up?" Sheri asked, leaning on the high edge of the reception desk where Beth sat.

"Of course it came up—I was there all night and we had to talk a *little*, didn't we?" Beth answered indignantly.

"Hah. You'd be surprised how little talking is required." Sheri smirked, gesturing for her to continue. "So what's he like?"

"Nice." *Okay, that sounded lame,* Beth thought, and tried again. "Protective. Sweet. Commanding." On the last one, she blushed even hotter. "Hot. Ex-Army. Smart. Funny. Hot. Did I miss anything?"

"I think you covered all possible attributes of a dream man, some twice. Now elaborate." Sheri fixed her with a stern glare.

Beth sat back in her chair, her eyes dreamy. "Well, he insisted on walking me home this morning before work. I didn't have any clothes other than what I had on last night to work out in and those were a little...damaged." She didn't meet Sheri's eyes when the other woman snorted with laughter.

"*Anyway,*" Beth stretched the word out. "He waited while I showered—okay, so he helped me shower." Her blush was not going away any time soon. "And then he was determined that he was going to walk me to the bus stop, even though I told him that I was perfectly safe at seven in the morning." Beth knew her smile was positively fatuous as she remembered the goodbye kiss he had given her when her bus had pulled up.

"Wow." Sheri's face had softened. "I do love a protective guy—as long as he's not crazy about it. Good for you, Beth—you saw the hill, you took the hill, in keeping with the military theme."

"I did, didn't I?" Beth was still a little awed by the success of her plan. Never in her wildest dreams had she thought that the dreamy gym guy she had basically been stalking would take her across his desk in his office and in his bed and on his floor and in his kitchen and in her shower—

She quickly broke off her line of thoughts when heat spread across her lower belly and her pussy dampened.

There was a whole day of work to get through before she could do Harry—*see* Harry, she corrected herself firmly—and agitating her already-buzzing hormones was not going to help.

Sighing, Beth glanced at her watch. Was eight-fifteen too early to call him? Probably, she decided, and blew out a resigned breath. It was definitely going to be a long day.

He couldn't concentrate. A stack of bills waited in his office but Harry wrapped his hands and pulled on his gloves instead. He headed for a heavy bag, forcibly keeping his thoughts away from Beth. His cock throbbed, hard and insistent, and thinking about her—the way she had looked during her last training session as she listened intently to him while he corrected her technique, her arms crossed beneath her breasts, pushing them upward, her bellybutton peeking out from under her tiny shirt—

He ripped his mind away.

Thinking about how she had looked in bed was worse— her expression as she came, her rosy nipples, swollen from his mouth's attention, his pink handprint on her ass—

Harry groaned. Pressing his gloved hands against either side of the punching bag, he leaned his forehead on the cool leather and squeezed his eyes closed. What was wrong with him? If he didn't get a grip on himself, he was going to come in his pants.

Glancing up, he saw Dominic eyeing him and laughing. Well, shit. Grimly, Harry began to hit the bag, concentrating on each strike, knowing that everyone in the gym was watching, amused, aware of just how horny, hard and desperate he really was.

Beth actually ended up working out that evening. Harry was training a wiry, middle-aged man when she arrived at the gym. Harry grinned at her when he saw her, a wicked, smoldering curve of his mouth that, even all the way across the gym, prickled her skin with heat. Simmering with a day's worth of sexual frustration, Beth decided that, since another hot bout of sex with Harry would have to wait, she might as well spend that time hitting something.

She watched him as she wrapped her hands, her eyes fixed on the way his t-shirt sleeves were stretched around his biceps. Harry was holding the heavy bag steady for his client's punches, watching the man closely and making an occasional comment that Beth couldn't hear. Every so often, Harry's gaze would flick up to find her.

"You two wanna get a room?" An amused voice yanked Beth's attention off Harry. Dominic was grinning at her.

"We're nowhere near each other," Beth protested, blinking innocently.

Dominic snorted. "You don't have to be. Those looks you're giving each other are about to set the gym on fire." He glanced down and grimaced. "What the hell did you do to your hands?"

"What?" Beth looked down at her wrapped palms. Sure, they didn't look *exactly* like when Harry had wrapped them for her but they weren't that bad, were they?

"Here, give me one." Dominic unwound the offending wraps and started again. "Watch me."

It was much easier to concentrate when Dominic was the one touching her instead of Harry. Even though Dom was a good-looking guy, Beth mused, he did nothing for her. Harry, on the other hand...just the thought of him made her palms sweat under the black wraps.

"Done." Dominic, unaware that she had just dissected his lack of sex appeal in her thoughts, looked pleased with himself as he fastened the Velcro on her left wrist.

"Thank you," Beth told him, admiring his neat wrapping job. She really had to learn how to do that, she decided.

"Anything for you, cookie girl," he said, patting the top of her head and ambling away to watch two men sparring in the ring.

With a quick glance at Harry, who was pulling on a pair of punching mitts, Beth grabbed a jump rope. Although she still tended to end up tangled in the rope, she was getting better, she realized. Feeling cocky, she threw in a crossover and immediately tripped. *Better stick to the basics*, she decided with a sigh, swinging the rope over her head to start again.

She was working on the speed bag when Harry's client left the gym. Beth twisted her head around to see Harry leaning against the front desk, chatting with Charlie. The speed bag, still in motion from her last hit, swung forward to smack Beth on her temple. She rubbed the spot as she bounced over to Harry.

"Hi," she chirped, leaning into his side for a quick press of her sweaty body against his. Harry's hand rested against her lower back and then skimmed up under her shirt, sliding easily on her hot, slippery skin.

"How was your workout?" he asked, smiling down at her.

"Great! I could totally kick your ass now." She put on her best tough face and took a fighter's stance but Harry just laughed and hugged her against his side.

"Do you want to go on a real date tonight?" he asked. "Seeing as we've never really been anywhere together except here?" The swing of his arm took in the gym and his loft above.

72

"Actually..." Beth thought of how to phrase it so she didn't sound like a *complete* slut. "I'm kind of sweaty and...hmmm...well, wired..."

Harry grinned in total understanding, lifting her a little off the ground as he turned toward the back wall and the stairs that led to his apartment. She squeaked and grabbed his arm. Beth didn't know if she would ever get used to how easily he could pick her up.

He let her walk in front of him to the stairs and she twitched her hips from side to side, just to drive him crazy. The back of her t-shirt was wet from sweat, clinging to her sports bra, and she could feel the cool air against the damp strip of skin peeking between her shirt and the top of her waistband.

As they neared the top of the stairs, Harry crowded against her, hurrying her steps. She laughed softly at his urgency, slowing her steps just to make him frantic. With a growl that only Beth heard, he used his body to herd her up the stairs and slammed the door to his loft open. Lifting her with a hard arm around her waist, he carried her inside.

Beth shrieked with laughter as her feet left the ground. She wriggled against him, loving the thick press of his erection against her ass. Groaning, Harry tightened his arm, increasing the pressure until she couldn't stand it anymore.

"Please, Harry," she moaned. The room flipped as he spun her around and tossed her over his shoulder in one movement. For a moment, she struggled to recover her breath in her upside-down state, bouncing against his back as Harry strode to the bedroom. Quickly realizing her prime position, Beth took full advantage and reached down to squeeze the firm globes of his buttocks. Harry retaliated with a swat across her ass.

Shivering with the tingles of pleasure that radiated from her upturned bottom, Beth squeezed again, digging her fingertips into the muscles that clenched beneath her greedy hands. Instead of giving her another spank, Harry tossed her onto the bed. She landed, bounced up and settled again on the mattress.

Harry stood above her, yanking his t-shirt over his head while toeing off his shoes. He pushed his pants and underwear down his legs, his socks coming off as well, and was totally naked before the bed stopped moving from Beth's airborne landing.

Her eyes were drawn to the deep red of his erection, standing stiff and eager against his stomach, and her mouth watered. She sat up abruptly, reaching for the hem of her shirt so she could pull it off, wanting to be as completely naked as he was, but Harry captured her wrists and crowded her back until she was lying flat again, staring up at him.

Beth was breathing in short pants, already wet and ready for him just from being tossed on the bed—that and seeing his naked body, his thick cock, his obvious eagerness for her. Shifting her hips, she let her legs fall open, frustrated by her clothes that blocked his entrance.

Still holding her wrists firmly, Harry pulled her arms to her sides and pinned them against the bed. He kneed his way in between her legs and leaned over her, his head lowering toward the small slice of exposed belly that had been teasing him for the past hour. Nuzzling her shirt higher, he licked her sweat-salted skin and darted into her bellybutton with his tongue, making Beth gasp as her stomach muscles contracted.

Moisture slid out of her body, darkening the fabric between her legs. Beth could smell herself, a mixture of exertion and arousal, of sweat and female heat. Pulling her hands above her head, Harry pressed her wrists in warning before releasing her.

"Stay or I'll tie you," he commanded and her pussy muscles spasmed at his rough order.

"Yes sir," she answered, her voice just as thick as his. Harry froze, his pupils dilating until all Beth could see of his irises was a faint ring of blue around deep, black pools.

"Fuck," he muttered hoarsely, yanking her shirt up over her head and taking her sports bra with it, leaving both tangled around her forearms. "I almost came when you called me that."

"You liked it...*sir*?" Beth's voice was a kitten purr. She liked being helpless with Harry but she also liked the power she wielded with her docility.

"Yeah. This is how much I liked it," Harry gritted, his eyes glittering as he pressed his inflamed cock against her fabric-guarded pussy, grinding against her heat and wetness. She whimpered, desperate to be filled with his turgid flesh, and pushed back against him, increasing the pressure until she thought she would explode.

He kissed her almost violently, his mouth taking hers, his invading tongue thrusting between her lips, teeth clashing together. As he nipped at her lips, his fingers slicked over her breasts, pinching the nipples into even harder points, tugging on the tips until Beth was almost sobbing with need, her hips pressing against his, her body begging him to enter her.

Instead, Harry pulled away. Beth instantly missed the throbbing pressure of his erection against her swollen, weeping folds. She tried to follow him with her hips but he held her still with one hand while the other reached to open the nightstand drawer.

"You have condoms everywhere," Beth teased breathlessly as he smoothed the protection over his rigid cock.

"You complaining?" he growled.

She opened her mouth, ready with a joking response, but was distracted when Harry lowered his head to her breast and sucked the tight nipple into his mouth. He played with it gently, rolling and sucking on the tip before using his teeth to tug firmly, sending ripples of sharp pleasure through her stomach and between her legs. Back arching, Beth moaned, all sensation centered on her wet nipple as Harry blew a soft stream of air on it, puckering the hard bud even more tightly.

As Harry moved to her other breast, Beth's head tossed restlessly. "Please..." she begged.

"Please what?" Harry's words blew another puff of air against her wet nipple, making her twist against the bed.

"Please fuck me!" Beth wailed, her hips arching into empty air, searching for his cock.

"Please fuck me...what?" he growled, sliding her workout pants down past her hips and over her legs. He knelt between her calves and tugged her socks off, massaging her feet with his wickedly knowing hands as he waited for her answer.

"Sir! Please fuck me, sir!" At her words, Harry was between her legs, shoving them apart, wider and wider, until she felt the pulling stretch in her thighs, sliding his cock into her welcoming heat, groaning at the squeezing-tight grip of her pussy. With his first plunge, he slid his hand between their bodies and rubbed his thick thumb against her clit, pinching the stiff, slippery nub of flesh and then tugging gently, sending Beth into a fierce orgasm that bowed her off the bed as she screamed her release.

Harry pulled out, his cock rock-hard and shiny with her juices, and flipped Beth over onto her stomach. Her body was soft and malleable after her climax and he tugged her onto her hands and knees with a steely arm around her waist. She obeyed and he placed a wide hand on her upper back, pressing her shoulders back to the bed.

Resting her head against her folded arms, her ass raised high, Beth felt tension return to her body—a mixture of nervousness and anticipation and arousal twisting together until she quivered against the calloused hand stroking her spine.

Kneeling behind her, Harry massaged her bottom with both hands, pulling the cheeks apart until Beth felt the cool air touch her pussy lips, still wet and swollen, and her clenching anus. He pushed her knees farther apart with his hair-roughened thighs, opening her even more until she felt totally exposed, completely vulnerable. A trickle of moisture slipped from her pussy to slide down her thigh. She hid her face in her arms, embarrassed by her obvious excitement at being spread open to him like this, being utterly under his control. She knew he saw the evidence of her arousal because he growled, a hot, excited sound, and stroked through the wetness with two fingers.

Without warning, Harry plunged those fingers into her pussy and her body welcomed him eagerly, tightening around the digits as he withdrew. He drew the wetness of her body back toward her puckered virgin hole, teasing it with a circling fingertip. Her hips pushed back at him, needing more, and he nudged at the opening, prodding gently until he had gained entrance, pressing his thick, slippery finger into her past the first knuckle and then the second. His other hand teased her clit, circling the swollen flesh with the lightest touch until it was standing at attention, begging for a harder contact.

Beth's body shook at the multiple sensations, the gentle attention to her clit, the invading digit sliding in and out of her ass. His first finger was joined by a second. The tight pinch of pain as he pushed past the initial resistance quickly faded to a burning stretch and then warmed to a hot, spreading pleasure. Beth liked the feeling of his fingers sliding in and out of her — liked it more than she expected. She wanted to feel his cock pressing into her there, filling her, taking her in a way she had never been taken.

Harry's breath hissed through his teeth as Beth pushed back against his fingers, taking them deep into her body.

"God, you are so hot and tight," he rasped. "Just the thought of being inside you is almost enough to make me come."

As he pulled his fingers free of her clinging flesh, Beth moaned at the withdrawal, protesting the needy emptiness of her body. She heard Harry moving around but Beth's lust-clouded mind couldn't figure out what he was doing until she felt the cool lube squeeze into her. Her hips bucked up at the sensation, meeting his fingers as they reentered her, sliding in easily, retreating too soon.

The slick, prodding head of his cock nudged at her entrance and Beth's nervousness, muffled by her pounding arousal, returned in a rush. Harry must have felt her stiffen, since he rubbed a soothing hand over one round cheek, sliding his fingers around to her belly and lower to brush against her clit. She jerked as his touch triggered a flash of pleasure and the movement pushed her against the blunt tip of his cock. With a low groan, Harry pressed into her, slowly but inexorably stretching her around his erection.

Beth had expected pain but she hadn't expected the drugging pleasure that swept over her as he filled her, the overwhelming sense of being taken, of being possessed by this man. The unfamiliar sensations swirling through her tangled with the twists of pleasure shooting from her clit as Harry played with her and another climax roared through her body, tightening her muscles around him just as he pressed the final inch of his cock deep into her ass. The quakes of her orgasm seized her, shocking her with their blinding intensity, as he thrust deep and hard, bracing his arms against the bed for leverage, his chest slick against her quivering back.

The feeling was intense—so intense that the tiniest corner of Harry's brain, the only part not overwhelmed with the nerve-frying ecstasy of plunging into the burning squeeze of Beth's ass, was totally freaked out. Tunneling deep into her back passage, he felt the clamp of her body close around his cock, gripping him so tightly that he couldn't breathe, couldn't think—he could just pump in and out of the hot, fist-like clutch of her ass. Thrusting faster, harder, the pleasure built, exploded, shooting hot lines of sensation along his spine, blanking his brain until there was only the feeling radiating from his cock as jets of release were yanked out of him.

With a final groan, he collapsed, somehow dredging up the presence of mind to topple sideways, pulling Beth with him so he didn't crush her beneath his weight. She was shaking and making small noises that took his pleasure-softened brain a minute to figure out.

"Shit—are you crying? What's wrong?" Panicked, he pulled free of her body, his partially hard erection reluctantly leaving her ass. Harry heard her breath catch as he slid out of her and his stomach clenched. He had been too rough—he hadn't been able to control himself. Wrapping an arm beneath her breasts, he pulled her back against his chest, stroking anything he could reach—her arm, her stomach, her hair and wet cheek. "Baby, did I hurt you?"

Beth shook her head, hiding her face with her hair.

"Talk to me, sweetie—tell me what's wrong." His stomach twisted in regret. He had been a greedy bastard to take her like that—wrapped up in his own pleasure. Petting her hair gently, he stroked the strands away from her cheek and tried to see her expression.

"Y-you didn't hurt me," she hiccupped. "Well, a little, but it didn't matter—I mean, I wasn't thinking about the pain." Harry felt her cheek heat against his hand and knew that she was blushing. "I don't know what's wrong with me...it was just...overwhelming. But I'm okay, really."

Now *she* was patting *him* soothingly on his arm. His stomach relaxed a little.

"I know what you mean," he admitted, playing with her hair. Harry loved how the strands looked colorless when he held them up one at a time but all together they blended into ten different shades of blonde. "It's pretty wild, isn't it—us, I mean."

"Yeah," she sighed. "I've never experienced anything like it before." Beth whipped her head around to look at him in a panic. "Wait—I didn't mean that in the girly way—I mean, the 'I've never felt this way before' way. I know we just met and it could just be a sex thing and—"

Laughing, Harry put his hand over her mouth. "I know, I know—I promise not to call you a girl!" Her eyes glared at him over the edge of his hand, making him laugh again. "It's more than just a sex thing. It's something big—I'm not sure what but I've had plenty of 'sex things' and I've never felt anything like this before. This was..." He blew out a breath. "Intense."

Beth nodded and he pulled his hand away.

"Scary," she added gravely.

"Very." Despite his sober tone, a smile tugged at his mouth. Beth answered with a grin that squeezed his heart.

After a shower that turned into a soapy free-for-all, Beth and Harry curled together in his bed, arms and legs and fingers tangled together, trying to touch as much of each other's skin as possible. The sun had disappeared and the room was dark, except for the faint glow of the streetlights peeking through the edges of the blinds.

"Can I ask you a question?" Beth asked as she idly played with his hair.

"Whenever someone asks that, you know the question is going to be good," Harry said wryly.

"Is that a no?"

"Of course not. If I said no, I'd be dying of curiosity, wanting to know what you were going to ask. Fire away, although I reserve the right to be evasive." His hand floated down her spine, feeling the bump of each vertebra.

"Have you ever...well, had that done to you?" Beth asked in a rush, as if she was trying to get the words out before her darkness-inspired bravery could slip away.

"Had *what* done?" he questioned, although he had a pretty good idea what she was asking. Harry knew he was stalling for time, time he needed to decide what he was going to tell her.

What the hell, he might as well be honest. If it freaked her out, it was better that he knew that now.

"You know..." Her voice trailed away. Even without seeing her, Harry knew that she was blushing. "Has anyone ever had you...here?" Her hand trailed over his hip and brushed shyly against his buttock.

"A man, you mean?"

He felt her shrug. "Well, a man, or a woman with...extra equipment."

"Isn't a woman with extra equipment called a man?" he teased and she smacked him in the arm. Harry yelped—she had good aim in the dark. Maybe she didn't need any more boxing lessons. She was pretty dangerous as is.

"Okay, okay," he surrendered. "The answer to your question is no."

"But?"

"What do you mean, 'but'?"

"You just sounded like you weren't finished. Like you were going to say 'no, but...'" she pressed.

"Huh." He was quiet for a moment. "You're pretty perceptive."

After another short silence, Harry continued. "I've never had sex with a man but there was this one guy. We were in the same unit in Afghanistan." He laughed a little, softly. "A meaner son of a bitch you'd never want to meet." Despite his words, he was smiling a little.

"Smart little bastard too. There was something about that kid..." Harry was quiet for so long that Beth must have thought he had drifted off to sleep because she poked him.

"What?" he yelped. "Woman, I'm going to have more bruises from sleeping with you than I get sparring with Dominic."

"Finish the story," she demanded. "You're killing me with curiosity here."

"Not much to finish. Nothing happened, but…well, we got really close. I mean, you connect with everyone in your unit, but Ky and I—we were really tight."

"Ky? Short for Kyle?"

"Malachi."

The way he said the name stirred up a few wisps of jealousy in Beth toward this man that Harry had liked so much. Surprisingly, arousal also curled low in her belly at the thought of the two soldiers, simmering sexual tension building between them… *Whoa, getting a little pervy here*, Beth thought, cutting off the mental image of Harry and the other man.

"So no action in the desert?" she asked, trying to keep her voice light.

"No. I don't think he had any idea what I was thinking. Plus there's no privacy there. Not that anything would have happened anyway. It was just a feeling—I don't know why I'm telling you all of this," Harry finished with an embarrassed laugh.

Beth found his face in the dark and stroked along his stubbly jaw. "I'm glad you did. In fact," she admitted, embarrassment for embarrassment, "I thought it was kind of hot." Although she blushed fiery red, she pushed through to boldness and slid her leg on top of his, opening herself against him and turning her hip so he could feel her wetness against the top of his hard-muscled thigh.

Harry jumped at the contact and she was close enough to his groin to feel his cock thicken and swell, electrified by her arousal. They fed off each other's excitement, lust building lust, heat flaming against heat. His hardness made her wet and her liquid heat made him even harder. *A perfect match*, she decided smugly.

As Harry rolled her over to her back—his weight pressing her into the bed—that was her last coherent thought for a while.

Chapter Six

୭

Beth sketched from memory, drawing in the lines of Harry's body that she was learning by sight and touch. The picture quickly took a rough shape—Harry in his loft, leaning back against his kitchen counter, his palms braced behind him, stretching the muscles across his chest and shoulders into vivid relief.

"That's really good," the rotund man sitting in the bus seat behind her commented, his comb-over flopping forward as he peered over Beth's shoulder.

"Thanks," she said, her pencil still moving.

"Your boyfriend?" the man asked.

"Something like that," she said, glancing back at him, smiling a little.

The stranger gave her a friendly pat on the shoulder. "Well, good for you," he told her, sitting back. "He's very good-looking."

He certainly is, Beth thought dreamily, tracing the outlines on her drawing with a light fingertip. The bus lurched to a stop and she looked up, startled to realize that she was already at her stop. Flipping her sketchbook closed, she snatched up her purse and hopped off the bus.

"Bye, Ed," she tossed over her shoulder with a grin.

Harry was waiting for her.

"You know that I can see the gym from here," she told him, hiding a goofy smile at the sight of him. Bouncing over to him, she gave him a quick, smacking kiss. Harry caught her around the waist and pulled her to him, turning it into a real embrace.

83

She pulled away, flushed and aroused.

"Are you here to make sure I walk the half-block to the gym safely?" she teased, still breathless.

Tossing an arm around her shoulders, Harry pulled her into his side. "Are you coming in today then?" he asked.

"Just to say hi," she told him. "Thought my body could use a break."

At Harry's raised eyebrow, she laughed and shook her head. "A break from working out," she clarified. "Although we must burn a ton of calories when we…umm." She glanced around, remembering a little late that they were in public.

He grinned at her. "Speaking of 'umm', how about we go out tonight?"

"Is that a euphemism?" she asked suspiciously.

Laughing, he squeezed her against his side and kissed her nose. "No, no euphemisms. Just standard, everyday date that we've never been on. You know, some food, some drink, maybe some entertainment?"

Beth felt a surge of excitement. "I'd love that," she admitted, bouncing a little in anticipation. "Pick me up at eight—I'm going home to get ready."

"Hang on." Harry caught her hand and reeled her back in. "I'll walk you."

Rolling her eyes, Beth told him, "You don't have to do that, you know—I'm not five."

"Still getting those notes?"

She nodded reluctantly.

"Yeah, I'm walking you home." Harry tucked her back into his side.

"Thanks for watching the desk tonight, Dom," Harry said, slapping the other man on the shoulder affectionately.

"Happy to help," Dominic grinned. "I'm just amazed you got up the balls to actually ask her out. Things are good then?"

Ignoring the slam on his manhood, Harry gave an affirmative shrug. "Yeah. Pretty damn great, actually."

"Figured that by the way you're wandering around here with that silly-ass grin," Dominic smirked. "Remember this the next time you decide to ignore my advice."

In too good a mood to take the bait, Harry just shook his head and headed for the door. As he drove the few blocks to Beth's building, he realized that he was smiling. *Damn*, he thought, glancing in the rearview mirror, *maybe Dominic's right about my constant, silly-ass grin.*

He was happy, Harry realized. Really happy. The only problem with the whole situation was that the more time he spent with Beth, the more he liked her. And the more he liked her, the more he worried about her. Pulling up to her building, he glared at the front door, propped open as usual.

He parked and went in, taking the stairs three at a time. As he headed toward her apartment door, he made a mental note to buy light bulbs. If the landlord wasn't going to replace the burned-out bulbs in her hallway, then Harry would, he decided. It wouldn't improve the lax security of her building very much, he knew, but at least it would help his peace of mind a little until he could get her to move to his loft.

Startled by the thought, Harry froze in place, staring at Beth's door. Was he actually considering having her move in with him? Was he nuts? He had only known her for a few weeks. This was their first actual go-out-and-do-something date. If he mentioned moving in together this early on, he was going to freak her out so much she'd run from him screaming.

On the other hand, if he had to think about her creepy admirer roaming freely in her poorly lit hallway too much longer, he was going to lose it.

Harry groaned, scrubbing his hands over his face. *Stop worrying*, he ordered his brain. He'd find a way to get her out of this building and into his. Somehow.

Beth opened the door at his knock and stared. Harry was gorgeous in whatever he wore—sweatpants, shorts, absolutely nothing—but tonight he was just...amazing. She was almost drooling. It was just dress pants and a button-down shirt, but still. With a shake of her head, she stepped back so Harry could come in.

"God, you look beautiful," he rasped, cupping her face in his hands so he could kiss her. She wriggled with pleasure at the compliment and then forgot everything as his mouth found hers.

Beth was dizzy by the time he raised his head.

"We should go," Harry rasped without dropping his hands. His eyes were lit with a hot, blue light, mesmerizing Beth. She couldn't look away.

"I'll get my purse," she breathed, not moving.

He closed the distance between them, his mouth just millimeters from hers when he stopped himself and pulled away, shaking his head.

"No," he stated firmly. "I promised you an actual date tonight."

Giving him a sultry smile, she said, "I wouldn't mind if you broke that promise."

He took a half step toward her before catching himself. "Nope, we're actually going to do this. Grab your purse and let's get out of here before I change my mind." He turned her in the direction of the door and gave her a light smack on her bottom.

Beth made a face at him over her shoulder. "Fine, fine."

They made it into the hallway without any other delays. As Beth locked the door, Harry scowled again at the useless light bulbs dotting the ceiling.

"Have you gotten any more cards?" he asked.

"Sure," she said, dropping her keys into her bag with a little more attention than was warranted.

"What does that mean?" Harry must have caught an uneasy note in her voice.

She tried to blink at him innocently. "The cards come every day," she told him, not mentioning the fact that today's card had been different—and a little scary. The card itself had been similar to the others, with a picture on the front of a moony pair of lovers lit by the glow of a fireplace, and a rhyming, preprinted verse on the inside. What had been done to it was the frightening part. Harry was protective enough as it was—if he saw the card, with the woman's face removed with a hole-punch and a single word, "WHORE", scribbled on the inside, he wouldn't let her out of his sight without an armed guard.

"Uh-huh," he grunted, still eyeing her suspiciously.

As they descended the stairs, Beth hooked her hand in the crook of his arm, deciding that a change of subject might be wise. "Who's watching the gym?"

"Dominic. It's his contribution to the cause." He grinned.

Looking at him curiously, she asked, "What cause is that?"

"Us," he answered. "You're the first girl I've dated who he actually likes."

She snorted. "That's just because I brought him cookies."

"No," Harry disagreed, holding the passenger-side door of his SUV open for her. Despite the step up into the vehicle and Beth's short skirt, she managed to swing herself into the seat without exposing too much skin. Proud of her accomplishment, she smoothed her skirt over her thighs and looked up at Harry, who was still holding the door open, staring as her hands straightened the silky fabric over her legs.

Clearing his throat, he shut the door and circled around to the driver's seat.

"He likes you because you're nice," he continued, as if there had been no pause in their conversation.

Beth made a face. "Nice?" she repeated. It sounded so...boring.

Hearing the disappointed note in her voice, he turned his head to smile at her. "I meant nice in a good way," he clarified. "And I believe Dom also mentioned that you were smoking hot."

That sounded better, she decided. "Why didn't he like any of your other women?"

He frowned. "When you put it like that," he complained, "it sounds like I have a harem. And he didn't like them because they weren't very likeable."

"Really?" Beth asked, pleased.

He laughed. "Really."

"Huh." She pondered that for a moment. "Why did you go out with them then?"

Shrugging, he twisted the steering wheel into a turn. "Dominic thinks it was so I wouldn't get hurt."

Beth turned a laugh into a cough and he turned toward her.

"What?" he demanded, pretending to be offended although his eyes gleamed with humor.

"Nothing. Just the idea of Dominic as a touchy-feely, advice-giving gal-pal." She cocked her head. "So you're saying that I could hurt you? I'll have to remember that next time I have the gloves on," she teased.

The light in front of them turned yellow and then red. Letting the SUV roll into a gentle stop, Harry reached across and took her hand. "You could rip out my heart," he said seriously.

Her eyes widened at his words, fear and exhilaration sending her stomach into a dive. "Oh."

Beth's tiny-voiced response didn't seem to bother Harry. He just kissed her hand and returned it to her lap.

"So how was it?" Sheri asked.

Beth looked up from the card she held with a frown.

"That bad?" Sheri made a sympathetic face.

Blinking at her friend in confusion, Beth shook her head and smiled as the question finally registered. "Of course not—it was great. Dinner, wine bar, a midnight walk across the Millennium Bridge, back to his place..." Her smile widened and her eyes lost focus.

Sheri snapped her fingers in front of Beth's face. "Stay with me here, girl. Don't be drifting off into some sickeningly sweet memory just when you're getting to the good part. So you went back to his place..."

Laughing, Beth tossed a binder clip across her desk at Sheri, missing her target by a good two feet.

Sheri shook her head. "I would hate to see you in any kind of organized sport. So if it wasn't your man, what's up?"

"What do you mean?"

Rolling her eyes, Sheri leaned against the desk. "Whatever. Do I have to beat it out of you?"

Beth chewed her lower lip as she eyed her friend. It would be a relief to share this with someone, she decided, and held out the card.

"What's this?" Sheri asked, turning it over so she could see the front. "A cheesy card? And what did you get on it—jelly?"

Shaking her head, Beth told her, "I think it's red paint. Read the inside."

Sheri complied, her frown growing. "This is sick," she said, holding the card in two fingers like it was contaminated.

"I know," Beth said, relieved that she wasn't overreacting. "Someone slid it under my apartment door last night. All the others he brought during the day while I was at work."

"All the others?" Sheri repeated, her voice sharp. "How long has this freak been bugging you?"

Shrugging, Beth guessed, "A couple months maybe? They were always sweet before though, and harmless. Now it's like he hates me."

"Hmm," Sheri looked thoughtful. "Think he's seen your Army boy hanging around?"

"You're right—that's probably it." Beth shivered. "It's so creepy to think about someone watching me."

Sheri rolled her eyes. "Like smearing red paint all over a greeting card and writing disgusting, violent stuff about what he's going to do to you isn't creepy?" she asked incredulously. "Wake up, Beth—you have a full-blown, unstable, pissed-off stalker on your hands!"

Beth swallowed hard and nodded. "What should I do?"

"Tell your muscle man—he's a boxer, isn't he? Might as well use that to your advantage." Sheri gave a bloodthirsty grin at the thought.

Even before the words were out, Beth was shaking her head. "Nope. He's protective enough without a stalker lurking around. He'd handcuff me to him."

"Mmm, that sounds interesting," Sheri murmured, making Beth laugh despite her worry.

"Really," she said, sobering quickly. "He'd go nuts. What's option number two?"

Sheri shrugged. "So don't tell him. Just hang around him a lot. Think he'd mind?"

As she thought about the wild nights with Harry, a feline smile touched Beth's mouth. "I think he wouldn't mind at all," she purred.

"God, you're making me miss sex," Sheri groaned. "I'm off to see if someone will get freaky with me in the supply closet. Don't worry about Mr. Creep-tastic—just make an effort to never be alone. I'll walk you to your bus stop after work and then just keep soldier boy in bed the rest of the time. Got it?" Walking backward away from Beth's desk, she pointed a stern finger.

"Got it," Beth grinned. When put like that, this stalker thing could actually be fun.

Chapter Seven

ഔ

Beth wiped her sleeve across her forehead, mopping at the sweat that threatened to run into her eye and sting like hell. She had just finished a grueling workout and looked a mess.

It's worth it though, she thought, grimacing at her reflection in one of the mirrors that lined the wall. She might be red-faced, her skin gritty from drying salt, but her arms were starting to show definition—nothing too bulky, just a firm, rounded line along her shoulders and upper arms.

Harry had been coaching her on the free weights during her training sessions, demystifying the torturous equipment that filled the gym. It was hard to remember her first intimidating moments amid the heavy bags and grunting men. Now she bounced around, exchanging nods and smiles with the regulars and a few smart-ass quips with Dominic, feeling like she actually fit in.

Flexing a little in front of the mirror, she had to grin at her reflection. *Try to get me now, creep,* she thought, cocky in the safe confines of the gym. She was spending almost every night at Harry's loft and any stalker worries had retreated to the back of her mind.

The cards continued to arrive each day, scattered on the floor for her to find when she stopped by her apartment to check her mail or collect more clothes. She gathered them up quickly, shuffling them in with her other letters and bills, but Harry would give her a look—that you're-not-fooling-anyone eyebrow lift—and walk a little closer to her on the way back to his place.

Automatically her eyes searched the gym, finding him quickly. He was giving a tour to what looked like a new member, a chubby man with awkwardly new athletic shoes. Beth realized that she was smiling just from looking at Harry. He glanced up at that moment and winked at her before turning back to his new client.

Her stomach rolled in excitement and Beth laughed at herself for being so easy. Even after having been together constantly for almost a month, he could make her soaking wet with just a glance or the light touch of his palm against her shoulder blade. The memory of his hand on her skin brought another surge of desire flashing through her and she pressed her thighs together. Shaking her head at her infatuation, Beth headed for the front of the gym for a fresh towel.

"Hey, Dominic," she called out as she passed him. Busy doing squats, he just gave a red-faced grunt and nod in response. The front door swung open as she reached for a towel and Beth turned, mildly curious. She was starting to know the regulars, especially the evening and weekend crowds, and she craned around the towel rack to see who had just entered.

It was a stranger. The man wasn't very tall but he was built hard. The sleeves of his ratty Army t-shirt strained to cover his thick biceps. Beth could only see the black buzz-cut back of his head until he turned in a slow circle, obviously looking for someone.

When she saw his face, she almost fell over. Catching her balance on the rack, her towel dangling forgotten from her fingers, Beth just stared.

He was beautiful.

Harry was gorgeous, of course, but this man was...unworldly. His skin was the color of creamed coffee and his slanting cheekbones narrowed his eyes, which were shadowed by the longest lashes, so thick and dark that Beth noticed them from fifteen feet away. His full lips had a sulky twist that just made him that much hotter.

Completely blown away, it took a moment for Beth to realize that he was staring at her. Staring at her staring at him. She shook her head a little to clear it, although it didn't make the man any less outrageously pretty, and headed toward him.

"Looking for someone?" she asked, a friendly smile curling her lips as she approached.

"Yeah," he grunted, his expression remote. His eyes dismissed her, wandering away to scan the room again.

"Anyone in particular?" *Okay, he might be a beautiful, beautiful boy, but he's an awfully rude one too,* Beth thought.

"Yeah." The silence stretched and the man glanced at her again. "I can find him on my own. Off you go, Barbie." He turned completely away from her, leaving her gaping.

"Barbie?" she repeated, startled and a little flattered— with her short, round figure, comparisons to a Barbie doll were few and far between. "Do you really think I look like Barbie?"

"Are you still here?" Annoyance flooded his voice. "Fine. *I'll* leave." Shouldering the strap of his duffel bag, he weaved in between equipment and people. Beth found herself admiring his tight, denim-covered ass for a second before she caught herself. She shook her head—what a shame. Such a good-looking outside and such angry innards.

Harry, new member in tow, emerged from the locker room and Beth hurried over to them. Harry gave her a quick smile, resting an easy hand on her lower back.

"Do you have any questions?" he asked the chubby man with the glowing new shoes.

"Nope, looks great—can't wait to start," the man enthused, flushed and shiny. He shook Harry's hand and smiled at Beth before heading for the front door.

"I bet you can see those shoes from space," she murmured.

Harry laughed. "Blinding, aren't they? Oh well, they'll get dirty fast enough and then the astronauts will have to find their own way home." He wrapped an arm around her shoulders and squeezed her in a sideways hug. "'Sup, my sweaty sweet pea?" he asked cheerily and Beth wriggled a little as she remembered what she had wanted to tell him.

"There's a super-hot and really cranky guy looking for someone and he won't tell me who and I'm dying of curiosity!" Twisting around, Beth spotted the stranger and pointed. "There! Do you know him? He called me *Barbie*."

Harry snorted a laugh. "Barbie? I bet that—" He broke off suddenly when his gaze locked on the man maneuvering his large duffel around the equipment. "Well, shit-balls," he breathed. His arm dropped off Beth's shoulders as Harry strode toward the stranger.

"Pokey!" Harry called out, a grin lighting up his face. The other man's head jerked around and the duffel hit the floor as he met Harry halfway for a back-pounding hug.

"Pokey?" Beth muttered in disbelief. "What kind of name is 'Pokey'?"

She followed Harry, trying to be unobtrusive but still curious about the gorgeous, rude stranger. Pokey was actually smiling and even more beautiful, beaming up at Harry as they gripped each other's arms in the macho version of a hug.

"Hey, Captain Morris."

"Harry," he corrected with a little shove to Pokey's shoulder. "We're in the real world now. Here, I'm just Harry."

Nodding, Pokey kept silent and his eyes drifted over Harry's shoulder to a hovering Beth. Following the other man's gaze, Harry turned his head and saw her. He grabbed her hand and pulled her forward while Pokey's smile disappeared as if it had never existed.

"Beth, this is Malachi West. I told you about him. Ky, this is my girlfriend." Harry beamed at both of them, oblivious to their stunned expressions. Ky was the first to recover, his face smoothing into blankness as he gave her a cool nod.

Beth knew her mouth was hanging open, but couldn't help herself. This was Ky? *The* Ky? Staring at the expressionless

95

man in front of her, Beth realized that, now that the initial shock was passing, she could better understand Harry's feelings. Ky was so gorgeous that it would be hard *not* to lust after the man.

"Wait—you called him Pokey?" She asked the first question that leapt into her mind.

Harry laughed. "Yeah, one of the guys, J.T.—he was from Texas—he once said that Ky was meaner than a rattler that had been poked by a stick. 'Rattler poked by a stick' is a bit long for a nickname, so it got shortened."

"Huh." Beth digested this. The amazing fact that the object of Harry's crush was actually here, right in front of her, was shoved to the back of her brain to deal with later. "So it has nothing to do with a bendy horse?"

Still chuckling, Harry gave her shoulders an affectionate hug. Ky's face grew even more still, as smooth and cool as a sheet of ice.

"Hey, how long are you going to be in Denver?" Harry asked, not giving Ky a chance to answer before bending over and shouldering the abandoned duffel. "You're going to stay with us, right?"

Ky shrugged noncommittally. Beth wondered if she had imagined the slight wince at the "us". Despite Ky's poker face, Beth was definitely getting the impression that Harry's feelings for his Army buddy had not been one-sided. She knew that she should consider Ky a rival but, being crazy about Harry herself, she couldn't help but be sympathetic.

"Of course he's staying," Beth jumped in and Ky gave her a sideways glance. "We're out of takeout leftovers though— let's order pizza." She gave an unmoving Ky a nudge toward the apartment stairs. When that didn't work, she tried a harder shove. Ky stiffened and, for a moment, Beth was worried that he might walk out.

Harry's fingers settled on his shoulder and the two men locked eyes for several brutally long seconds. When Ky finally dropped his gaze and took a step toward the stairs, Beth sucked in air, only then aware that she had been holding her breath.

"Come on!" Beth gave him another small push and Ky turned to glare at her. "No wonder they call you Pokey," she said, making Harry laugh. Ky led the way up the stairs to the door of the loft, urged on by Harry's hand on his back and Beth herding up the rear like a Border Collie.

"Better move," Harry told Ky, his eyes sparkling. "When the woman gets hungry, she gets mean," he whispered loudly, glancing mischievously back at Beth, who smacked his butt in retaliation.

They piled into the apartment and Beth called dibs on the shower. It might not make her the best hostess but her need was desperate—she stunk. As she ducked into the bathroom, she couldn't resist glancing back at the two men, both so beautiful that, together, they took her breath away.

Harry grabbed two beers from the almost empty fridge and offered one to Ky, who accepted it with a nod. They sprawled into kitchen chairs, slouching against the backs and stretching their legs, unwittingly mirroring each other.

Ky glanced around. "Nice place," he said.

"Thanks. It's handy. When I opened the gym, it was just me—five a.m. to eleven at night. Having this place saved me. No commute—just drag my tired ass up the stairs and I was home."

Harry couldn't stop staring—he just couldn't believe that Ky was actually here.

"Shit, it's good to see you. What's it been—a couple years?" Harry asked, taking a pull of his beer.

"Two and a half," Ky corrected. At Harry's raised eyebrow, he dropped his eyes to his beer.

"I emailed you," Harry mentioned casually, trying to not make it sound like an accusation. "Called a few times. I even tried writing an actual letter."

97

His eyes still lowered, Ky rubbed the back of his head. "Yeah."

"Didn't think about emailing back—letting me know you were alive?" Harry asked mildly.

Ky just shrugged. "Seemed...easier not to."

"What have you been up to?" Harry had a pretty good idea where Ky had been—he had the watchful, jumpy energy of someone fresh out of combat.

"Iraq," Ky confirmed. "Just finished a six-month stint. Spent a week with the old man in Chicago." He focused on his beer bottle, picking at the label with his thumb. "That was plenty, so I thought I'd visit Denver. See some old friends."

Harry grinned and kicked Ky's foot. "Glad you did. Seriously, you need to stay awhile. I have plenty of room here. It's close to a pretty kick-ass gym too."

"Girlfriend might have something to say about that," Ky muttered, his mouth twisting.

"Beth's cool," Harry assured him. "You saw her. She pretty much shoved you up here."

Ky just shrugged again, his eyes back on his beer.

"Hey, Cap'n," Beth called, peering around the bathroom door. "Order the pizza—I'm starving!" A glimpse of her bare shoulder sent Harry's cock to instant attention. He gave her a suggestive grin and an acknowledging wave of his beer.

"Thanks." She had obviously caught his drift, because she winked before disappearing back into the bathroom.

"You guys pretty serious then?" Ky asked, drawing Harry's attention away from the closed door that hid a naked Beth.

It was Harry's turn to shrug and flush a little. "Yeah, I guess. I mean, it's just been a month—not even—but...it's different. *She's* different." He took a drink of his beer and then pondered it, turning the bottle in his hands. "I never thought about...you know, settling down and all that shit. Beth...Beth makes me think about it." Shooting a look at Ky, Harry shook his head, embarrassed. "What about you? Was there someone waiting for you to get home?"

"No. I thought that maybe..." Ky shook his head. "Never mind. I was stupid. Aren't you supposed to be ordering pizza?"

"Right." Harry could tell that a deeper conversation was going on, that more was being said than just the words that were spoken, but he wasn't sure how to bring the undercurrents to the surface. *Time for the deep shit later*, he thought. "What do you want on your pizza?"

They were all a little loopy. It was getting late and the three of them were sprawled in the living room, empty beer bottles collecting around them. Harry slouched in a chair, reminiscing with Ky about their Army days. Beth, sitting on the floor by his feet, her back propped against his legs, was taking full advantage of his loquaciousness. Usually he was tight-lipped about his experiences in Afghanistan, releasing only tiny snippets and clues, so she listened intently, eager to fill in the gaps.

"You mentioned a guy from Texas—who was he?" she asked.

"J.T.," Harry laughed and Ky's expression lightened at the name.

"What was that short for?" Beth glanced between the two men.

"Justin Timberlake," Ky answered, deadpan.

Eyeing him uncertainly, not sure if he was setting her up for a punch line, she asked, "Really?"

"Honestly," Harry chuckled, reaching down to muss her hair. "His name was actually Michael Schwartz but he had deluded himself into thinking he looked just like Justin Timberlake. He was this scrawny, homely kid with these ears that stuck straight out—didn't look a thing like the real J.T. but the nickname stuck."

"He was always singing too," Ky added. "Sounded like a pig being tortured."

Harry nodded. "God, he did, didn't he? He was lucky none of us shot him just to end our misery."

"Especially Hammer—I thought he was going to take J.T. out one of those days." Half a smile pulled at Ky's mouth.

"Hammer, as in MC?" Beth asked in disbelief. "Did you all have musicians for nicknames? Were you the boy-band unit?"

"Hammer as in hammerhead shark, dumbass," Ky scoffed, hurling a throw pillow at her head. Beth ducked, grabbed the pillow and chucked it back at him.

"Okay, sorry, sorry," she laughed. "Tell me the rest of the nicknames."

"Well," Harry began. "You know Pokey's. Then there was Jughead—no mystery there—he just had a really, really big head—"

"Physically or are you talking enormous ego?" Beth interrupted to ask.

"Actual, real-live, huge head," Harry confirmed.

"Huh." Beth pondered that for a moment. "Who else?"

"Our medic, Barney—that was just a shortened version of his last name, Barnowzky." Harry sobered and when Beth glanced over at Ky, she saw that his face had drawn tight.

"Have you heard from any of the guys?" Harry asked Ky, who shook his head.

Harry frowned. "Me neither—not for months. I need to call them up, get together or something. Hammer's just outside Colorado Springs, you know—we could get to his place in an hour." Both men were silent for a few moments until Harry spoke again. "What was your Iraq unit like—were you guys tight?"

Ky took his time answering, draining his beer and carefully placing it with the other empties on the coffee table. "They were okay—good guys, I guess. They all thought I was an asshole." He paused for so long that Beth opened her mouth to ask a question when Ky spoke again. "It was different, after Barney. You get your guts ripped out once, you aren't too excited about setting yourself up for a second time."

Beth glanced up at Harry, who looked sad and far away. "Yeah. Losing Barney was harsh."

Sucking in a breath, Beth's eyes grew huge. "Was he…?"

"Killed?" Ky finished harshly. "Yeah. Shot right in front of me. Yelled at me to get back and then bam—the back of his head is gone."

Beth recoiled, making a small, horrified sound.

"Knock it off, Ky," Harry ordered gruffly. "She doesn't need to hear it."

"It's okay, Harry," she told him, swallowing hard. "You guys had to see it. I shouldn't be a big baby about just hearing the words."

Harry reached down to stroke her hair and Beth tipped her head against the side of his knee. The silence lengthened and Beth, sleepy from the beer, felt her eyelids slide closed.

Pushing to her feet, Beth swayed a little then caught her balance. "I'm off to bed. Hey, Cap'n—can I sleep over tonight?"

"As if you haven't been sleeping over for the past month," Harry snorted, snaking an arm around her hips and pulling her toward him. "Might as well move in here."

"This place is just so convenient—it's close to my gym," she giggled as he tugged her into his lap with a growl. The room spun around her as she tumbled over the arm of the chair and sprawled against him. "And you have a really big bed. That's nice."

"I'm a big guy—I need a big bed." Harry kissed her, a quick peck that caught and held, turning longer and deeper, until Beth gave a low groan and twisted off his lap, landing on her knees on the floor.

"Bed," she stated firmly. "You guys talk. Good night, boys." After giving Harry a quick, smacking kiss, Beth crossed to Ky and, with beer-inspired courage, bent down to give him a peck on the cheek. As she approached, he looked alarmed and froze under the brush of her lips. She looked down at him for a second, thinking that, despite his constant snarly mood, there was something of the little boy lost about Ky.

With beery sentimentality, Beth reached a hand down to ruffle his hair—or at least rub his buzz cut, since he didn't have much hair to ruffle—but Ky jerked his head away from her with a scowl, glaring at her hand like it was a poisonous spider.

Instead of being offended, Beth grinned evilly and lunged for him. "Give us a big hug, Ky," she cooed, trying to wrap her arms around him. He ducked and rolled out of his seat, easily gaining his feet and dodging behind Harry's chair.

Harry laughed and covered his head with his arms. "Don't use me for protection, man," he warned. "She may look soft and squeezable but Beth can totally kick my ass."

Beth advanced on them, plotting her attack. She decided that the quickest way to her goal was a straight line—and shot up and over Harry. Hard hands grabbed her before she made it to Ky and Harry hauled her down until she was sitting, laughing, straddling his lap.

He shook his head at her sternly. "How many times do I have to tell you? No jumping the guests." His fingers were curled around the cheeks of her butt, tugging her firmly against his groin. Beth wiggled against the hard bulge at the front of his pants and felt, more than heard, his deep groan. She would have touched him, pressed her hands against his cock to feel his heat and hardness, but Beth glanced up and saw Ky watching them with an unreadable expression.

"Sorry," she grinned at him, giving Harry a final quick kiss on the nose and a surreptitious press of her hips, making his eyes flare with need. "I'll really go to bed now."

Clamoring out of his lap, she gave them a flip of a wave and headed for the bedroom. Just the short press of his erection against her pussy had made her heart race. She could feel the wetness of her arousal soaking her panties and Beth wished that Harry would hurry up and come to bed. She needed him inside her.

Gritting her teeth against a silent moan, she stripped off her clothes and slid between the sheets, feeling the cool fabric as it teased her erect, aching nipples. She settled in for a frustrating wait but, thanks to the beer, fell asleep almost instantly.

"You're safe now, she's gone." Harry was still smirking, although he was as hard as hell, thanks to that little bump and grind from Beth.

Ky warily lowered himself to his chair. "She's...affectionate."

"Definitely that," Harry agreed. "So tell me about this girl—the one you said you thought would be waiting."

Silence stretched through the room. Ky finally looked up, meeting Harry's eyes with a fierce contact. "I didn't say it was a girl," he stated, never dropping his gaze.

Harry started. "Oh. A...guy then?" he asked, holding himself still, not allowing the uncomfortable squirm.

Ky smiled but there was no humor in it. "Yeah. A guy." His smile dropped away. "I told my dad. That's why he kicked me out."

"Shit, Ky," Harry said softly but Ky shook off his sympathy.

"Didn't expect anything different, really. I mean, Dad's a cop, a real hard-ass, macho guy. Queers aren't his favorite group of people." He leaned his head back against the chair and closed his eyes. "Fuck."

"You're his kid though. He'll get through it."

"Yeah, right," Ky agreed, but when he looked at Harry, his eyes were blank, empty of hope.

Harry stood up. "You need to get some sleep. Things'll look better tomorrow." *Christ*, he thought, *I sound like fucking Little Orphan Annie.* He held a hand out to Ky, who stared at it for a second before grasping it and pulling himself up. Harry kept pulling, using Ky's momentum to tug him into a hard hug. After a stiff second, Ky relaxed slightly, allowing his head to fall forward and rest against Harry's collarbone.

"Shit," Ky muttered thickly, shoving Harry away abruptly. "How about this for high drama? I think that's enough emotional crap for one night."

Harry watched him quietly but Ky avoided his eyes.

"Come on," Harry said gently, steering the other man with a hand on the back of his neck. Ky braced against the touch, as if he was going to throw Harry's hand off, but eventually accepted the light pressure.

"I think Beth even changed the guest-bed sheets after her shower," Harry chatted easily. "One of the pluses of kind of living with a woman." Ky grunted in response.

Harry flicked the light switch, bathing the guest room in a yellow glow. Both men blinked, accustomed to the dimness of the living room.

"You know where the bathroom is. Otherwise, just let me know if you need anything—I think I could unearth an extra toothbrush or whatever..." Harry's voice trailed off to silence and his hand fell away from Ky's shoulder. "Well, good night then."

"Night," Ky grunted. Harry turned to leave the room but stopped when Ky grabbed his hand in an awkward grip. "Thanks," Ky muttered and dropped the contact, turning away in embarrassment.

"Anytime. Stay as long as you'd like." Harry slipped into the hallway, pulling the door almost closed behind him. His forehead was worried as he headed for his own room and the drowsy, warm woman who waited for him.

Chapter Eight

The shouts jerked Beth awake and she was halfway out of bed before she even realized what woke her. Harry pressed her gently back down into the covers.

"Shhh, go back to sleep," he whispered, pulling the sheet over her. Beth looked at him standing by the bed, her mind still foggy with sleep.

"What's going on?" she asked, whispering as well, just because he had.

Harry pulled on a pair of pajama bottoms as he answered. "It's Ky—sounds like a nightmare. I had some hellish dreams for months after I was discharged. I'll be right back."

His gentle tap on the guest-room door elicited no response, so Harry turned the knob and pushed the door open. The bed was rumpled and empty. Ky stood at the window, silhouetted by the nocturnal lights of the city.

"Hey, can I come in?" Harry asked quietly and saw the dark form shrug. Padding up behind Ky, Harry looked over the other man's bare shoulder out into the artificially lit night.

"Nightmares?" he asked.

Ky didn't turn around. "You didn't have to come running in here. I'm not a five-year-old with a monster in his closet."

His surly tone almost made Harry want to smile. "After I got back," he said quietly, "I think I stayed awake for two weeks. Couldn't sleep—not without anyone to watch my back. Couldn't even pace with my blown-out knee. All I could do was sit on the couch in my shitty apartment. Watched more of the shopping channel than I care to remember. Almost bought The Sandwichator too."

That brought a snort from Ky. "What the hell is The Sandwichator?"

Harry grinned in the dim light. "You haven't heard of The Sandwichator? You put your bread on it, and cheese or meat or whatever, and it seals it into a handy little grilled snack."

"That sounds pretty nasty," Ky scoffed but Harry could hear the amusement in his voice.

"Yeah, probably," he agreed, his eyes wandering out the window again. "It's funny what you'll do at three in the morning just to hear another person's voice."

Ky was silent for a few moments. "Now I'm hungry," he finally announced, startling a laugh out of Harry.

"Come on then. I don't have The Sandwichator but I do have that amazing cooking invention called a 'pan'—and I make a pretty kick-ass grilled cheese," he offered, hooking an elbow around Ky's neck as if to drag him to the kitchen. Instead of tossing off the playful arm, Ky leaned into Harry, bare back against bare chest, turning his cheek against Harry's shoulder.

Arousal hit Harry like a sandbag to the stomach, unexpected and hard. He couldn't prevent his arm from pulling the other man closer, his breath coming fast and heavy. Harry had thought he was over this, that his dreams of Ky had just been a symptom of too few women and combat stress, but here he was, erect and wanting, Ky glued against his chest— and Beth just a thin wall away.

It was one of the hardest things he had ever done, to force his arm down and to step back, away from the only man he had ever wanted. He did it though, thoughts of Beth helping him to release Ky, although he couldn't stop himself from first lowering his head and pressing the briefest of kisses against the other man's temple.

"Come on," Harry said again when he was standing clear, several feet from temptation. His voice, rough and unsteady, didn't even sound like him. He cleared his throat and tried again. "I promised you a sandwich."

For endless moments, Ky kept his back to Harry. His dark figure, so solitary and still, cracked Harry's heart.

"It gets better, you know," he started but Ky turned to face him, shaking his head.

"Never mind," Ky told him, his voice drained of emotion. "Let's eat."

For once at a loss for words, Harry silently led the way to the kitchen.

By the time Harry slipped back into bed, Beth was dozing. She was awakened by the gentle bump of his body against hers as Harry curled around her.

"Mmmm..." she murmured, tucking her bottom more firmly into his groin. Her body was malleable from sleepiness but Harry's body was hard-wired, muscles tight, his cock fully erect, searing the skin of her backside. His arousal stirred her own desire and a melting glow began to build in her belly. Beth wiggled against him again, nestling his erection between the cheeks of her ass, enjoying the feel of his silky heat against her bottom.

Groaning softly, Harry's hips jerked involuntarily, smearing the wet tip of his cock against her tailbone and trailing back into the dark crevice. Pleasure spread from Beth's stomach, reaching lazy tentacles of warmth throughout her body. *This is nice*, she mused, the sleepy, meandering arousal slowly heating her from the inside out.

Just as she let the thought slip away, Harry's patience snapped and Beth found herself flipped onto her belly, his cock buried deep in her pussy. She was startled, although not uncomfortable—she had been soaking wet and he had slid right in. She almost expected to hear a click, they fit together so perfectly.

Tugging her hips off the mattress so that they were tilted up toward him, Harry pulled out until only the head was lodged inside her and then slammed home, filling her up so completely that Beth gasped. Thrusting faster, Harry covered her back with his hair-roughened chest and just the prickling softness against her skin, together with the sensation of being surrounded, enveloped in his masculine body, sent Beth spiraling higher. As her inner muscles tightened around his driving cock, he plunged faster, harder, until he exploded deep inside her, catching her shoulder with his teeth at the same moment and biting down, just hard enough to send her over the edge with him.

They fell asleep seconds later, with Harry still inside her.

Beth stumbled into the kitchen, barely having had the presence of mind to pull a pair of pajama pants and a camisole top on before leaving the bedroom. She bounced off the doorframe and fumbled for a chair, lowering herself on it with infinite care.

"Coffee," she croaked, squinting at the two grinning men — okay, one grinning and one smirking.

"You had what? Two whole beers last night?" Ky asked, not moving toward the coffee pot at *all*, the bastard. Beth scowled. Luckily, a way-too-happy-looking Harry was headed in that direction. *Harry is wonderful!* her coffee-craving brain declared.

"Three," she corrected defensively. "And I'm not hung-over — I'm *sleepy.*"

"Uh-huh." Ky sounded skeptical and Harry gave her a commiserating smile as he handed her a blessedly steaming mug of coffee.

"I am. Someone kept waking me up last night." She took a sip and closed her eyes with pleasure. There was nothing like coffee after four hours of broken sleep. Opening her eyes, she caught Ky's tight-faced expression.

"Oh not *you*," she clarified, gesturing to Harry with her coffee mug and almost slopping the hot liquid all over. "Him." Then she blushed, realizing what she was admitting.

Laughing, Harry bent to give her a kiss. "*He* very much appreciated those sleep interruptions," he told her, his voice low. He wickedly nipped her lower lip as he drew away. Beth's face flushed brighter and her lower belly warmed. She shook her head, amazed that, even hung-over and sleep deprived, she could get aroused in an instant by Harry's touch.

Red-faced, she turned away from the Harry-shaped temptation and concentrated on Ky, catching a glimpse of such a lost, heartbroken expression that Beth's stomach twisted in pity. Ky's face blanked so quickly she had to wonder if she had imagined it.

"So what do you guys want to do tonight?" She forced a cheery tone. "Do we want to go out?"

"Can't," Harry said in a glum tone. "Charlie asked for tonight off—I have to work until closing, so I'm stuck downstairs until after eleven." Beth knew that whenever Harry worked late, all he wanted to do was crash—well, have wild sex and crash.

"I could pick up some DVDs after work," Beth suggested, the caffeine kicking in and making her feel halfway human.

"Where?" Harry's eyes narrowed and his voice was stern.

Knowing what was coming, Beth rolled her eyes. "The rental place a few itty-bitty, short, little blocks from here."

Harry was shaking his head before she even finished. "No. It's getting dark early now and I don't want you wandering the streets alone."

"It's not like I'll be wandering aimlessly. How am I going to try out my boxing skills if I can never leave the gym alone?" she asked plaintively, although she didn't mind his protectiveness. *Don't mind it at all*, she thought, squirming a little against the hard seat of the kitchen chair. His narrow-eyed glare and dictatorial tone had made her soaking wet, actually.

"You can try out your boxing skills when I'm dead. On second thought, no, you can't." Harry looked perturbed at the thought. "If I die, you just can't ever leave the house."

"Yeah, that'll work." Ky was smirking again.

"Why are we making post-death plans? Weren't we talking about movies?" Beth asked, trying not to laugh. "How about this—why don't I stop back at the apartment, pick up Ky and a-renting we will go? That way, if necessary, I can use my self-defense skills over *Ky's* dead body?"

"Sounds good," Harry agreed over Ky's indignant, "Hey!"

"In fact," Harry added, looking at Ky, "why don't you meet Beth at the bus stop and you guys can go from there."

With a deep sigh, Beth gave Ky a long-suffering look. "He won't even let me walk home from the bus stop. It's the one right outside. About a half-block away. That third-graders walk home from. That perfectly safe, well-lit bus stop."

A corner of Ky's mouth turned up as he responded to Harry's suggestion with an affirmative shrug.

"Since I am obviously not needed here," Beth announced, pushing herself to her feet, "I'm going to get ready for work." She frowned at Harry. "Speaking of work, who opened the gym this morning?"

"Charlie switched with me so he could have tonight off," he explained as he stretched and yawned. Beth promptly forgot what she had asked at the sight of his naked chest muscles pulling tight under his hair-dusted skin, his drawstring pajama pants barely clinging to his hipbones. She noticed that Ky was watching too, his narrow eyes hot and intent.

Feeling a mix of possessiveness and empathy, Beth gave Harry a pat on his hard stomach and a quick kiss on the chin in passing. She wanted to climb that ripped body and really

111

kiss him but it seemed cruel to be overly demonstrative in front of Ky, taunting him with what he couldn't have, like eating cookies in front of a starving person. The memory of Ky's lost expression filled her mind and Beth couldn't help sneaking in a quick pat on the arm and kiss on the cheek before Ky could duck away, scowling.

She knew that she should be offended by Ky's reaction to her affectionate gestures but it was actually kind of fun to try to slip in under his guard with a kiss or hug or even just a pat. Despite his cranky personality, she couldn't help but like Ky, to feel a camaraderie with him—maybe because they were both in crazy, wild love with Harry.

As she headed for the shower, much more cheerful than she had been when she first dragged herself out of bed, she glanced back to see Ky glowering at Harry, who grinned.

"Way too affectionate," Ky growled. Harry just laughed.

As Beth got off the bus that evening, her eyes immediately caught on Ky, who was slouching, legs sprawled, on the bench. Her stomach jumped at the sight of him, her heart speeding up way more than was justified by the short walk from her seat to the sidewalk.

This isn't good, she thought, trying to shove the reaction away. *I love Harry and Ky's gay, for God's sake! And in love with my boyfriend*, she told her disobedient body sternly. He was just so freaking beautiful. She sighed silently, unable to stop staring.

His slanting eyes were unfocused as he gazed off into space, his arms crossed over his chest, tightening the fabric of his shirt across the definition of his upper arms. His face was all sharp angles except for the sulky curve of his lips, a mouth so full and sullen that it made Beth want to bite it.

Stop, she commanded her brain, swallowing hard against the threatening drool and squeezing her thighs together, as if she could push back the arousal that had soaked her panties.

How can two men turn me on so quickly? she wondered, firming her spine and plastering a friendly smile on her face as she walked toward Ky.

He glanced at her and focused, a half-smile kicking up one corner of his mouth for a fleeting second before his habitual scowl replaced it. That flash of a smile was enough to twist her heart and she moved behind him to hide her expression, slipping an arm around his neck in a playful headlock.

"Hey," she greeted him, sneaking in a quick kiss that bounced off his ear as he pulled away from her and stood in one smooth motion. "This will be fun—I haven't been walked home from the bus stop since I was six and Nancy Sawyer threatened to beat me up. She was eight and quite a *large* girl, so I was understandably terrified."

"Are you ever quiet?" Ky asked grumpily as he walked beside her.

"Actually, I'm usually pretty shy. Especially when I first meet someone," Beth chatted on, not at all offended.

He made a disbelieving noise. "You weren't quiet around me."

Shrugging, Beth considered that for a moment. "You don't seem like a stranger—I mean, Harry talked about you so much that it was like I knew you, and then when I learned your nickname was Pokey—how can you be nervous around someone named Pokey?"

With a growl, Ky knocked against her with a light bump of his shoulder. "The nickname is not common knowledge. I had to threaten the guys in my unit to get them to keep quiet. Cap'n never could keep his mouth shut." He glanced at her sideways, obviously trying to hold his indifferent expression. "So...what did he say about me?"

"Harry?" Beth asked.

"No, the fucking mailman. Who do you think?" Ky growled, kicking at a small piece of concrete that had crumbled off the edge of the sidewalk.

"Manners, Pokey, manners," Beth tutted, holding back a grin at his glare. "My, you're a surly one. Let's see…what did Harry mention…"

"Fuck it—just forget it," he muttered, walking faster.

Beth laughed but relented. "I'm just kidding. He said—" She broke off abruptly, wondering how much to share with Ky. The DVD rental store was just ahead and this probably wasn't the best conversation to be having in a crowded aisle. Serious now, she grabbed his arm and tugged him toward a low wall bordering a parking lot. "Let's sit."

Ky looked at her askance but allowed himself to be pulled over to the wall. "That bad?" he asked, not really sounding as if he was joking.

"No, just…private." Beth pushed herself up to sit on the brick ledge and watched her dangling feet as she put the words in order in her head. Ky leaned against the wall next to her, watching her face warily. She took a deep breath and plunged in. "I asked him one night if, well, if he had ever been with a man." Her face was already bright red and she couldn't meet Ky's eyes, so she stared at her sensible black heels, took a deep breath and continued. "He said he hadn't but…"

"But?" Ky's voice was tight and Beth could actually *feel* his eyes boring into her.

"Well, he said 'no' but then started talking about you." She snuck a quick look at his stunned expression. "About how close you guys got and how you were together in Afghanistan—not in that way—" *God*, she thought, flushing even more brightly, *this conversation is full of minefields.* "And there wasn't any privacy and maybe nothing would have happened anyway but there was something between the two of you. I believe he also called you a mean son of a bitch, but it was in an affectionate tone."

There was silence and Beth bumped her heels against the wall. *Probably scuffing them*, she thought ruefully.

"Why are you telling me this?" Ky finally asked.

"I have no idea," she said. And then admitted, "Okay, maybe one or two ideas. Before I actually got the balls, so to speak, to walk into the gym, I had been walking by the place twice a day just to stare at Harry. I mean, I had to get to the bus too, so it wasn't *just* to stare at him, but I guess what I'm trying to say is that I know what it's like to want something that seems unobtainable."

"And you want me to obtain him?" Disbelief coated his words.

Beth shook her head. "I don't want to lose him, if that's what you mean. I love him. It terrifies me to think that someday he might not want me anymore or find someone else or..." Her stomach was clenching just talking about it, so she stopped. "It's just that I love him and I like *you*—even though you can be a total asshat—and I know what it's like to be crazy about him and I can't imagine how it feels to love him and not have him, that's all."

The words fell out of her mouth in a chaotic tumble, dropping off into complete silence. She risked a glance at Ky's face and saw a dozen emotions pass through before his expression settled into its usual unreadable lines.

"Shit," Beth groaned, pressing her hands to her flaming cheeks. "You must think I'm insane. I didn't mean to tell you all of this. Just forget I said anything." She hopped off the wall.

"Right, just like that." His smile held no humor.

"I won't say anything to Harry about it—how you feel, I mean," she promised, searching his face for a reaction, any reaction. *God, he's hard to read*, she thought.

Ky nodded and took a step toward the rental store and then stopped. "Just for the record, I think you're okay..." He trailed off in a mumble.

"Wow—okay. I'm...flattered?"

He shot a look out from under his eyelashes. "No need to get all sarcastic." He ignored her indignant sputters at that pot-calling-the-kettle-black statement and continued. "You're good for him. Not all girly and annoying."

Beth had to grin. "You're the king of damning with faint praise, aren't you?"

Scowling at her, Ky turned and started walking away. "Fine, I won't say anything then."

Laughing, Beth chased after him. "Kidding! I'm kidding! Come on, tell me nice things about me."

"They're not that nice," he grunted but stopped walking so she could catch up with him and latch onto his arm.

"Fine—tell me okay things about me," she wheedled, blinking up at Ky as innocently as possible and drawing a reluctant half-smile from him.

"I don't know," he started with a shrug. "You're just...what you see is what you get. You're not all manipulative and makeup-y and frou-frou. You're more like a guy—well, a guy who smells good."

Beth beamed at him. "You think I smell good?"

Hunching his shoulders up to his ears, Ky shook her hand off his arm and strode toward the store. "Jesus Christ, Barbie—you're like fucking Rainbow Brite. Are we going to get a movie or not?"

"Language, Pokey!" Beth called after him. He flashed a glare over his shoulder and stormed into the rental store. Smiling to herself, Beth followed more leisurely. A scowling Ky was waiting for her just inside and they both made their way to the new-release section.

"Hey, I want to see this one." Beth grabbed an action movie from the shelf. "It's supposed to be mindless yet entertaining—my favorite."

"See!" Ky said triumphantly. "You're a guy. You just proved my point." Beth stuck her tongue out at him as he pulled the DVD case from her fingers and put it back on the shelf. "I've had enough explosions for a while. Let's get this one."

Standing on her tiptoes to read the back cover of the movie in Ky's hands, Beth groaned. "Please. A romantic comedy? That's so gay." Although she clapped her hand over her mouth, a giggle still escaped.

"It's supposed to be good." Ky put it back on the shelf sulkily.

"Fine," Beth gave in, rolling her eyes. "But only if we can get this one too." She held up a martial arts film. "All the violence is punching and kicking, so there will be no explosions or firing of guns. I might even learn something about self-defense too — it's educational," she finished primly.

"Fine." Although he pretended to give in grudgingly, Beth could tell that he was pleased with the movie selection. She had to be careful — making Ky happy could prove to be addictive.

When Harry finally locked the gym and flicked off all but the security lights, he wearily climbed the stairs and let himself into the loft. Beth and Ky were sprawled on the couch in the darkened living room, watching the martial arts movie. Beth was stretched across the entire sofa, her legs tossed casually over Ky's lap. Surprisingly, Ky hadn't shoved the offending limbs away but instead draped one arm across her knees and had his other hand absently wrapped around her bare foot.

Harry watched them for a few minutes, warmed by their careless intimacy. He liked seeing them together, he realized. It was comforting to see the two people he loved more than anything else in the world so relaxed and safe. He wanted to freeze the image in his brain, to extend the moment forever, before reality got in the way.

Beth glanced up and smiled when she saw him in the doorway. She shifted, attempting to sit up to make room for him next to her. Instead, Harry climbed over the back of the couch, lifting Beth onto his lap as he settled next to Ky, who grunted a distracted greeting, his eyes never leaving the screen. Beth curled against Harry's chest, her soft curves molding against him, stretching her legs across Ky's lap again.

Harry watched the movie for a few minutes and then glanced at Ky. "Beth's choice, I presume?"

The corner of his mouth twitching up, Ky nodded. "I see why you don't let her go to the video store by herself."

"Yep," Harry grinned down at Beth's indignant face. "Bloodthirsty little thing."

"And here I thought you were concerned about my safety, not your movie selection. You should have seen what Pokey here picked out," she retorted, her eyes returning to the TV.

"Hey," Ky protested, throwing a pillow at her. "You liked it. You even *cried*."

Beth threw the pillow back. "I did not—I *told* you that I have *allergies*!"

Rolling his eyes and smirking, he gave Harry a look. "Whatever."

Grinning, Harry relaxed against the back of the couch. He stretched the arm not wrapped around Beth across the back of the sofa behind Ky, who gave him a quick sideways look before his eyes fastened back onto the television. If Harry didn't know him better, he would have thought that a hint of a smile touched Ky's mouth.

The curve of Beth's ass nestled in his lap. That, combined with the heat from Ky's thigh radiating along the length of his, hardened his cock.

Despite his arousal, Harry was happier than he could remember being in a long time. Dropping a kiss onto the top of Beth's head, he settled in to watch the movie.

"Strip," Harry commanded once they had reached the privacy of his bedroom. Beth had felt how hard he had been through the majority of the movie. From the rough edges of his voice as he barked out that single word, she could tell that his patience had worn thin.

Immediately, Beth began to melt, that strict tone sending shockwaves of arousal through her body and a trickle of moisture from her heating pussy. Although it wasn't very modern-woman of her, she loved when Harry used that stern voice with her. Obeying, albeit slowly, she grasped the hem of the camisole top she had changed into after she and Ky had gotten back from the rental store.

A fraction at a time, her fingers pushed the fabric higher, revealing the shadowed hollow of her bellybutton, the peach sheen of her skin. By the time Beth's hands had traveled high enough to let the bottom curves of her breasts peek out, Harry was breathing hard, his chest heaving with the need for air.

"Off. Now." His voice was gritty, his eyes fixed on the gradual unveiling of her skin. Beth pulled the top over her head, her full breasts naked and swaying a little from her movement. Tossing her camisole to the floor, she stood in just her drawstring pajama pants. They were pink with tiny white poodles on them and Beth had never thought of them as especially sexy but Harry was staring at her in a way that made goose bumps rise on her naked skin.

"Everything," he said hoarsely, unblinking. With a tiny smile, Beth turned her back to him, revealing the smooth line of her back. Untying the ribbon that held the pajamas in place, she loosened the fabric, running her fingers just below the waistband. Just that small touch on her skin increased her excitement and she could feel the dampness spreading between her legs, seeping into the soft, cotton fabric.

The loose pants clung for a bare second around her hips but a small wriggle made them slip to the floor, exposing the round curves of her ass. Beth peeked over her shoulder, creaming at the sight of his enraptured expression, his eyes fixed on the generous flesh of her bare bottom.

She knew he loved her ass—loved to look at it, knead it, fuck it, smack it—a shiver ran through her at the thought of his broad hand spanking her, reddening her cheeks until they were so sensitive that just a brush of his fingers was almost enough to make her come. She was so caught up in the memory of that sexy punishment that his voice made her start.

"Bend over," he rasped, moving toward her. Harry was still fully dressed, and for some reason this made her nakedness seem even more arousing.

Obediently, she bent over at the waist, resting her hands on the bed, arching her back and moving her feet well apart so that everything was revealed to him. The cool air struck the wet tops of her thighs as she separated them and the sound of Harry's indrawn breath when he saw her glistening folds made even more moisture seep from her inner core.

"Christ, you're beautiful," he muttered and Beth jumped again at the closeness of his voice. She was always shocked by how quietly he moved. It must be something they learned in the military, Beth figured, since Ky had that same silent glide to his walk, that same awareness of where he was in relation to everything else at all times. The two of them made Beth feel like a clumsy hippo in comparison to their jungle-cat slink.

The roughened palms of his hands settled on her lower back and all rational thought dissolved, leaving only sensation and need and heat. With a low moan, Beth arched into his touch as his fingers passed over her skin, smoothing around the sensitive sides of her torso and up her slightly rounded belly. Moisture leaked from her as her inner muscles tightened on emptiness when his hands cupped her breasts. His chest was so close to her back that she could feel his radiant heat even through his clothes. She involuntarily arched her hips, pushing them toward the hard cock that she knew was hovering just out of reach.

Harry trapped her nipples between his fingers and tugged, almost painfully, dragging another needy moan from her before he stepped back, breaking the contact. Beth moaned again, this time in protest, fighting her hungry body's demand that she stand up, turn around and *force* him inside her if she had to. Although she shook with arousal and her fingers clenched around handfuls of the comforter that covered the bed, she stayed in place, bent over with her feet spread, and was rewarded by a gentle stroke down one cheek of her bottom.

"Good girl," Harry murmured, gently petting her with both hands now. "Now tell me what you want."

"You," she panted, pressing back against his hands, only to receive a light, reproving slap that made the flesh of her ass quiver.

"What do you want me to do?" he asked and Beth bit her bottom lip against a wail of frustration. He was going to make her say it, she realized, before he gave her what she wanted — what she *needed*. She felt like she was going to spontaneously combust if he didn't touch her soon, if he didn't cram her so full of his iron-hard erection that she could feel the head of his cock butting up against the entrance to her womb.

"Fuck me," she growled, her all-consuming desire erasing any last inhibitions, the last coating of civilization, leaving her stripped down to her basest needs. Her rough words were rewarded by the thrust of two hard fingers into her weeping pussy and she tightened around the digits immediately, trying desperately to hold them inside her.

"Here?" Harry asked, obviously not done tormenting her yet. "Or here?" Pulling his fingers from her slippery, grasping depths, he pushed them into her tight ass. Her muscles tightened around the intruders but he plunged his slick fingers deep. The stretching pull of her back entrance shot rivulets of pleasure up her spine and through her jealously clenching pussy.

"Either! Both!" Beth tried to pump her hips against his hand, to lodge his fingers even more deeply into the tunnel of her ass, but he caught her hip with his other hand, stilling her effortlessly. With a sob, she twisted against his grip, desperate for relief. "Anything…please!"

As his hand left her hip, she heard his short, breathless laugh. "I like the 'both' answer," he said, his voice thick, all of his previous control and teasing evaporated. Harry shoved at his pants and underwear, jostling his thick fingers that were still buried inside her ass. Finally, she felt the wet head of his cock brush against her folds and nudge against her swollen pussy lips and she angled her hips, trying to urge him inside her. Instead, she felt the burning hot cock slip against her, sliding easily to bump against her eager clit.

It was so sensitive, so ready for his touch. Beth gave a startled cry that lowered to a moan as his fingers pulled almost all the way out of her ass before plowing back in. His other hand reached around to gently pinch the stiff nub of flesh, the light flick of his thumbnail contrasting with the smooth rub of his slippery cock. One more squeeze and tug of his fingers and Beth felt the contractions of her orgasm begin.

As her muscles tightened in climax, Harry thrust his cock deep into her pussy, groaning at the exquisite squeeze of her inner muscles. Angling his fingers so that he felt their pressure against his cock, he plunged into her, withdrew and plunged again, the added sensation of his fingers making the blood pound hard in Beth's ears.

She was thrust right into another orgasm, his double invasion swamping her senses. The image of Ky thrusting into her ass as Harry fucked her pussy, their cocks rubbing against each other with only the thin membrane separating them, flashed into her mind, blinding her with an unexpected rush of pleasure, making her scream.

As her fierce climax overtook her, her inner walls clamped around Harry's cock and fingers in a squeezing grip and he shouted his release only seconds after the sound of her scream faded from the room.

Beth's arms shook with fatigue and she slowly unclenched her aching fingers from the comforter. As Harry gently pulled his fingers and semi-erect cock free of her body, she felt the same sense of loss that she always did, a need to keep Harry buried inside her, to feel him surrounding her from the outside and the inside. Sighing, she tumbled toward the bed, curling on top of the covers and letting her eyelids sink shut.

Harry's rumbling laugh floated in her semiconsciousness and Beth felt herself being lifted, tucked beneath the covers. He must have stripped off, because she felt his naked body wrap around hers just seconds later. As she slipped toward unconsciousness, she felt the brush of his lips on her ear and heard, "I love you."

Beth murmured, "Love you, Cap'n," asleep almost before the words had left her mouth.

In the room next door, Ky lay wide awake, staring at the ceiling, the aftershocks of his own climax still shuddering through him. He had heard the noises that Beth and Harry had been making, heard the final shouts of completion, and Ky's fist had grasped his own erection as he imagined what they were doing, where they were touching. With a quiet groan, he had spilled into his own hand, feeling lonelier than he had ever been in his entire life.

Chapter Nine

ഏ

Beth was jolted out of her dreamless, heavy slumber by shouts from Ky's room.

"Fuck. Third time tonight," Harry muttered under his breath but slid toward the side of the bed, pushing himself to a sitting position and heaving to his feet.

Still fuzzy with sleep, Beth rolled to face him and propped herself on an elbow. "Just bring him in here," she said in a voice froggy from sleep.

"In *here*?" Harry asked in a whisper.

"It's a king-sized bed so there's plenty of room. Saves you from having to get up—you can just throw an arm over him or something. Besides, having other warm bodies around might keep the ghoulies away." As she woke up a little more, Beth felt a warm tingle start to invade her lower belly. What began as a platonic suggestion from her sleep-hungry brain was opening up other, more sexual possibilities.

Harry looked at her, his face serious. "Sure?"

She nodded, her stomach clenching with nerves and budding arousal.

Shrugging, Harry headed for the door. "I'll ask him. It would be nice to get at least a few hours of sleep."

Wide awake, Beth collapsed back into the pillows, her heart pounding. A low murmur of voices came from the other room and she strained to hear the words. Panic shot through her as they fell into silence and she closed her eyes, faking sleep. The echo of her hammering heart almost drowned out the click of the latch as the door to their room opened. Beth cracked her eyes, only to squeeze them shut again when she saw the men. They were both shirtless—Harry in the sweatpants he had thrown on before heading to the other man's room and Ky in boxer briefs.

The mattress jounced slightly as someone climbed into bed—Harry, Beth realized, as he spooned against her, the soft fabric of his sweatpants pressing to the back of her legs. He was aroused, she realized, his erection hot and hard against her ass even through the material covering his groin. She couldn't help a small wriggle of her bottom against his stiff cock, pressing the ridge into the naked crease of her ass. His arm tightened around her waist—as a protest or a request for more, Beth wasn't sure.

The bed dipped again as Ky slid beneath the covers. Beth could feel Harry's heart pounding as quickly as her own, and the buzz between her legs began to ache as wetness seeped from her pussy to slick the tops of her thighs. She just hoped that neither of the men could smell her arousal, realize how excited she was, just from having them both in the same bed with her. Shifting, trying to press her legs together to muffle the throbbing pulse, Beth bumped against Harry's rigid cock again, felt him stiffen along the entire length of his body.

What is wrong with me? she wondered. It couldn't be right to want both men so much, to wish for this crazy love triangle to come together. Beth felt like she was feeling all the wrong emotions for the situation—she was supposed to be jealous of Ky, not soaking wet from wild thoughts of both men filling her, front and back, or of Harry thrusting his cock into her eager mouth as Ky took him from behind. *You have to stop,* she commanded herself desperately, her skin flushed and prickling with sweat from the vivid images.

With the press of Harry's erection against her ass and the knowledge that Ky was probably in the same rigid condition just inches away from Harry, banishing her depraved thoughts was impossible. *It's going to be a long night,* Beth realized with a silent groan.

She eventually must have fallen asleep because when she opened her eyes, the clean, rosy sunlight of early morning was pouring through the windows. The three of them were tumbled together like a litter of puppies, arms and legs twisting around each other until she didn't even know which ones belonged to her. Someone—or maybe all of them—had kicked off the covers and the cool morning air tightened her nipples to hard points. Harry was still behind her, his front pressed to her back, although he must have gotten up at one point to go to the bathroom, since Beth was now in the middle of the bed.

Ky's head was nestled close to her breasts, his sleeping breath brushing against her nipple with each exhalation. One of his arms supported his head, while the other crossed both Beth's and Harry's hips. Her eyes traveled over the corded transition between shoulder and neck before sliding down the smooth definition of his chest to his stomach, dark in contrast to the white fabric of his boxer-briefs. *God, he's so beautiful it hurts*, Beth thought, pressing her hand against her stomach, as if the pain were an actual, physical ache.

Her gaze fell lower, to the large bulge behind the cotton fabric of his underwear, and she swallowed. Beth's hand itched to tug the fabric down, to expose his straining erection, and felt another rush of guilt. Even with all the good-looking, ripped guys who worked out at the gym, she had never even looked at anyone except Harry until Ky walked in. As greedy as it was, she wanted them both.

The realization that she was ogling another man as Harry lay behind her was enough to propel her out of bed. Beth eased out from their octopus arms without waking either man, although Harry shifted, grumbling in his sleep, before resettling into slumber. She watched them for a few moments, entranced by the sight of the two men, so gorgeous, sleeping facing each other in unconscious imitation. Beth felt a rush of emotion—possessiveness and love and longing—so intense that she forgot to breathe. A swarm of tiny lights swam in front of her eyes, forcing her to suck in a quavering breath.

Beth was just about to get out of the mesmerizingly warm spray of the shower when Harry opened the door and stuck his head in. She shrieked.

"Have you learned nothing from *Psycho*?" she demanded, swatting him with her net pouf. "It's the golden rule — don't pop in on someone in the shower without a warning!"

Harry grinned, unabashed. "I don't think that's the golden rule," he corrected, climbing all the way in and crowding her to the back of the small shower stall, closing the door behind him.

"Oof," she grunted, pushing against his wall of a chest. "Well, it should be. I don't think we both fit in here," she added, giving his immobile form another shove.

"We'll make it fit," he growled suggestively, pressing her flat against the cool wall. "I've been hard all night and not able to do anything about it. I'm not waiting any longer." His erection burned against Beth's belly, turning her insides to warm goo but also reminding her of the long night of frustrated arousal.

"Can I ask you a question?" Her voice was reduced to a breathy gasp as Harry palmed her hips, his wide palms and long fingers wrapping around her ass cheeks.

He lifted one of her legs up over his hip before answering. "Only if I can fuck you while you ask it," he gritted, sliding his hand up her slick thigh until his fingers found the entrance to her eager pussy, opened to him by her raised leg.

"Okay." Beth could hardly remember her question now that Harry's fingertips were penetrating her, slipping easily through the moisture that leaked from her, mixing with the spray from the shower. He pulled away his teasing hand, to her disappointed moan, and lifted her higher against the wall until she could wrap both legs around his waist.

127

The head of his erect cock nudged at her pussy and Beth tilted her hips, wanting him to take her. She had been waiting forever, all through the endless night. She desperately tightened her legs around him to pull him into her.

Harry held back, ignoring her frantic efforts, and commanded, "Ask."

Staring blankly at him, having forgotten everything except the need to have him inside her, filling her, Beth vaguely remembered having a question. It didn't seem to matter now and she tried to pull him into her again, murmuring, "Please?"

"Ask your question," Harry repeated through clamped teeth, his erection still barely touching her.

Why did I bring up the stupid question in the first place? Beth wondered hysterically. Taking a deep breath, which did nothing for her clarity of mind, especially because it pressed her breasts against Harry's hair-roughened chest, she struggled to remember what she wanted to ask.

"When you..." she started, trailing off when Harry began to push into her. He stopped when the words stopped and Beth almost cried.

"When you were...hard," she began again, desperately grateful that Harry's invasion of her also continued, "was part of that..."

The progress of Harry's cock halted again when her voice fell away. Frantic for more, Beth just blurted out the words, tact and self-consciousness unimportant.

"Were you hard because you wanted Ky?"

When Harry stopped his thrust this time, it was because of shock at her question instead of any teasing game. "You think that I don't want you?" he asked finally, prodding his enormous erection farther into her in emphasis.

"Of course I know you want me—" She broke off with a gasp when he nudged his cock in another bare inch. What a conversation to be having with Harry halfway inside her, Beth marveled, sucking in a short breath to continue. "But I think you want him too."

Instead of answering, Harry drove his cock into her, flattening her against the shower wall with his thrust. Beth's hands scrabbled for purchase, finally digging into the hard muscle of his shoulders. He snarled as her nails pressed crescents into his skin.

Pulling her thighs up and apart, he plowed into her, forging through the tight clutch of her pussy until his cock was lodged, pulsing, deep inside her clenching heat. An entire night of silent, desperate arousal, hours of listening to Ky and Beth breathe, when all he wanted to do was fuck them both — desire poured out of Harry until he was blind and mindless with it. Her small gasps drove him wild, made him thrust harder, faster, until his hips pounded against hers, technique forgotten, only raw need driving him.

When he exploded, his bad knee gave out, almost dropping him to the shower floor. Harry caught himself with each hand on an opposite wall as Beth clung to him, legs and arms wrapped tightly around him.

"You okay?" croaked Beth, looking dazed.

"I'm fine," he said shortly, reality bringing the bitter taste of self-disgust. Just because he didn't want to face his true feelings for Ky didn't mean he had to act like an animal with Beth. "The question is, are you okay?"

"God yes," she breathed, her heartfelt words startling a laugh from Harry.

"Really?" he asked. "I wasn't a brute?"

Beth kissed his chin. "A bit of a brute, but that was the fun part. And I kind of started the whole thing by asking you about Ky."

Gingerly testing to see if his knee would support his weight, Harry felt secure enough on his feet to take his hand off the wall and wrap it under Beth's hips. "No," he said slowly, picking his words carefully. "You had a right to ask. Your timing, however—"

Beth laughed and swatted the backside of his head.

"Ow!" Harry made a mock-pained face but quickly sobered. "You know I would never cheat on you, right?"

"Of course I do, but that's not why I asked. *Do* you have a thing for Ky?" she pressed.

Harry frowned. "What does it matter? I told you that nothing would happen."

Shrugging, Beth focused on a point on Harry's neck as if she was unable to hold his gaze. "It's just…I mean, I guess I just…well, if you did feel something it would make me feel less like a perverted slut," she finally finished in a rush, her face pink.

"What?" Harry shook his head. "Now I'm really confused. Why are you a perverted slut?"

"Because—" Beth broke off with a short laugh. "If we're really going to have this conversation, you need to put me down. Your poor knee!"

"It's fine." Shrugging off her concern, Harry didn't take his eyes off her face. "What were you going to say?"

Beth shook her head, her face set in stubborn lines. "Down," she demanded and Harry rolled his eyes.

"Fine," he conceded, allowing her to slide to her feet. "Here, we might as well get out." Reaching down, he turned off the shower and opened the door. Beth stepped out after him and Harry wrapped her in a towel. Snagging a second one, he toweled her head briskly.

"Enough, enough!" she cried, her laughter muffled. Harry pulled the towel free and Beth shoved her wild blonde curls out of her eyes.

"Okay, now talk," Harry commanded, leaning against the sink and swiping the towel over his own shorn head.

"Right." He watched as she took a deep breath, as if she was steeling herself. "You're not the only one who's thought about it."

He jerked in shock. Of all the things he thought might come out of her mouth, that had not been one of them. "You mean…"

Chewing on her lower lip, Beth shrugged, her gaze bouncing nervously around the bathroom, landing anywhere except on Harry's face. "Oh, you know. About you and Ky together. About you and me and Ky together." She finally glanced at Harry and quailed at his stupefied expression. "Oh God, now you think I'm a perverted slut, don't you?" she wailed, covering her eyes with her hands and almost losing her towel.

With a choked laugh, Harry pulled her into a hug. "Of course not, I just…I mean, it's just—great, now I'm sounding like you." He laughed again when Beth poked him reprovingly in the stomach. "Just give me a minute, okay? This is a lot to take in."

"Okay," Beth mumbled against his chest.

"I never thought this thing with Ky—whatever it is— would ever actually be anything." Harry paused, running an absent hand down to the small of Beth's back. "I didn't even plan on telling anyone, much less acting on it."

"You don't have to," Beth told him. "I'm happy with just you, you know."

Harry chuckled and rubbed her rumpled head. "I'm happy with you too—so happy it freaks me out sometimes."

"If you *wanted* to though…"

Blowing out a hard breath, he leaned against the sink again and stared at the ceiling. "I don't know what I want," he admitted. "Except for you—I know I don't want to lose you. And I know that I love having Ky here and that seeing you together…" He paused, pressing a fist against his chest. "I know that just looking at you makes me harder than a rock.

And that lying in bed with both of you last night…that nearly killed me."

Beth let out a strangled laugh. "You and me both, Cap'n."

"I'm just so amazed…" Harry said, tipping her chin up so he could look directly at her. "You would really be okay with this?"

"I don't know," she admitted, shrugging. "I've never done this before. I want it, I do know that, but I'm not sure about the aftermath. If you end up liking Ky better, I might have to kill you both."

"Not going to happen," he assured her, hooking an elbow around her neck to pull her in for a quick kiss. "I can't believe that you're up for this. You're either the best girlfriend in the world, or the worst."

"I'm voting for the best, in case you're doing a poll," she said and then pushed back from him. "And I have to get going or I'll never catch my bus."

"I'll give you a ride," he promised, giving her an affectionate swat on her towel-covered bottom. "If my nose doesn't deceive me, I think that Ky's cooking breakfast."

Beth's mouth dropped open. "Someone's cooking? Here?" She gave Harry a shove toward the bathroom door. "I have to hurry—it might be pancakes. Did I ever tell you that I *love* pancakes?"

"Better get ready fast then—because so do I. There might not be any left by the time you get out there." Harry winked at her as he backed out of the door and shut it behind him.

Beth finished getting ready in a flurry and rushed into the kitchen—where she slid to an amazed halt. Ky was at the stove, spatula in hand, cooking what looked to be, happiest of all happy days, pancakes. Beth swooped in on his unsuspecting back and hugged him from behind.

"Pokey, did I mention how much I love you?" she asked.

"Down, Barbie, down," Ky shook free of her clinging arms. "Let go or it's cereal for you."

Beth dropped her arms immediately at the threat, ducking her head around his arm to peer at the heavenly-looking pancakes. "Are those blueberries?" she asked reverently.

"Fresh blueberries," Harry confirmed from his seat at the island, his mouth full. "Ky shopped."

Looking at him in awe, Beth went in for a second hug. Ky jumped back, using the spatula to fend her off. "Sit!" he ordered, pointing at the stool next to Harry.

"Whatever you say, O mighty pancake god." As she obediently plopped herself down, Harry leaned over to give her a sticky kiss on the cheek.

Picking up a fork, Beth tried to sneak a bite off Harry's plate but he pushed it out of reach.

"I thought you loved me!" she wailed. The heartless bastard just grinned unrepentantly through a mouthful of pancake.

With a sigh, Beth resigned herself to waiting. "What are you two doing today?" she asked.

"I have the day off," Harry told her between bites. "If Ky's interested, we could go on a hike outside Boulder." He glanced at Ky, who shrugged his assent.

It's funny, Beth thought, *how I can already translate Ky's shrug vocabulary.*

"Day off?" Beth queried in surprise. "Doesn't Charlie have class today?"

"Yep, but Dominic's going to pick up a few shifts. He's already here all the time, so he figured that he might as well get paid for it. Charlie's going to take over at three after his classes, so I'm free," Harry crowed. Beth scowled at him.

"You don't have to sound so happy about it," she grumped. "Some of us still have to go to work."

"What do you do?" Ky asked.

"I'm the receptionist and all-around butt monkey at Anchor Paper. It's a decorated-paper company—you know, for scrapbooking and invitations and crap like that," she explained.

"Really?" Turning from the pan to glance at Beth, Ky raised a curious eyebrow. "I thought you had some art degree."

"Yep, sure do," she confirmed glumly. "That and five bucks will buy me a cup of coffee. Speaking of coffee—did you make some?"

Harry pushed his cup toward her. "Here—have some of mine. Why don't you do anything art-related?" he asked.

She took a blissful sip. "Dunno. My apartment isn't really set up for painting. I sketch on the bus. Drawing's easy—you just need a pencil and paper. Painting, now, painting's messier. And scarier."

"You could paint here," Harry offered, shoving another bite in his mouth.

"Thanks. I should start up again. I think I just get lazy— that and it's easier not to paint anything than to risk not being any good," she admitted.

"Who cares if it's bad?" Ky asked. "If it sucks, you can just chuck it. You don't even have to show us."

Taking another swallow of Harry's coffee, which he wasn't about to get back anytime soon, Beth pondered that. "You're right. Thanks." After another sip, she added, "Speaking of jobs, what do you do, Ky?"

"Shoot at people. Blow things up." He tossed some pancakes on a plate and thumped it down in front of Beth.

"Ah, thank you, wonderful Pokey." She trailed lines of syrup over the stack. "I meant, what will you do now?" A horrible thought occurred to her. "Unless you're going back— you're not, are you?"

Concentrating on pouring perfect circles of batter, Ky shook his head. "Can't, even if I wanted to. Pretty much flunked the psych exam."

Harry's head came up. "PTSD?" he asked.

Ky shrugged affirmatively. "That or just good old-fashioned combat stress. Either way, the diagnosis is BSC."

Beth screwed up her face, trying to figure out the acronym. "Huh?"

"Bat-shit crazy," Harry translated.

"Oh." Beth chewed silently for a moment. "So what are you going to do?" she asked again.

Ky eyed her in exasperation. "You are a fucking bulldog, aren't you, Barbie?"

She copied one of his shrugs and looked at him expectantly.

He blew out an impatient breath. "I don't know, okay? Don't really know anything except how to kill people."

"You can pick up some shifts at the gym if you want," Harry offered. "Do some training even."

"I don't know. I heard the owner's a real asshole." Ky looked at him sideways, the corner of his mouth twitching up.

Harry tossed a balled-up napkin at his head. "Very funny. You'd a good trainer. Boot-camp style is popular right now — people would pay you to scream obscenities at them and make them run laps."

"Ooh, you'd be good at that, Pokey," Beth teased.

Ky flipped the pancakes. "I'll think about it," he said.

"Sorry to run, kiddos, but I'm going to miss my bus if I don't leave now," Beth told them, hopping off her stool after one last sip of Harry's coffee.

"I'll drive you," he protested but Beth shook her head.

"That's okay — I don't mind the bus." She gave him a kiss goodbye that tasted like syrup and coffee before bringing her plate to the sink. Ky watched her warily, obviously expecting her to lunge for him at any moment.

"Have fun hiking," she told them. "Don't worry about me, slaving away to support this family. Just enjoy yourselves." She gave them her best dejected eyes but Harry snorted with laughter and Ky just rolled his eyes. Seeing that no sympathy was forthcoming, she jostled Ky with her shoulder. "See you, Pokey," she said. "Thanks for the ab fab pancakes." He grunted.

"Such a sweet boy," Beth cooed. On her way out, she mouthed, "Talk later," to Harry, who nodded and waved. Rushing through the door and down the stairs, she waved at Dominic as she ran past. *What a morning it's been*, she thought, amazed. It wasn't even eight o'clock and already she'd had wild shower sex with Harry, talked about having a threesome with Ky and ate homemade blueberry pancakes. *What else could happen today?* she wondered, running for her bus.

The city of Boulder stretched out before them in miniature, the reservoir looking like the smallest puddle.

"Nice," Ky breathed.

Harry glanced over at him. "I know, right? I love this hike."

Ky nodded. "I felt like I was in the back of beyond but then—wham! Here's the city."

Grinning, Harry drawled, "The back of beyond has groomed trails?"

Ky gave him a good-natured shove. "I'm a boy from Chi-Town. It's the back of beyond to me," he defended himself.

Finding a seat on a not-too-uncomfortable rock, Harry took a drink from his water bottle. "Next time, we'll really go into the wilderness. Camp for a couple nights, scout for mountain lions and bears—and then run away if we see any."

"Sounds...interesting," Ky responded, flinching a little at the mention of big, hairy animals with teeth and claws. "Does Barbie camp?"

Harry laughed. "We'd just tell her we were going for ice cream. That'd get her in the truck."

"Yeah and then she'd kick both our asses once we got to the campsite." Ky grinned at the thought and Harry felt like he'd been kicked in the stomach. *The kid is lethal when he smiles,* Harry thought, trying to catch his breath.

That morning's conversation with Beth replayed over and over again in his mind, alternately exciting him and scaring him half to death. Should he bring it up to Ky? How the hell did he start a discussion like that? Beth had, but she tended to just open her mouth, let the words roll out and damn the consequences. Harry couldn't do that. What if it scared Ky off, pushed him to leave? Harry's stomach clenched at the thought.

"Is it okay?" When Ky spoke, Harry jumped, worried that he had actually said his thoughts out loud. "Me staying with you, I mean?" Ky didn't turn around as he asked, his voice carefully casual.

"What? Of course it is," Harry reassured him, surprised. "I love having you — *we* love having you. If you tried to leave, I think that Beth would tie you to the bed." As soon as the words passed his lips, Harry winced. He definitely had sex on the brain. The thought of Beth tying a compliant Ky to the bed made him swallow hard.

"I know I should be...well, planning my future or something, but — " Ky broke off with a shake of his head.

"Is that what started this?" Harry pushed himself off his rock and stepped toward Ky's stiffly erect figure. "The whole career-counseling session at breakfast?"

Shrugging, Ky remained silent.

"That wasn't a hint," Harry assured him. "If I wanted you out, I would tell you to get out. And you know that Beth wouldn't hesitate to kick you to the curb if she didn't want you there. I just brought up the whole working at the gym thing because…well, the gym is what got me out of the black hole I fell in after leaving the Army. Not sleeping, not eating, just limping around on my fucked-up knee, pissed at the world and watching too much late-night TV."

Ky gave a humorless huff of laughter. "Been there. Only it's not my knee that's fucked up—it's my brain."

Walking over to stand behind Ky's rigid back, Harry wrapped a hand over the shorn skull in front of him. "Your brain's fine," he said quietly. "It's what happened over there— that's what's fucked up." He wrapped his other arm around Ky and pulled him into a loose embrace against his chest. Harry rested his chin on the back of his hand, still spread over Ky's head.

They were both silent for so long that small animals nearby began to move, rustling in the underbrush. A pair of trail runners panted by, looking at the two men curiously, which shook Harry and Ky out of their stillness. They both turned to watch the runners' progress, winding up the switchbacks of the narrow trail.

"Jesus, doesn't that remind you of basic training?" Ky asked, stepping a few feet away from Harry.

Nodding, Harry grimaced at the memory. "Hell yeah. We ran so much that I had nightmares about running—nothing chasing me, just endless running."

"And it was always a hundred and ten degrees."

"In the shade," Harry added, deadpan, and then grinned at Ky. "We get to go downhill now. At a walk."

"Halleluiah," muttered Ky and they headed back down the trail.

Chapter Ten

ಏ

Beth sighed, bored. It had been a long, dragging day at work, especially when she thought about Harry and Ky enjoying their free day. The air seemed to press down on her, stifling, as she shoved away thoughts about her conversation with Harry that morning. When five o'clock finally arrived, she jumped up and almost ran out of the office, not able to sit still for another second. She couldn't even concentrate enough to sketch on the bus ride home.

She felt restless, shivery in her skin, and the thought of her usual workout just made her sigh again. She had been hoping for a training session with Harry or, even better, dragging him into his office for some hot desktop sex but he was working with a new member. Beth recognized the client as the chubby man with the very white shoes who had been in for a tour the day that Ky had arrived. Harry was demonstrating a jab in slow motion, his body moving with such liquid fluidity that watching him magnified Beth's restive feelings to almost unbearable levels.

Turning away, she saw that Ky was working at the uppercut bag, his sweat-dampened shirt outlining the muscled grooves in his shoulders and back. With an impish grin, Beth made her way toward him.

"Hey, Pokey," she greeted him. Ky glanced at her sideways and then ignored her, attacking the bag with renewed fervor.

"Come on, Ky, can't you hit harder than that?" she teased. If she couldn't concentrate on her own workout, she reasoned, she might as well be disruptive to someone else's—especially if that person was so fun to disrupt.

He didn't even glance at her but Beth saw his jaw tighten. She bit back a triumphant grin. "Put some effort into it!"

That did it. Resting his gloved fists against the still-bouncing bag, Ky turned toward her with exaggerated patience. "Did you want something?"

"I'm bored."

Rolling his eyes, Ky turned back to the bag. "So go bother your boyfriend," he growled, his punch tossing the bag on its chains.

"He's working," she told him. "Come on, Ky—teach me something. I don't want to do my usual workout today."

"So go to the mall instead."

"Please, Ky?" she wheedled, giving him her best big-eyed, pleading look, which was totally wasted since he wouldn't even glance at her. "Please, please, please?"

"God, you're annoying, Barbie," he grumped, although he gave up on hitting the bag. "How does Harry stand you?"

She shrugged. "He has the patience of a saint. Come on, Ky—it'll be fun. It'll help you decide if you want to be a trainer."

"Are you going to leave me alone if I say no?" he asked.

Beth, sensing victory, just grinned at him. With a defeated sigh, Ky stripped off his gloves.

"Come on, Barbie," he commanded, "into the ring."

Maybe this isn't such a good idea, Beth thought nervously as she trailed after Ky. "Um, I haven't actually sparred with anyone yet," she told him.

Ky bent over to slip between two of the ropes. As he straightened, he raised a taunting eyebrow at her. "Chicken?"

"Of course not," Beth denied, although her tentative tone belied her words. "I just don't really want to be in a situation where…I mean, I wanted to wait until…"

Ky made an impatient, spit-it-out gesture with his hand.

140

"I don't want to be hit until I know I won't cry," she admitted. "I mean, how embarrassing to be in the ring, bawling like a baby after the first punch?"

"Oh for the love of fuck, Barbie, I'm not going to hit you! Now will you get your ass in the ring?"

"Oh." She eyed him a little suspiciously before climbing into the ring. "Okay."

"So what do you know?" Ky asked.

Raising her fists and falling into her stance, she glanced at her ungloved hands and then up at Ky. "Should I—?" she began, but he cut her off.

"No gloves. You won't get to hit *me* either," he told her.

With a shrug, Beth began to shadowbox for him. He watched impassively for a few moments.

"Stop."

She obeyed, her hands dropping to her sides.

"Sit down."

"Okay," Beth acquiesced, plopping down. *Ky looks very tall from here*, she thought as she watched him from her seat on the mat, waiting for his next command.

"Now get up."

She clambered to her feet and looked at him curiously. "Do we fight, fight, fight now?"

"What?" Ky asked, baffled.

"It's a cheer. You know, stand up, sit down, fight, fight, fight—yay?" Her words faltered as he stared at her.

"Of course you were a cheerleader," he groaned. "Never mind. If you could restrain from *cheering*," Ky put a world of disgust in that one word, "we could continue."

"No need to get cheer-hostile," she muttered under her breath.

"What?" Ky snapped.

141

"Nothing!" Beth chirped, her most innocent smile in place. "By all means, continue."

Eyeing her a little suspiciously, he gave a short nod. "It took you about five minutes to get up."

"I wouldn't say—" Beth began to defend herself but was cut off by the sharp, slicing movement of one of Ky's hands.

"Watch," he ordered and sat down, a casual arm resting on his bent knee. In a blur of motion, Ky was on his feet in a fighter's stance, moving so quickly that Beth took a startled step backward.

"The enemy won't wait for you to get up before attacking," he told her.

"What enemy?" Beth asked, confused.

"The enemy about to attack you," Ky explained with exaggerated patience. "Sit down."

She sat.

"Are you right-handed?" he asked. Beth nodded. "Okay, put your weight on your right hand and your left foot, swing your right leg through and plant it behind your right hand."

She struggled to follow his directions, feeling like she was playing Twister with a drill sergeant.

"Behind your hand! Your knee should be right behind your arm," he barked at her. Beth shuffled her foot over behind her hand, lost her balance and fell backward.

"Again."

With a sigh, Beth started over. She had gotten herself into this, she acknowledged. What had she been thinking, asking Ky to train her?

After a few attempts, though, she was starting to get the hang of it. Beth wasn't gaining her feet as quickly as Ky had but it was much faster than her initial wobbly try.

"Better," Ky told her with a short nod. Beth grinned in triumph. For Ky, that was huge praise. "Don't get cocky—

you're not that good." Her smile dropped away. "Okay, on your back."

"Really?" she asked doubtfully. Ky just waited until Beth lay down on the mat. He knelt over her, straddling her body, his knees up close to her armpits. *Okay, when did this turn into a naughty game of Twister?* Beth wondered, her heartbeat speeding up.

"Everything is about leverage," he told her. "How do you get leverage?"

Beth shook her head.

"Dominant body position," Ky explained. "You're little and weak—"

Offended, Beth interrupted, "Who are you calling weak?" She flexed her arms as well as she could in her current flat-on-her-back position. "I'll have you know that's two tickets to the gun show right here."

Ky gave a crack of laughter, startling Beth into an answering grin.

"You're nuts," he told her. "Now pay attention. Which one of us is in the dominant position right now?"

"Um, that would be you," Beth answered, leaving the "duh" left unsaid.

"Right. So take it."

Beth tried. She pushed on his shoulders, twisted her hips, but he restrained her easily, holding her pinned on her back. Struggling harder, she felt a twist of panic low in her belly, the instinctual fear of helplessness, of loss of control that comes from being held down by a bigger, stronger male.

"Don't panic." Ky must have caught the change in her, her struggles morphing from playful to deadly serious. "Panic takes away your ability to make decisions, to take control."

Beth forced herself to stop struggling and lay still beneath him, breathing hard. As the panic cleared, she realized that arousal had slipped in, liquefying her lower belly. *Just ignore it,*

143

the logical side of her brain ordered. It was just her body responding to the situation, that was all. Instinct—it was only instinct. A hot man straddling her—of course her body would react.

"Are you ready to listen?" Ky asked and Beth nodded, shoving the disconcerting heat spreading through her to the back of her mind.

"Ready," she said, setting her jaw firmly.

"Okay, I'm going to pretend to strangle you," he warned and wrapped his hands lightly around her throat. Beth swallowed as she shoved back another rush of panic and adrenaline-fueled lust.

"Grab my right arm with both hands." Ky nodded when she obeyed. "Now put your foot over mine—no, not on top, over. Right. Now push straight up with your hips and follow me as I fall."

As she followed his directions, he toppled to his right, unable to hold himself in place with his right hand or leg. Beth rolled with him and ended up on top, flushed and pleased with herself.

"Yes!" she crowed, both fists held over her head as she straddled *him* now. "I'm on top! You are my bitch!"

"Okay, watch it," he said dryly.

"You do realize that you're creating a monster here, don't you?" Harry's amused voice made both Beth and Ky look over to where he watched at the side of the ring. Although he was smiling, his cheeks were flushed and his eyes were hot, making Beth suddenly and intensely aware of the movement of Ky's rib cage beneath her thighs.

"Enough for today." Ky's voice had a raspy edge to it as he turned his gaze back to Beth. His eyes, warmed to molten gold, mesmerized her for a moment, until Ky arched his back beneath her, unbalancing her seat on his chest. "Off, woman!" he commanded.

144

She climbed to her feet, her legs shaky. Beth purposefully did not think about *why* they were unsteady and offered a hand to Ky.

"Right," he mocked with a snort of amusement, ignoring her hand and easily rolling to a standing position in the effortless way that Beth now envied.

"Whatever," she waved a dismissive hand at him. "You're still my bitch."

Harry laughed. "I told you, man—a monster."

Over the next few days, they settled into an odd sort of routine. Ky was still sleeping with them but that's all that was happening—sleeping. Actually, Beth acknowledged, the only thing that was happening was her *not* sleeping. Instead, she was just lying there, hot and aching, for endless, frustrated hours.

On Sunday afternoon, Beth had to get outside. Harry and Ky filled the loft with their big male bodies and a thick undercoat of sexual tension until she couldn't think straight.

"I'm going for a walk," she announced to the guys, who were sprawled at either end of the couch watching a Broncos game.

"Sounds good." Harry pushed himself to his feet. "I've eaten way too many cheese puffs. See? I'm orange." He held up his cheese-stained fingers as evidence and turned to Ky. "Want to walk?"

Shrugging, Ky clicked off the TV. "Might as well. This game sucks anyway." He stood up, stretching his arms to the ceiling.

"Um..." Beth wasn't sure how to say it tactfully, so she went for straight on. "Actually, I was hoping to have a little, well, alone time." The guys just looked at her blankly. "By myself. Without either of you. Alone."

"You're not walking by yourself," Harry told her. Usually Beth thought his protective streak was endearing and sweet but now it was just annoying.

"Yes," she clipped out, "I am. I'll see you guys in an hour." She turned to leave but Harry had maneuvered so that his towering frame blocked her exit.

"God, you're fast," she muttered. "Now move."

"No. It's not safe for you to be walking alone." He didn't budge.

Beth was moving from irritation to outright anger. "It's a perfectly beautiful, sunny afternoon. I am not five years old. I can walk around the fucking park if I want to." She poked the hard chest in front of her at each snapped-off sentence.

Harry's face was as hard as stone. "And I can walk around the fucking park too. So go." He stepped back to let her pass. With a suspicious glare, Beth moved toward the door. Harry followed.

"If you even think about walking behind me," she threatened, "I swear I will...I will..." Her mind blanked of all fitting punishments.

"You'll what?" The amused note in Harry's voice was the last straw.

"I'll move back to my place," she hissed and slammed the door behind her. The satisfying echo reverberated through the high-ceilinged space of the gym, even over the music, and the few members working out looked up, startled. Embarrassed, she hurried down the metal stairs to the gym floor.

"Hi, Charlie," she greeted the lanky kid when she passed the front desk, receiving a casual grin and wave in return.

"Hey, Beth," he said. "Which one of those two meatheads managed to piss you off?"

She had to smile at that. "Both of the meatheads."

"Ah," he nodded, giving her a commiserating nod as she headed for the door.

Once she was outside, her anger cooled quickly, allowing guilt to creep in. The image of Harry's stricken expression when she threatened to move out was plastered on her brain, poking at her conscience. With a sigh, she resolved to apologize to him when she got back.

It was a cool day but the late afternoon sun warmed her bare arms and the top of her head as she walked the four blocks to City Park. She waved to a family basking in the sunlight on their front porch as she dodged two kids speeding down the sidewalk on bikes. A smile touched the corners of her mouth. The beautiful day made it impossible to stay mad at anybody, even two gorgeous, extremely aggravating meatheads.

As she meandered through the park along the sun-dappled path, Beth felt the rest of her bad mood fall away. She passed the playground, glancing over when a little boy shrieked in excitement as his dad pushed him on the tire swing. The dad looked up at her and smiled, eyeing her with interest. Beth gave a quick wave and hurried on. She had enough guy problems without adding any more males to the mix.

She walked to the front of the pavilion and sat by the lake, idly watching the fountain in the center shoot water high into the air. A pair of Canadian geese stalked her, hoping for a tasty handout.

"Aren't you supposed to be migrating soon?" she asked them. They circled away warily at the sound of her voice. "Although I suppose Colorado, even in the winter, is a balmy place when you're from Canada."

Apparently deciding that she was not going to provide any food, the geese waddled off across the grass. Beth watched them go, a little jealous of their simple lives. *I bet they never have longings for threesomes with a hostile ex-soldier goose,* she thought, and then shook her head and pushed to her feet. This was her time alone, when Harry and Ky were not allowed along — and that included not permitting them to take up space in her brain.

She crossed through the park, past the delivery entrance to the zoo and the back side of the science museum. Late afternoon thunderclouds were gathering, blocking out the warming sun, and Beth shivered. She should probably head back, she realized, reluctant to return to deal with the consequences of her mini-tantrum. *Apologizing sucks*, she thought morosely, making a face.

With a sigh, she turned toward home. She had just taken a few steps when a fat raindrop plopped onto her arm. Peering at the ominous sky, Beth sped up to a jog as the rain began to fall in earnest, cold spatters hitting her face and shoulders, leaving wet circles on her t-shirt.

"Ow!" A small pellet of hail had smacked against her cheek and she broke into an all-out run toward the street bordering the park. Spotting a bus-stop shelter, Beth angled her path to meet it. Ducking inside the glass enclosure, she flopped down on the bench, struggling to catch her breath after her rain-drenched sprint.

A trickle of water ran down Beth's temple. She brushed it away with the back of her thumb. The rain and hail hammered against the shelter and ran in rivulets down the glass sides, blurring her view to outside. When her breathing had slowed, she stood up to peer through the water-streaked glass at the kaleidoscope of cars flying by.

Her breath fogged the glass in front of her face and Beth absently drew a heart with her finger. Inside the heart, she wrote "H + B", paused for a second, then added "+ K".

"Are you twelve?" she muttered under her breath with a huff of self-conscious laughter and started to lift her fist in order to scrub out the entire heart.

"Excuse me?"

The man's voice startled Beth and she whirled around to face the stranger who had joined her, unnoticed, in the shelter.

"Sorry—didn't mean to scare you," he told her with a smile. Beth, not reassured, nodded distantly and moved to stand closer to the opening.

"Waiting for the bus or just trying not to get wet?" he asked, undeterred by her standoffish demeanor.

"The latter," Beth eventually answered, unable to be rude enough not to respond at all, even though the man creeped her out. He was perfectly nice looking, with blond hair plastered to his forehead by the rain and straight white teeth, but something about him made all her instincts shriek that she should get away. She bit her lip, eyeing the downpour, debating whether to leave the shelter and brave the weather or stay and brave the stranger.

"Don't run away," the man wheedled. "I don't bite—unless you want me to." He laughed at his own tired joke, flashing his oversized teeth at her again.

Beth felt a flare of irritation. She had found a perfectly good way to stay out of the rain—and do a little doodling—and this annoying guy had to ruin it by making her all uncomfortable. "I should get home," she muttered, scowling out into the rain.

"Why? Is there a boyfriend waiting for you there?" His voice was greasy, she decided, greasy and false.

"Two," Beth threw back at him over her shoulder and darted into the rain. The wet weather definitely seemed like the preferred option now. The rain soaked her again, running uncomfortably through her hair and down the front of her tank top. Hail bit at her bare arms and the back of her neck as she tucked her head and ran along the muddy trail that paralleled the road, heading in the general direction of home. Glancing behind her, she saw the stranger had left the bus shelter and was following her. She sped up.

"Beth!"

She squinted through the downpour at a white van that had pulled over to the side of the road. *Who do I know who owns a van?* she wondered. The driver had lowered the passenger-side window and was leaning across the seat, gesturing for her to come over. She hesitated, throwing another glance over her shoulder. The stranger was only twenty feet away and moving closer. Taking a few steps toward the van, she recognized the man — it was Ed, her bus driver.

"Hop in — I'll give you a lift," he called, pushing the door open. "Hurry up — the seat's getting wet."

She swung into the dry haven of the van, pulling the door closed behind her as Ed closed her window with a button on his door. Beth looked out the window at the soggy, disappointed stranger and felt a surge of relief. That had been a little scary. If Ed hadn't come along, she really might have had to try out her self-defense skills.

She shivered and water trickled down her collarbone. "I'm afraid that I'm going to get your seat even wetter than leaving the door open would have," she apologized, buckling her seat belt before pushing soaked strands of hair out of her face. "Do you have a towel I could sit on?"

Ed shook his head. "Don't worry about it. What were you doing out in this weather anyway?" He turned the heat up and Beth sighed with pleasure as the air warmed her chilled skin. It was cozy inside the van, with hail clattering on the roof and the rhythmic whoosh and thump of the windshield wipers.

"Oh, I argued with my boyfriend —" She cut herself off before she could make it plural. "And went out for a walk. I guess I wasn't watching the weather."

Ed didn't respond except for a short nod.

"Thanks for picking me up," she babbled into the uncomfortable silence. She had never really had a conversation with Ed that went past pleasantries, so she searched her mind for something to say. "It was lucky you were driving by. Where were you headed?"

"The zoo," he told her and Beth looked at him in surprise. He had never struck her as the animal-loving type but, then again, she really didn't know him.

"I hope you were able to spend some time there before the rain started," she said.

He shook his head. "I never got there. Waited too late, I guess."

Beth's eyebrows met in a puzzled frown. When he pulled over to pick her up, he was headed away from the zoo, not toward it, she realized. An uneasy prickle started in her belly. Why would he lie about something as silly as that?

"Here's my street—turn right." She rushed her words, suddenly anxious to get out. The cozy security of the van now felt stifling and claustrophobic. "In fact, the rain is lightening up. Why don't you just drop me off here and I'll walk the rest of the way. Good exercise, you know." She gave Ed a forced smile but he didn't see it. He stared straight ahead and drove past the turn.

Craning her neck to look back at the missed street, she felt the uneasy feeling explode into straight-up fear. "Ed, let me out. Now." She tried to make her voice forceful but a nervous quaver had snuck in.

"Can't do that," he said neutrally.

"Sure you can," Beth told him, wincing at the shrill note of hysteria in her voice. "Just turn at the next street and loop around. It's coming up fast—okay, now turn..." She twisted in her seat, gesturing at the missed intersection, beginning to panic as familiar landmarks of her neighborhood grew tiny in the rearview mirror and then disappeared.

"Ow!" The sharp pain in her thigh brought her head whipping back around. As Ed pulled his hand back, something glinted between his fingers.

"What did you..." The words felt fuzzy in her mouth. She turned her head toward her door and the colors in her vision blurred. She couldn't focus her eyes or her brain but she could

151

still feel the frantic need to escape. Her fingers scrabbled against her seat belt buckle, desperate to find the release button.

Ed caught her hand, stopping her clumsy struggles. "Relax," he told her, his voice oddly gentle. "Just let yourself go."

She stared at the pale blob of his out-of-focus face. *Why is he doing this to me?* she wondered plaintively just before her world went black.

Chapter Eleven

🕰

Harry was pacing. Ky had been watching him wear a track across the floor for—he checked his watch—eighteen minutes. *Two more minutes before he goes after her*, Ky estimated, glancing at Harry's set face. *Or less.*

"Was I unreasonable?" Harry asked him, jerking to a stop and planting his fists on his hips.

Ky shrugged. What could he say? He didn't blame Harry for wanting to protect Beth. Fuck, Ky had already fallen into bodyguard mode around her and he had known her—what, a week? Normal people didn't understand it, though, didn't recognize that danger was everywhere, that injury and heartache and death could easily be around the next corner.

"Well?" Harry demanded, obviously not placated by a shrug.

Ky gave him a look. "Why are you asking *me* what's reasonable?" he asked.

"I don't know." Harry scrubbed his hands across his head. "I want to go after her but—" He looked at Ky, his normally cheerful face tight. "Do you think she'd actually do it?"

"Do what—move out?"

Harry winced at the words. "Yeah. You should see her apartment building. No security, no *light bulbs*, for fuck's sake—she has a stalker, you know."

Ky's head came up in surprise.

"Yeah—some asshole who drops cards at her place while she's at work, sends her flowers." Harry resumed his pacing. "She thinks learning to fight is fun, a hobby, something she'll

153

never have to use. She doesn't understand that not everyone's *nice*."

Ky pushed himself to his feet. "Let's go," he said, heading toward the door.

With barely a pause, Harry followed.

Two hours later, Harry was almost insane with worry. They had walked the neighborhood and City Park until the downpour had forced them back to the gym. Beth was still not there. They gave a wide-eyed Charlie strict instructions to call the second that Beth walked in the door before they took off in Harry's SUV to continue their search. No one said *if* she walked through the door. Harry couldn't even consider the possibility. *No,* he told himself, *she's taking a really long walk. She got caught in the rain and ducked into a coffee shop or something.* He tried to picture her, safe and warm, sipping a latté and reading the paper, oblivious to the time.

His eyes ached from peering through the windshield into sheets of rain. They had crisscrossed the park over and over, curving around the ridiculously meandering roads and roundabouts until Harry had lost patience and turned into the muddy grass, making his own paths through the deserted park.

It was almost fully dark when Harry pulled up to her apartment building, stopping the SUV with a lurch that jerked Ky into his seat belt. As he approached the entrance, Harry saw that the front door was propped open with a brick. He kicked it aside with restrained violence.

"See?" he demanded. "It's just left open all the time!"

Ky just nodded impatiently and shoved him through the doorway.

Ignoring the grinding pain in his knee, Harry ran up the stairs and through the dim hallway to Beth's door. Harry hammered his fist against it, even as his twisting gut told him that no one was inside her apartment. His pounding echoed back with no response, no opening swing of the door, no annoyed Beth telling him to be quiet or he'd upset the neighbors.

Ky grabbed his arm, stopping the fall of his fist.

"She's not here," he told Harry, giving his arm a little shake. Harry set his jaw and tried to yank free, determined to pound on the door until Beth answered it or it fell down, but Ky held on, using his other hand to grip the back of Harry's neck, forcing him to look at Ky.

"She isn't here," Ky said again and Harry finally met his eyes.

"Then where the fuck is she?" He heard his voice crack halfway through. His anger was slipping and he grabbed for it, preferring rage to the bewildered terror that rushed in to replace it. Beth wasn't warm and dry at a coffee shop somewhere—she was too considerate for that, too conscious of his constant worry.

Ky tugged on the back of his neck and Harry slumped forward, pressing his forehead against the broad shelf of Ky's shoulder.

"We'll find her," Ky said and Harry nodded without raising his head. They would find her. Harry had to believe that or he would lose his mind.

Beth woke to darkness. She was used to the constant twilight of city nights, the glow from streetlights and buildings and car headlights warming the sky to a red glow. This was different—this was a true, complete blackness. The dark pressed in on her, not letting air pass into her lungs, choking her with fear.

Don't panic. She forced her breathing to slow and deepen as Ky's words from their training session echoed in her mind. Forcing herself to ignore the darkness, Beth focused on what her other senses could tell her, examining each tiny detail in order to hold back the terror that threatened to envelop her, to overwhelm her brain and leave her helpless.

She was alive. That was good. When she tried to move her arms, she realized that her wrists were bound behind her. That was not so good. Contorting her hands, her fingers slipped across a smooth surface covering her wrists—duct tape? *It really is the all-purpose tool*, she thought, grimacing at her gallows humor.

When she tried to shift her legs, Beth could feel that her ankles were taped as well, stacked on top of each other as she lay curled on her side. There was carpet beneath her—short, prickly nap that smelled like dust and gasoline.

Fabric, rough and musty, brushed her arm when she moved. Beth blinked and felt her eyelashes bump into something. It was almost a relief to realize that she had a blanket covering her. That explained the suffocating darkness.

The floor was shifting beneath her, vibrating and bumping against the side of her head. She must still be in the van, she figured, hearing the hum of the engine, the *whump-whump* of the tires crossing seams in the road.

Where is he taking me? she wondered. Beth could feel the hysteria building in her chest, wanting to bubble out of her in a scream. *No*, she thought, fighting the urge. There is no point in yelling while still in the van. All that would do is let Ed know that she was awake.

Oh God, Ed. Her bus driver. The guy she had greeted cheerfully twice a day, who she'd always thought of as shy and sweet and harmlessly odd—*he* was her stalker. All those cards, the flowers—she jerked, pulling painfully at her bound hands. The notes had changed after she'd met Harry, she remembered. The cards had gotten cruel and angry once Harry had started walking her to the bus stop and giving her a kiss goodbye, after Ed had seen them together.

How stupid I've been, she thought, giving her head a thump against the carpet. She should have sensed something was off about Ed. Instead, she had been completely oblivious. And getting into his van—even five-year-olds knew better than to get into a car with a stranger. A van, especially—how many horror movies had she seen? A van was always the serial killer's transportation of choice.

She shivered. *Stop it,* she told herself sternly. He hadn't killed her yet—wasn't that a good sign? Maybe he just wanted to...keep her. Beth shuddered again. She was breathing in shallow gulps and she could feel her heart fluttering like a captured bird's. *Be brave,* she told herself. *Harry and Ky will find you.*

Beth shook her head, the scrubby carpet scratching her cheek. She couldn't wait for the guys to save her, like some helpless woman tied to the railroad tracks in an old, silent movie.

A plan. She seized on the idea. She needed a plan. Her brain wouldn't focus and she let out an almost silent groan. She had always been terrible at improv.

Okay, she commanded herself. *Think.* What would she be yelling at the screen if this was a movie? She needed a weapon. No, first she needed her hands free so she could hold a weapon. *Good,* she commended herself, relieved to have something to focus on other than the possibilities of what Ed might do to her once the van stopped.

Twisting her hands, Beth investigated the tape holding her wrists together as thoroughly as she could, discovering to her disappointment that she could only brush the slick surface with her fingertips. There was no chance of getting the kind of grip necessary to tear the tape. She needed something sharp.

Feeling as far as her arms would reach, which wasn't very far, Beth discovered only more dirty carpet. When she tipped slightly toward her back, she was able to explore a fraction farther but it still wasn't enough. Pushing her hips over, followed by a tiny shift of her shoulders, she moved backward, just a bare inch, but it felt like a huge, obvious movement to her. Fear that Ed might notice, might guess what she was doing, shot through her. Her heart pounded so loudly that she was sure he could hear it.

The van's engine slowed and labored as the tires dipped into ruts in the road. She tried to hold her head clear of the carpet but her face smacked into the floor several times.

It must have been a winding road as well as a bumpy one, since Beth could feel her weight shift with each curve that the van navigated. She used the momentum to slide across the floor until she could touch the side of the van. Her backside pressed against the lump of the wheel well as her hands touched everything they could reach, searching for a sharp edge but finding only smooth metal beneath her fingers.

As she felt along the side of the van, Beth tried to keep track of the turns but her head was still fuzzy from whatever drug he had given her to knock her out. She guessed, *left, left, right just a little, then…another right?*

Her plan to free herself flew out of her mind when she felt the van slow. With a final lurch, the vehicle stopped completely. Her heart hammered and nausea pressed against the back of her throat as she heard the driver's side door slam. Were they at a gas station? A rest stop? Should she scream?

She almost shrieked involuntarily as another door was jerked open, this one close to her feet, but she managed to strangle the sound before it reached her throat. He grabbed her ankles and pulled her toward him, burning her bare arm against the carpet. It was nearly impossible to stay limp, to pretend unconsciousness, but Beth did her best.

"So you're awake." *Obviously, I'm not that great of an actress*, she thought as her shaking returned. Although she tried to hold her muscles stiff to fight the shudders, her body ignored her efforts until she was almost vibrating.

"You might as well do the work then, and save me from carrying you in." Ed's voice was muffled through the blanket that still covered her head but she could understand what he was saying well enough.

Not a gas station. She felt the tape around her ankles tighten and then he pulled it free. It didn't hurt, since her jeans and socks protected her legs, but the tearing sound made her squeeze her eyelids together.

What should I do? she wondered frantically, frozen not through intent this time but in panicked indecision. The only movement she made was her uncontrolled quaking. Ed yanked the blanket off her and Beth blinked at the night sky, pinpoints of light blacked out by Ed's looming silhouette.

"Up you go," he said, grabbing her arm and dragging her out of the van, holding her upright until she found her feet. Beth was surprised by the strength hidden in his lanky body.

The moon was only half-full and vaguely illuminated the rocky, scrubby ground peppered with evergreens. They were obviously high in the mountains—the air felt thin and cold, and her panting breaths dried her mouth. Ed had pulled the van next to a drooping cabin with small, dark windows that frightened her more than anything else had during the entire horrifying day.

"Ed." Her teeth chattered, clicking together as she spoke. She clenched her jaw, trying to force back the shudders. Seeing his face, so familiar and innocuous, feeling the tight grip of his big-knuckled fingers around her arm, the same hands she had seen on the bus' steering wheel a hundred times—her idea of Ed did not fit with what was happening. Beth said his name as if she were checking to see if he was really there, if her eyes were to be trusted. She wanted him to laugh, to say that none of this was real, that he hadn't stalked her or kidnapped her or tied her up in the back of his van.

But he didn't say any of those things. Instead he grunted, "Come on," and pulled at her arm, urging her toward the crooked front door of the cabin.

"Wait," she told him, instinctively leaning back away from the pressure.

Ed turned to face her, grabbing her other arm as if he was going to toss her over his shoulder in a fireman's hold. As he bent toward her, Beth swung her head forward, not planning, not thinking—and cracked her forehead against the bridge of his nose.

He yelped, dropping her arms to clutch his face. Beth paused for a moment, almost as startled by the head-butt as Ed was. *Run!* her brain screamed and she did, pivoting around and bolting, her feet sliding in the loose rocks as she scrambled down a slope toward a wall of trees that promised dark shadows and hiding places. Rocks and spiky plants tripped her up and her hands, still taped behind her back, couldn't offer balance. If she fell, she was fully aware that nothing would stop her from landing on her face.

The trees were getting closer and Beth ran faster, fixing her eyes on the ground in front of her, trying to distinguish the actual obstacles from the shadows created by the moon. She didn't dare glance back, didn't want to know if he was right behind her. He could very well be breathing down her neck— Beth couldn't hear anything except her own labored breathing and the thud of her feet hitting the ground.

So close, she thought, flying over the final few feet of bare ground before the trees. *So* –

She hit an invisible wall, sharp lines of pain running across her midsection and thighs before she bounced backward and fell to the ground. Immediately, Beth rolled to her side and then her knees, dragging in ragged breaths, fighting to regain her feet and her air as her eyes searched for the barrier that stopped her headlong flight.

She saw the narrow, dark shape of a fencepost and something in her mind clicked. Wire fencing, hidden by the darkness, must have blocked her way and knocked her backward. Dropping to her belly, not even feeling the pain as she hit the ground hard, Beth pushed herself along with her feet, wriggling on her stomach beneath the lowest wire.

The wire grazed her hands and she sucked in a sobbing breath. *Halfway there,* she thought...

But then hands wrapped around her ankles for the second time that night, wrenching her back away from escape, scraping her stomach on the rocky ground as her tank top was dragged up under her armpits.

When her body was clear of the fence, Ed hauled her to her feet by her trussed arms, jerking a shriek of pain from her. His arm wrapped under her chin and pressed against her throat. Beth struggled, kicking backward and twisting her body in his hold, but everything went black for the second time that day.

When they got back to the gym, Ky could tell from one glance at Charlie's face that Beth hadn't returned. He wanted to check the loft anyway, to see for himself that the unthinkable was happening. He moved quickly toward the stairs but Harry still beat him to the door, swearing at the keys that shook and jangled together in his hand.

"Give me those," Ky ordered, trying to take them from him but Harry shouldered him away.

"I've got it," Harry snapped, forcing the key into the lock and twisting it violently. The door swung open, revealing the dark, empty loft.

"Beth?" Harry called out as he strode inside but her name echoed, unanswered. His face emptied of hope for a bare, heartbreaking second before he jerked back to action.

"I'll try calling her again," he said, heading to the living room to resume his pacing while he pulled out his cell. A phone rang behind Ky, making him jump and whirl around, half expecting Beth to be standing in the kitchen with a mischievous look on her face.

It was just her purse sitting on the counter. Ky crossed to it, digging out the phone and silencing it. It showed forty-two missed calls. He stared at her wallet, tucked inside her purse, and swallowed hard.

"Harry," he called out, holding up the wallet, but Harry was already right beside him, staring at the purse. *She's out there with no cash, no credit cards, no ID*, Ky thought grimly. The last hope that Beth was tucked away somewhere, pissed at them but otherwise fine, faded away.

Ky pulled his own cell from his pocket and Harry looked at him.

"I'm calling the cops," Ky explained.

Harry shook his head. "I called them already. They won't do anything. Not until she's been missing for two days. Two fucking days!"

Shrugging, Ky found the number and hit "send" as his mouth curved in a humorless smile. "I have someone on the inside," he said, his stomach twisting as he listened to the phone ring on the other end.

"West here," barked a voice and Ky felt the words ball up in his throat. *Beth*, he told himself. *She needs you to do this.* The thought helped, loosening the knot enough for him to speak.

"Dad." He closed his eyes, turning his face away from Harry's view. "I need your help."

The darkness was back. No moon, no stars, just the same dense black that she had woken up to in the van. Beth blinked, squeezing her eyelids together and then staring into the emptiness, as if she could see through sheer will alone. Nothing.

She was on her back, her arms at her sides—not taped anymore, she realized, and jerked her hands toward her face, feeling for a blanket, a blindfold, whatever was creating this thick blackness.

Her eyes were uncovered. Somehow, that was scarier.

Touching her wrist with her other hand, Beth could feel the sticky residue on the slightly swollen area where the tape had been yanked off, leaving her skin hairless and hot. It was the only place on her body that was warm. A horrifying idea occurred to her, making her jump and grab at her middle, relief rushing over her at the feel of her tank top beneath her fingers. Her jeans were still on as well, she discovered.

What are you doing? The strident voice in her brain, the one that was so determined to survive, had suddenly woken up. Beth shook her head, wincing at a throb of pain beneath her skull. She realized that she was just lying there, helpless, as if her hands and feet were still bound, when Ed could be back any minute.

Get up, the voice ordered. *Get out.*

Rolling to her side, Beth ignored the twinges of her sore muscles and followed the giving surface of whatever she was lying on—a mattress of some sort, she guessed—until her fingers curled over the edge. She slid toward the side, the rough denim of her jeans making a soft noise as it brushed against the mattress.

Beth froze, panic locking her in place as she wondered whether Ed was already here, wherever "here" was. Was he standing in silence, listening to her move? She swallowed her fear, forcing herself to shift to the edge of the bed.

Just don't think about it, she ordered herself. If she let herself imagine him, think about him standing in the darkness, waiting for her to bump into his motionless figure... Gritting her teeth together, Beth found the cold, smooth floor with her hand. Pushing herself off the mattress and onto her knees, she tried to steady herself as dizziness swept over her.

As her mind cleared, she was able to stand, straightening carefully while holding a hand above her head in case the ceiling was low. *The last thing I need is a concussion,* she thought with a grimace, but neither her head nor her hand met anything except air. The complete darkness and lack of solid contact disoriented her, as if she was twisting in a murky pool of water. She swayed, not completely sure for a moment which way was up.

She extended her arms but only felt empty space. Moving across the floor with shuffling steps, she crisscrossed her arms in front of her and then extended them to her sides, sweeping the air with wide gestures. After six careful steps, her fingers caught on a wall—concrete blocks, she could tell, feeling the square outline and the bumpy texture of the surface.

When her hand met the wall, she hesitated, unsure about what to do next. She knew she should move, should find a way out, but after making actual, physical contact with something besides air or musty mattress, she was reluctant to take her hand off the concrete.

Moving slowly, she slid her feet carefully along the floor, her fingers never leaving the cold comfort of the wall. Counting her steps, Beth felt along the rough blocks, hoping to seize on the edge of a doorway, the frame of a window—hell, she'd settle for a light switch.

Beth remembered hearing somewhere that the way to escape a maze was to keep one hand on the wall and just follow it out. If it worked for a maze, surely it would work for a room as well. *There has to be some kind of opening, right?* she thought a little desperately.

Her heart was speeding up again, the single-minded focus on each step splintering, allowing panic to creep in around the edges.

"Stop it." Her words were quiet but they echoed in the darkness. Beth clamped a hand over her mouth, too late to hold back the sound. She heard something—footsteps?—above her and she stared into the dark, her eyes unblinking, so wide that tears gathered around the edges but didn't fall.

Another noise, a rattling, scraping sound, came so close to her that she jumped, trying to refocus on where it originated, but one spot of darkness was the same as the next. Her breaths rushed in and out, crowding her throat, as her nails dug into her bare arms.

A square of the ceiling fell away, framing a black silhouette against the barely lit background, only visible to Beth because of the complete absence of light a few seconds before. She heard a soft click and was blinded by a flood of brightness across her eyes.

"What did he say?" Harry asked even before Ky could end the call. Harry had barely restrained himself from grabbing the phone away from Ky during the endless conversation. Harry glanced at his watch—okay, so it had been an endless four-minute conversation.

"Well?" he demanded when Ky didn't immediately answer. A part of Harry admired him for making the call, for reaching out to his dad, but the rest of him couldn't focus on that, couldn't concentrate on anything except Beth.

"Can't do much," Ky said, staring blindly at his cell phone. "No point running her credit cards, no plates to check. He'll put her description in the system, let us know if he gets any hits. He has a buddy with DPD—he's going to give him a call in the morning, see if anything strange went down today—yesterday," he corrected himself, finally focusing on his phone and noticing the time.

The same wave of emotion rushed over Harry, an equal mix of terror and frustration and helplessness. "We have to do *something*," he said, wincing at the pleading note in his voice.

Ky dropped his gaze. "He said to start calling hospitals."

Harry stared at him. "Fuck."

Throwing an arm up to protect her eyes from the glare, Beth stumbled back a few steps, the light hitting her like an actual blow. All her bravery, all her plans dissolved in one bright flash and all she could do was cower.

Her eyes finally adjusted, although she still had to shield her gaze from the light. Ed was still just an outline, this time because the light was in front rather than in back. He must have descended a ladder or stairs, as he was on her level now instead of above her. He still hadn't said anything, not a word, and for some reason, this sparked a surge of rage that freed Beth's tongue.

"What do you want?" she demanded. Despite her anger, Beth's voice wavered halfway through.

Ed didn't answer.

"Damn you!" She sucked in a sobbing breath, felt it rough against her throat. "What do you want?"

When he remained silent, her tears began in earnest and Beth sank to her knees, doubled over with the force of her sobs. She hated each tear that forced its way out of her, furious that her body was betraying her this way, that he had the power to make her cry. Eventually the tears stopped, leaving only the dry heaves of sobs.

"We had to be together."

Ed's voice made her jump and jerk her head up. She had forgotten about the powerful flashlight and blinded herself again.

"This was the only way."

"No." Beth shook her head and then couldn't stop. "No. This is not the way. This is the *insane* way."

Ed balanced the flashlight on one of the steps of the angled ladder. She could see now that the light wasn't directly in her eyes but she almost wished that she couldn't. The indirect illumination cut strange shapes into Ed's face, making him harsh and strange and scary—*scarier*, Beth thought, tightening her arms around her middle.

She looked away, glanced around the small room. It was empty except for the mattress in the middle of the floor. Concrete surrounded them, floor and walls, the only wood the exposed ceiling joists and the ladder that descended into the space.

"You were straying," he said, drawing her startled gaze back to him.

"What?" She climbed to her feet slowly, feeling vulnerable on her knees, trapped and unable to run.

"Those men," he said in the same calm voice. "I saw you kiss them. Hug them. They were making you dirty."

He's crazy, Beth realized and then felt stupid. *Of course he's crazy,* she told herself. *He just kidnapped you, dumbass.*

"It wasn't dirty," she said slowly, trying to feel her way. She wasn't sure what would get through to him and what would just make things worse. "They're my boyfriends."

"No!" he snapped, taking a step toward her. Beth retreated instinctively and felt the rough wall against her back. Obviously, that had fallen under the "make things worse" category.

"Okay," she gasped, trying to force her brain to work. "They're not my boyfriends?"

"They're pretty boys," he sneered, his calm demeanor shredding before her eyes. "They expect everything to fall in their laps. They don't know how to work for something — don't know how to earn anything."

"So you *earned* me?" Although terror still thrummed through Beth, she felt a small spark of indignation when he nodded.

"All those cards, all those days of watching out for you on the bus, making sure no one bothered you, the flowers — I was patient. I knew we belonged together and I was just waiting for you to realize it." The shadows on his face shifted as he scowled. "And then you just threw it all away."

"There is nothing between us," Beth told him. "You don't even know me."

Closing the space between them in two long strides, Ed cupped her face in both hands, holding her head still when she tried to flinch away. "I know everything about you. I know that we belong together."

Beth shook her head as well as she could in his grip. "No. We don't. You need to let me go. Just let me go now and I won't tell the cops or anything. We'll just take it as a learning experience—you've learned not to kidnap women and I've learned not to get into strange men's vans—"

She broke off with a gasp when Ed thumped her head back against the wall. "I'm not a strange man," he said. "I'm your soul mate."

Despite the pain bouncing around her skull and the fear that gripped her, Beth said stubbornly, "No, you're not. You're a stranger—a *crazy* stranger!"

"Stop it!" He dropped his hands to her upper arms and shook her, hard. "We need to be together—you'll see." Lifting her off the floor, Ed tossed her sideways across the mattress. She rolled to her side immediately but he had followed her down and twisted her onto her back, pinning her easily with his weight.

"You'll see," he repeated, his voice thick.

No, no, no, no, her brain repeated over and over, knowing what came next, remembering this from every nightmare she'd had since she was old enough to realize that she was female and vulnerable.

Ed tried to kiss her and she bit him. Rearing back with a yelp, he slapped her so hard she saw actual stars.

"Why are you denying this? It was meant to be." He held her down with one hand on her throat as his other fumbled with his pants. Hysteria whipped Beth's head against the mattress, made her twist her body, fighting his.

A sense of déjà vu crept in, sneaking in under her terror. Another man pinning her down, his hands gentle on her throat even while he barked orders. Ky. Harry watching, his eyes lit with blue fire. What had Ky told her? She tried desperately to remember.

Grab his arm with both hands. She heard Ky's voice as if he was in the room with her. Her fingers circled Ed's wiry arm. Foot over his. That one was harder but she managed. Now hips straight up — hard.

Even in the strange light of the flashlight, she saw his eyes widen in surprise as he toppled to the side, Beth following him down. She hesitated for a second once she was above him and then scrambled into action, shifting over until her knee rested squarely in his crotch.

She ground down with all of her weight, all of the strength she could muster, watching his face as it went slack with shock. His body snapped into a ball, tossing Beth unnoticed to the side, as he dragged in agonized breaths, keening in pain.

Beth rolled to her feet, not sparing another glance back as she grabbed the flashlight and shot up the ladder. She emerged in the main room of the cabin, pulling herself through the square opening on the floor. Freedom beckoned but she only took two steps toward the front door before spinning back to the black hole in the floor.

The trapdoor was heavy but adrenaline helped her slam it shut and shoot the metal bolt home, trapping Ed in the cell he had prepared for her.

Ky hammered the heavy bag with his fists. The gym was closed, empty except for him, the dim security lights providing the only illumination. He didn't know how long he had been attacking the bag. All he knew was that it was long enough to make his arms quiver and turn his knees to water, but it wasn't long enough to quiet his brain.

His glove slid off the bag on his final right hook and he toppled sideways, barely catching himself with a couple of staggering, sideways steps. Bent over, arms braced against his shaking thighs, he gasped for air.

"Where the fuck are you, Barbie?"

Chapter Twelve

When Ky finally made it back up the stairs to the loft, he saw Harry hunched over on the couch with some kind of notebook in his hands. Ky moved to stand next to Harry, close enough to see what he was looking at.

It was Beth's sketchbook, the one she always kept in her purse so she could draw during quiet moments — on the bus, in line at the DMV, on one of her rest days at the gym as she waited for him or Harry to finish working out. Harry was staring at a sketch of him and Ky. Beth had caught them in an unguarded moment when they were messing around after a sparring session. Harry had Ky in a playful headlock, grinning in his happy Harry way, and Ky was smiling up at him.

To Ky, his adoration of Harry blazed from the page and he had to glance away from the picture, embarrassed. He looked at Harry instead, and his gut clenched at Harry's expression — so afraid, so lost. Ky was used to Harry being the strong one, the Cap'n, always prepared and always laughing, not scared of anything.

"This is how she sees us, Pokey," Harry said, his voice raw from worry and lack of sleep. Ky couldn't say anything — no reassurances, no hope, just no words at all. All he could do was flip the pages of the sketchbook over to another picture, this one of a stranger, a drawing that didn't show love in every pencil stroke. Ky cupped his hand around the back of Harry's skull and pulled the other man's head against his sweat-soaked stomach in a rough embrace. Locking his arms around Ky's waist, Harry burrowed his face against the hard abs.

Ky tightened his fingers behind Harry's head and closed his eyes at the pain in his heart.

Once out of the ugly little cabin, Beth ran to the van. Grabbing the driver's door handle, she threw her weight backward, nearly pulling her shoulder out of its socket when the door refused to open. Staring at the handle in utter disbelief, she gave it another jerk. *Who locks a car in the middle of nowhere?* She took a single step back toward the cabin and then turned and ran in the opposite direction. The keys might be somewhere in the cabin and Ed might still be locked safely beneath the floor, but Beth just couldn't force herself to go back into the hulking structure.

The road was barely two tire tracks, disguised by the darkness. She stumbled and fell several times when her toe caught on the uneven footing or a rock shifted beneath her. She lost the flashlight on her second fall, spent precious seconds searching for it but then fear caught her and she had to run again.

Each time she fell, she ignored the pain in her knees and palms, pushed herself up and took off into the darkness. A small part of her brain told her that it was stupid to blindly tear around the mountain—she had gone off the road in her panicked flight—but she couldn't help it. She had to get away from Ed as fast as she could.

When she finally stopped, sucking in painful breaths of the thin air, she realized that she was very, very lost. Dawn was turning the blackness around her a light gray but everything still looked the same, no matter which direction she turned. The trace of a road had completely disappeared. Sweat evaporated almost instantly from her skin, leaving her shivering in her thin tank. It was freaking cold in the mountains.

Although she had lived in Colorado all her life, she had never been an outdoorsy kind of person. Camping was not something she considered fun—the beds were hard and she always felt dirty. An occasional hike was fine, as long as it was on a groomed trail, lasted no more than a few hours and was followed by a shower and lunch at a restaurant. She had never been in Girl Scouts, had never wanted to learn how to start a fire by rubbing two sticks together and, even if a compass had magically appeared, she wouldn't really know what to do with it.

In Denver, she always knew which direction she was going because the mountains were to the west. Here, to her disgust, the mountains were on all sides. She turned in a full circle and the pink edge of sunlight creeping over one of the peaks caught her eye.

The mountains might be all around me, she thought with a small, triumphant smile, *but the sun only comes up in the east.* East was good — that was the direction of civilization.

A full-body shudder overtook her. Walking would help keep her warm, she decided, and headed toward the rising sun.

By dawn, Harry had pulled himself together. Losing it wasn't going to help Beth, he told his red-eyed, stubbly jawed reflection. He turned away from the mirror to see Ky in the bathroom doorway, watching him warily.

"What'd your dad say?" Harry asked, his heart sinking when Ky shrugged and shook his head.

"He had nothing."

Pulling his shoulders back, Harry pushed aside the disappointment. "Okay. You take the neighborhood, spiraling out from here, and I'll take the park."

Even before the words were out of his mouth, Ky had given a short nod and left.

"Okay, Beth," Harry said to the empty bathroom. "Time to get you home."

No one had seen her. Harry had crisscrossed the park over and over, asking every person walking a dog, biking, running or sitting under one of the big trees drinking out of a paper-bag-wrapped bottle if they had seen her.

He had brought a picture, one of his favorites of her, taken one day when Beth had just finished working out. When Harry had called her name, she had glanced over her shoulder and smiled at him, giving him just enough time to take the picture before she noticed the camera and ducked, laughing, out of range, giving him hell for taking her photo when she was, in her words, "a total mess". He thought she looked beautiful.

He was losing his voice from asking over and over, "Did you see this woman here yesterday?" and losing heart at every "no" or head shake.

"Are you sure you didn't see her?"

The woman pushing a stroller shook her head and hurried away, giving Harry a quick, uneasy look over her shoulder. He blew out a frustrated breath and ran a hand over his face, feeling the rough stubble. *Great*, he thought. Now he was scaring people. It was probably an entirely different crowd at the park on a Monday morning than had been there on Sunday afternoon, he knew. The odds of talking to anyone who had seen her were slim.

Depression and dark fears threatened to overwhelm him but he shoved them back, striding over to a man pushing his toddler on a swing. The man flinched as Harry approached. Harry tried to lighten his grim expression but didn't think he was very successful, judging by the man's wary look.

"Did you see her yesterday?" Harry asked the same question he'd been asking all morning, thrusting the photo in front of the man's startled face.

The man glanced down automatically and smiled. "Yeah," he said. "I remember her — pretty girl."

Harry blinked at him for a second, so accustomed to "no" that a "yes" took several moments to register. "Really? You did? Where? Was someone with her? Which way was she headed? Was someone following her?"

"Um." The man took a half step back at the barrage of questions. "What?"

Taking a deep breath, Harry restrained the urge to beat the answers out of the man. "Where did you see her?" he asked, speaking slowly with a great effort.

"Right over there." He waved toward a path parallel to the playground.

"Was she alone?"

The man nodded.

"Was anyone following her? Was anyone who looked suspicious lurking around?" Harry sucked back the next question when the man started looking panicked again.

"Is she okay?" he asked, lifting his fractious child from the swing. "Did something happen to her?"

"She's missing," Harry told him impatiently. "Was someone there?"

"Not that I noticed," the man said slowly, squinting a little as if trying to remember. "I wasn't really paying attention though—if I look away from Tyler for a second, he's gone." He gestured toward his little boy, who was already running off toward a slide. His dad hurried to catch up as Harry followed close behind.

"Which way was she going?" he asked.

"Toward the lake—or pond or whatever. The one next to the pavilion."

Harry gave a short nod. "Did she look worried, anxious—anything like that?"

The man grinned. "Nope. She looked pretty content, like she was just out for a stroll." His smile dropped away. "Sorry. I forgot that she's missing. I hope you find her."

"So do I," Harry told him, wincing at the massive understatement. He dug in his pocket and pulled out one of his cards for the gym. "Call me if you think of anything else."

The man studied the card. "Sure."

"Thanks," Harry tossed over his shoulder as he hurried toward the pavilion, digging his cell phone out of his pocket.

"Someone saw her," he said when Ky answered. Talking to someone who actually remembered her had left his heart pounding so hard he could barely hear Ky's response.

"Give me ten minutes—I'll meet you," Ky was saying. "Where?"

"The pavilion by the pond."

Harry waited through a second of silence and then glanced at his phone. Ky had already hung up.

No one else had seen her. Harry didn't know what he had expected—a trail of breadcrumbs? A neon sign with an arrow? The surge of excitement Harry had felt after talking with the man on the playground was quickly deflating.

"Hammer's on his way," Ky said.

Harry's head whipped around. "You called him?"

He shrugged. "He's a PI. Thought he could help."

"Good idea." Rubbing a hand across his head, Harry turned in a slow circle, taking in the pavilion, the pond, the trees scattered across the green expanse. "Where did she go?" he asked, half to himself.

"It wasn't that way," Ky pointed back toward the playground. When Harry raised a questioning eyebrow at him, Ky explained, "That guy who saw her—he noticed her. Thought she was cute?"

Harry clenched his teeth together and gave a short nod.

"He was watching for her then—would have known if she passed him again."

"Good point." Harry looked out over the park, thinking. "There aren't any roads in that direction."

It was Ky's turn to lift an inquiring brow.

"If someone," Harry swallowed hard, "took her, they would need a car close by. It's hard to get a fighting, screaming woman a few feet, much less across a park. Someone would notice."

Ky looked across the pond, his face and voice tight as he asked, "Could she still be here?"

The idea hit Harry in his stomach like a punch. "No," he snapped immediately. And then repeated more slowly, "No. People are crawling all over this park. It's been almost sixteen hours. Someone would have...found her." He could feel his hands shaking and shoved them into his pockets.

Ky gave him a quick glance and then nodded. "Okay. So, perimeter?"

"I'll take that," Harry said quickly, grateful that Ky had let it go. There were some things that he just couldn't think about without falling apart. "You check out the interior roads through the park. Keep an eye out for tire tracks through the grass too."

Giving him a sideways look, Ky clarified, "Tracks that aren't ours, you mean."

"Yeah. Someone else had to have seen her, right? People don't just disappear."

Ky didn't answer. He just gave Harry a rough squeeze on the arm and headed off across the park.

"Stupid mountains."

Beth was hot. The sun was high in the sky and her bone-deep shivers during the night seemed impossible. How could she have been so cold when she was burning up just a few hours later? She was also thirsty. Incredibly thirsty. Each breath of dry, thin air felt as though it sucked the last drops of moisture from her.

Although she was trying to walk in a straight line, boulders and steep drop-offs blocked her way, forcing her to make frequent detours. Even when her path was clear, Beth wasn't quite sure she was still headed east. It was easy when the sun was coming up and she could just keep walking toward it. Now, with the sun up above her, it would be all too easy to wander in the wrong direction.

A scrubby evergreen cast a pitifully small shadow and Beth sat down in the measly bit of shade to rest for a moment, shifting around as she tried to find a comfortable seat on the stony ground. After a few moments, she gave up and attempted to ignore the hard press of a rock in her rear.

She eyed a small cactus that squatted close to the ground. Living in Denver, surrounded by sprinkler-fed lawns, she often forgot that the lush, green grass wasn't natural for Colorado. Still, it was strange to see a cactus.

Beth looked around, half expecting to see Ed approaching. Despite her paranoia, the panicked rush of fear that had kept her moving through the night had dulled and now she just felt thirsty. Thirsty and bone-tired. Her feet were bruised from the rocky ground, even with the cushion of her athletic shoes.

With a soundless sigh, Beth wrapped her arms around her updrawn legs and rested a cheek on her scraped knee. She could still see the cactus, although it looked sideways now from the tilt of her head. She had a vague memory of watching something on TV about how cacti stored water. The thought of moisture made her try to swallow but her throat was so dry that she gagged. The cactus was starting to look better and better, and she imagined breaking off the top and watching water shoot into the air, as if the cactus was an open fire hydrant. The only problem was that she couldn't remember if her sketchy knowledge of the cactus's water-holding ability came from a *Nature* special or if she had seen it on a cartoon. She shrugged—either way, it was worth a try.

Pushing herself to her knees, she reached for the flat, round cactus and then hesitated. It looked a little dangerous to touch. Beth tried to grasp in between the sharp spines but sliver-thin needles worked their way into her skin, making her fingers itch and burn. Gritting her teeth, she twisted it hard. The cactus was surprisingly resilient, bending instead of breaking. Beth struggled with it for a few seconds before releasing the spiny plant with a frustrated huff.

She stared balefully at the small green thing as she stood, giving the cactus a final, aggravated kick and immediately feeling guilty.

"Great," she muttered. "No water and I've probably killed the poor thing."

Beth realized that, while she had been fighting a cactus, Ed could have been tracking her, might even be over the ridge right behind her. Swallowing down a surge of panic, she forced herself to sit back down on her uncomfortably rocky seat. Stumbling around during the day was only going to dehydrate her further. Beth knew that she had to rest sometime—it was better to walk at night, when the sun wasn't sucking everything that resembled liquid from her body.

Trying very hard not to think about Ed, Beth sat on her rock and waited for darkness.

Harry really wanted to hit something. He had circled the park over and over, asking everyone he passed whether they had seen Beth. No one had. The day was slipping by and the typical afternoon storm clouds bunched in the western sky.

"Shit," he muttered. Rain would clear out the park and he would be left by himself with only a soggy picture for company.

He blinked. *Wait*, he thought. Rain—it had been pouring the previous day. What if Beth had been caught in the storm?

Where would she have gone? Harry broke into a trot as he started his umpteenth pass around the park, this time looking for possible shelter.

He dismissed options as he passed — the overhang on that building was too narrow, that tree wouldn't have blocked the wind tossing rain and hail into Beth's face. When he saw the bus shelter, he ran faster, knowing in his gut that this was it, that this would have been the prime place for her to wait out the storm.

One older woman was sitting in the shelter when he pulled up, breathing hard from his sprint. She looked at him curiously.

"No reason to run. The bus won't be here for five minutes at least," she told him.

He just nodded and pulled out Beth's picture. "Did you see her here yesterday?"

The woman was shaking her head even before she looked at the photo. "Didn't take the bus yesterday. My sister drives me to church on Sundays."

Even after the thousand "nos" he had heard that day, Harry still felt a pang of disappointment. "Thanks," he muttered, sitting heavily on the bench. *So what if she had been here?* he wondered, discouraged and exhausted. What would the shelter tell him?

His head tilted back until it bumped the wall behind him. The clouds were closing in on the sun but a few bright rays escaped around the edges, highlighting the dirt that coated the glass of the shelter. Harry stared sightlessly through the dingy panels, trying to beat back the overwhelming dread. Could it be too late? Was she already —

He broke off the thought immediately but nausea still rose in his throat.

He tried to clear his mind, focusing on the glass in front of him. The sunrays emphasized the grime layered across the window and Harry's mood sunk even lower. Was this dirty, depressing sight the last view that Beth had?

"Knock it off," he growled out loud and the woman darted a nervous glance at him and shifted down the bench, away from him. Harry looked straight ahead. *What's my next step?* he wondered. He had always been cool under pressure, ready with Plan B when Plan A didn't work, or Plan Z just to take everyone by surprise. Beth's disappearance had hamstrung him, taking away his calm, his ability to think, and replacing them with hysterical worry.

"Fuck," he sighed under his breath, glancing through the sunlit glass again. Harry's gaze sharpened when he noticed a clean smudge, an arched line through the dirt. Shoving himself to his feet, he moved toward the glass. He bent a little, his eyes so close to the mark on the window that his nose almost touched it.

There.

It was two curves and a point below—a heart, he realized. Harry's heart pounded and his breath came quickly, fogging over the glass and bringing out the shape more clearly. There were letters—a "B" and an "H" and a "K"—connected by plus signs.

Harry's shaking hand came up, as if to touch, but he carefully held his fingers away from the heart, not wanting to smudge this message that he knew was from Beth, who had taken shelter here from the rain, who was always sketching...

Who loved both "H" and "K".

Ky told Harry that he'd meet Hammer at the gym and they'd drive over to the bus shelter. Harry paced, alarming the waiting woman again. The bus finally pulled up with a squeaky groan and several people piled out.

Harry pounced, thrusting Beth's picture under one startled face and then the next, but he only got head shakes and blank looks. With a frustrated exhale, he turned away from the departing bus to see a passenger he hadn't questioned. The man was hurrying away, his head tucked low.

Harry jogged after him, calling out, "Excuse me?" When the man just moved faster, Harry yelled, "Hey! Stop!"

Sprinting forward, Harry caught the stranger's arm and pulled the man around to face him. "Didn't you hear me?" he demanded and then held out Beth's picture. "Did you see her yesterday?"

The man ducked his head and shrugged, mumbling, "I gotta go." He tried to pull away but Harry held fast.

"Look at it," he ordered. The man's eyes darted to the picture. "Did you see her?"

Harry saw him swallow. Sweat was beading across the bridge of the stranger's nose. "Listen, I didn't mean anything by it. It was just harmless flirting, you know —"

Harry grabbed his other arm and hauled him off his feet. The man yelped in panic.

"You saw her? Where is she?" Harry gave the man a hard shake. "What the fuck did you do to her?"

"Nothing! Nothing!" Harry could feel the man quaking in his grip. "I was just being polite! She said she had a couple boyfriends already and then she left. I didn't touch her, I swear! Ask the guy who picked her up if you don't believe me."

"What guy? Who picked her up?" Harry pulled him up another few inches and the man gave a terrified whimper.

"Some guy in a van. She climbed right in, so I figured he was her boyfriend."

"*I'm* her boyfriend, asshole," Harry growled. "What'd this guy look like?"

"I—I don't know. It was pouring and—" His teeth clicked together as Harry gave him another hard shake. "Just a guy— white guy. Blond, maybe? Short hair. Skinny. Kind of goofy-looking—even through the rain I could see that his ears stuck way out."

"Tattoos? Scars? Birthmarks?"

The man just shrugged as well as he could in Harry's grip. "Not that I noticed. Sorry, man."

"License plate?" Harry's heart sank when the man just looked at him helplessly. "Okay. What color?"

"White—one of those service vans, like painters or plumbers use. You know—no windows in the back."

Harry nodded and released the man, who took a few stumbling steps backward before he caught his balance. "If you didn't do anything wrong, why'd you run?" Harry asked him.

"Figured you were the pissed-off boyfriend. All I did was hit on her a little, though—I swear."

Narrowing his eyes, Harry debated punching the man but restrained himself. He had more important uses for this guy. "Come with me—you need to give a description to a sketch artist."

"You mean cops?" the man asked, shaking his head and backing away. "Uh-uh, no cops. I told you everything I know." He whirled and darted away. Harry started to chase after him.

"Harry!"

The shout made him pause and look back to see Ky and Hammer hurrying toward him. With one last glance at the fleeing man, Harry let him go and waited for Ky and Hammer to catch up to him.

"She got in a van with some skinny white guy with ears that stick out. Blond. White van—he didn't get the plates. She knew him—got right in."

Ky stared at him. "How'd you know she was here?" he asked.

Harry gestured toward the shelter. "She drew a heart on the glass with her finger—put all of our initials in it."

"Always drawing," Ky said quietly.

"Yeah." He turned toward the other man. "Hey, Hammer. Thanks for coming."

Hammer just nodded. "No problem, Cap'n. Was that your witness running away?"

Blowing out a frustrated breath, Harry nodded. "He bolted when I mentioned going to the cops to do a sketch."

"Wait—you said his ears stuck out?" Ky asked.

"Yeah. Said he was kind of goofy-looking."

"Short hair?"

Interest caught, Harry looked at Ky intently. "Really short—what's up? Do you know this guy?"

"No, but we already have a sketch of him."

Chapter Thirteen

꙰

"Her bus driver." Harry held Beth's sketchbook open to the page with the skinny, goofy-looking driver who saw Beth every day, a guy Beth would have known, would have trusted enough to get into his van during a rainstorm.

"Thanks," Ky said into his phone, holding it against his ear with his shoulder as he scribbled something on a piece of paper. He ended the call and immediately made another.

"Ed Worlsby," he told Harry and Hammer while he waited for the person on the other end of the call to pick up. "He never showed up to work this morning." Shifting the phone back up to his ear, he said, "Dad. I need you to run a guy named Ed Worlsby. W-O-R-L-S-B-Y. Address, priors, every fucking jaywalking ticket he's ever gotten." As Ky listened, his face lost all expression, twisting a knot into Harry's stomach.

"Hang on." Ky grabbed his paper and pen. "Okay, go ahead."

The room was silent except for the scribble of Ky's pen for what felt to Harry like an endless time. As he shifted his weight, blowing out an impatient breath, he felt a hand settle on his shoulder. Turning his head, Harry looked at Hammer, who just gave him a nod and a squeeze on the shoulder. Returning the nod, Harry felt a little calmer. Hammer wasn't a big talker but he got things done. It was good that Ky had called him.

"Okay." Ky dropped his phone into his pocket as Harry's attention snapped back to him. "This guy was arrested six years ago in Kansas City but the charges were dropped."

185

"What charges?" Harry asked, pretty sure he knew the answer.

Ky met his eyes. "Menacing."

"Hard to prove," Hammer commented. The other men looked at him and he elaborated. "Stalking. Menacing. Whatever. Usually doesn't get to trial 'til someone's dead."

Silence surrounded the three men until Hammer winced slightly. "Sorry."

"She's not dead," Ky and Harry chorused.

Shaking his head, Ky continued, "He rents a room over in the Capital Hill area—one of those hot plate and shared bathroom kind of places."

"Not somewhere you could stash someone," Harry said, closing his eyes for a brief second before pivoting toward the door. "Let's go."

"Wait," Ky told him. "He also owns a hunting cabin and some land in the mountains just west of Jefferson."

"That's it." Harry was out the door, Ky and Hammer close behind.

"Were you able to get the exact location?" Hammer asked Ky as they pounded down the stairs.

"Better. Dad's going to call once he gets the GPS coordinates."

Hammer gave an approving grunt as he followed the other two men out of the gym.

The drive took an eternity. They took Hammer's SUV, since it was equipped with all the tools of the trade, including a GPS mapping system. Hammer drove, pushing eighty despite the twists and drop-offs of Highway 285, and Ky navigated, leaving Harry with nothing to do except go insane with worry.

"Can't you go faster?" he grumbled, wedging himself between the two front seats so he could see the speedometer.

Hammer shoved him back with an elbow to the chest. "Put your seat belt on, dipshit."

Muttering to himself, Harry complied.

"I brought a few things I thought you guys might need," Hammer said, accelerating as he passed a mammoth RV, squeezing in front of it just in time to dodge an oncoming car. "Beneath the seat."

Harry reached under and hauled out a duffel bag. He unzipped it to reveal an assortment of guns.

"Shit," he said. "You got hand grenades in here too?"

In the rearview mirror, Harry saw the corner of Hammer's mouth twitch. "They're in the other bag."

Harry jumped and started to bend over to check under the seat before catching himself. "Very funny." Hammer just shrugged.

Ky twisted around to examine the duffel's contents. "Got a nine mil?" he asked.

"What is this, a drive-thru?" Harry asked but handed him the gun and ammunition.

As Ky loaded the gun, he shook his head as his mouth twisted in a humorless smile. "Thought it'd be a little longer before I was armed again."

Harry looked at him closely. "Okay?"

"Shouldn't you ask me that before you give me the gun?" Ky asked mockingly but Harry's gaze didn't waver.

Ky shrugged, dropping his eyes to the weapon. "Yeah, I'm fine. Let's just find the son of a bitch and get Beth home."

When the cabin came into view, shadowed dark gray by the early evening sun, it seemed almost unreal. They had driven through so much uninhabited wilderness that the sight of the man-made structure was jolting.

Hammer had slowed the SUV to a crawl as he navigated the rocky terrain and he stopped completely when he saw the cabin.

"Go," he told the other two men but they were already out, carefully closing the vehicle doors so that they latched silently. Harry and Ky disappeared almost instantly into the shadows. Hammer put the SUV into reverse, backing up until he was out of the line of sight from the cabin windows, and then circled around, following the faint remains of a logging trail through the evergreens behind the cabin.

When a lopsided metal gate came into view, Hammer stopped the SUV and got out, swearing under his breath. The gate completely blocked the path. He was relieved to see that, although a chain wrapped through the gate and around the wooden post, there was no lock. He untangled the chain and pushed at the gate. It didn't budge, having sunk so low over time that it was resting on the rocky ground. Lifting the end of the gate as high as it would go, Hammer forced it open, wincing at the protesting creak of metal. He froze and listened, his arm muscles quivering as he held the gate motionless. When no warning shout came from the direction of the cabin, Hammer began to breathe again. He muscled the gate the rest of the way open and wedged it between some rocks protruding from the ground.

After climbing back into the vehicle, Hammer continued along the rock-strewn trail into the trees, wincing as the evergreen branches scraped both sides of his SUV.

"Cap'n's paying for a new paint job," he muttered. Figuring that the vehicle was as well hidden from the cabin as it was going to get, he turned off the ignition and slipped out, pulling his gun from his shoulder holster.

Carefully picking his way through the trees, he almost ran into a wire fence. Swallowing a curse, he bent and slid between the second and third strands, counting his blessings that it wasn't electric.

The rest of the way to the back of the cabin was empty of cover, so Hammer moved fast, closing the distance between trees and cabin wall as quickly as he could without tripping over a rock or one of the scrubby plants. He pressed his back to the logs of the cabin, glancing around the corner before he shifted to the side. There was only one entry—the front—and none of the windows were big enough for a child to get through, much less a guy as big as he was.

With his gun held in both hands, he crept along the wall toward the front, crouching as he passed the windows. A movement caught his eye and he went still, gun extended, his finger ready on the trigger. It was Ky, Hammer realized, relaxing his finger a fraction.

Ducking around the corner to the front of the cabin, Hammer saw that both Ky and Harry were already in position on either side of the rough, wooden door. He gave a soundless sigh. With four inches and about forty pounds on Harry, Hammer figured that he would get the privilege of kicking in the door. He was always the one who had to kick in the door.

Before he could move in, Harry held up a hand—*wait*—and pushed on the door. It swung open easily and Ky pivoted into the dark opening, staying low. Harry followed him in. Hammer felt the clear focus of battle, his pulse even, breathing steady. *Jesus, I've missed this.* With a grin, he ducked through the doorway after them.

The cabin was a typical hunting cabin—a single room with stacked bunks against one wall, a bare-bones kitchen against the other and a wood stove in the center. Enough light was still filtering through the windows to make it obvious that no one was there. Hammer saw Harry's shoulders slump in defeat and felt his own stomach twist in sympathy.

Ky bent to check the space under the kitchen counter. When he stood up and turned, Hammer took a step toward him. He had been in enough firefights with Pokey to know that look—the narrow-eyed glare, skin drawn tight over his cheekbones. As Hammer eased forward, moving into position to restrain Ky if necessary, a dark spot on the floor drew his eye.

With a sharp gesture, he caught both men's attention and pointed. As they moved closer, Hammer could see that it was a latch to a trapdoor cut into the floorboards. Harry crouched down and soundlessly slid the bolt clear. He gripped the metal pull and counted down with his fingers—three, two, one—jerking open the door as Hammer and Ky trained their guns into the hole.

The thin face from Beth's drawing stared up at them, his face a white blur in the darkness below.

Hammer heard a roar as Harry disappeared through the opening in the floor. There was a cut-off shriek and a thud and Ky shoved his gun into his waistband before climbing down into the hole.

"Fuck," muttered Hammer. Stomping to the trapdoor, he holstered his gun and followed the other two men through the dark opening.

Ky was closest, so Hammer grabbed him by the back of the shirt and tossed him to the side. Harry was straddling Ed's chest, hammering the skinny man's face with his fists. He was harder to pull free but Hammer finally managed to knock him sideways off a dazed and bloody Ed. Yanking his limp form off the floor, Hammer pinned Ed against one of the concrete walls with a wide hand around his thin throat. Blood poured from Ed's nose and dripped onto Hammer's forearm.

"Where is she?" Hammer asked almost conversationally. He saw a blur to his left and swung his free arm up to clothesline a charging Ky, knocking him to the floor. "Settle. You kill him and we don't get information." He refocused on the gasping man in his grip. "Now, if we just hurt him a little..."

Ed was clawing at Hammer's hand, trying to talk. When the grip loosened slightly, he croaked, "Now there're *three* of you? Leave her alone! She's *mine!*" His eyes bugged out as Hammer clamped his fingers around his neck.

"That's not what I asked," Hammer chided him gently. "Where is she?" He squeezed until he could see Ed's face darken, even with only the dim light filtering in from the opening above. After a few moments, Hammer relaxed his grip. "Where?" he prodded.

"I don't know," Ed gasped after sucking in a few rough breaths. When Hammer's fingers twitched against his throat, he blurted frantically, "No, really, I don't know! She attacked me and locked me in! I don't know—I don't!"

Hammer eyed the other man's desperate face for a long moment. Without releasing Ed, he looked over his shoulder at Harry and Ky. "Better go find her," he told them. "There's water and flashlights behind the backseat. Take one of the radios—it has built-in GPS. Grab a couple of jackets too—it's going to get cold."

Taking a step toward Ed, Harry growled, "No, I—"

"Go," Hammer barked. "I'll clean up."

With a final enraged glare at Ed, Harry complied. Ky hesitated.

"Sure?" he asked.

Hammer nodded. "Go find your friend," he said in a gentler tone and Ky followed Harry up the ladder.

After Ky's feet disappeared through the opening, Hammer turned back to Ed's terrified face. He abruptly pulled his hand from the skinny man's throat and Ed dropped to the floor. Without a word, Hammer strode toward the ladder.

"Wait!" croaked a frantic voice behind him. "You can't just leave me in here!"

Hoisting himself through the opening in the floor, Hammer didn't pause. "Wanna bet?" Not waiting for an answer from Ed, he slammed the trapdoor shut.

He felt a surge of satisfaction as he drove the bolt home, locking Ed in the dark hole. After a quick trip out to the SUV for gloves and a flashlight, Hammer began to efficiently search the tiny, dim cabin, running his fingers under every ledge, lifting the mattresses off the bunks—even sifting through the ashen remains of the fire in the potbellied stove. He checked the walls next, pausing when a piece of chinking between the logs next to the front door gave beneath his fingers. He worked out the loose chunk, revealing an old chewing tobacco can. The lid came off easily, as if it was opened often.

Inside lay four tiny locks of hair, all different shades of blonde and each tied with a thin ribbon.

His stomach twisted as he carefully replaced the tin and the chinking. He left the cabin and scanned the terrain.

"Can't dig on a mountain," he muttered to himself. "Did he take them someplace else?" He dismissed that idea immediately—why risk being seen with a body when Ed had such a perfectly isolated place right here? Hammer walked as he thought, spiraling out from the cabin. He halted at a twenty-foot dropoff north of the cabin, staring down the cliff. In the last of the evening light, he saw the dim shape of a pile of rocks below.

"Fucker," he muttered. Although the base of the cliff was too far down for the flashlight beam to reveal any details, Hammer knew in his gut that this was where Ed had dumped the women, where he had tossed their bodies to be picked apart by animals and covered by rocks and dirt from the crumbling cliff face.

Hammer turned away from the edge and walked back to his SUV.

"Any luck? Over."

After a short pause, Ky's voice came through clearly on the radio. "Picked up a trail. Woman's easier to track than a drunken elephant. Over."

Relief flooded through Hammer. "Good. Almost at the sheriff's office. I'll see what I can do but the search and rescue guys probably won't get out until morning. Over."

Ky's answer was just a grunt. "Over."

Hammer's mouth twitched. "Let me know when you find her. I'll get in as close as possible. Over."

"Got it. Over and out."

Hammer placed the radio in one of the cupholders between the seats, feeling lighter than he had before talking with Ky. They had a trail, which meant Beth was alive and moving—or at least had been a short while before. He turned into the parking lot of the small square building that housed the county's law enforcement.

A young deputy visibly started when Hammer walked in.

"Can...can I help you?" the man stammered, looking as if he wanted to bolt from the building. Hammer wasn't surprised by the deputy's reaction—there weren't many enormous black men in mountain towns like this and his fucked-up face didn't help with first impressions.

"Got a serial killer for you," Hammer said conversationally.

The deputy paled. "You?" he squeaked, fumbling for his gun.

"No, dipshit, *I'm* not the killer," Hammer told him in exasperation, his gaze firmly on the other man's gun. "Careful with that thing."

"Drop your weapon!" The deputy was visibly shaking.

Hammer sighed. "It's a radio."

"What's going on, Collins?" a new voice asked.

Both Hammer and the deputy looked toward the main entrance where an older man stood in the open doorway.

"Sheriff!" the deputy gasped with relief. "This man's confessing that he's a serial killer!"

Hammer sighed. "*I'm* not a serial killer. I want to *give* you a serial killer. He's all locked up and everything. And one of his victims is lost in the mountains."

The sheriff looked at Hammer calmly. "Well, good thing I stopped back in this evening then. Why don't you come talk with me, son?" The sheriff waved Hammer toward an office door, not even looking at the deputy as he ordered, "Collins, put that gun away. You could hurt someone with that thing."

Hammer liked the sheriff already.

It was fucking cold again and Beth was pissed. Pissed at Ed for dragging her out here, pissed at the mountains for making her sweat all day and shiver all night, pissed at Harry and Ky for not finding her yet, pissed at all bodies of water for not appearing in front of her when she was so *fucking* thirsty. She kicked at a rock and yelped when her toes connected with the unyielding surface.

Her little temper tantrum had warmed her up a little but the chill soon resettled on her bare arms and she shuddered. Beth knew she should keep moving but the thought of walking any farther made her want to cry and she was afraid that if she started crying she wouldn't be able to stop.

Besides, what a useless waste of water.

She wanted sleep with a drugging, bone-deep longing. She *needed* sleep almost as desperately as she needed water. The daylight hours she had spent sitting, alert, ready for Ed to come around the corner at any second, now seemed like a terrible, terrible waste when she could have been sleeping. As she trudged along, she daydreamed about curling up on the rocky path and disappearing into oblivion. If she slept, was it cold enough to freeze to death? It seemed better not to find out.

If she found shelter, a hole to crawl into that would keep her warm, what if some other animal had taken residence already? Last night, she had been mindless with fear and the need to escape, so thoughts of bears and mountain lions and rattlesnakes hadn't been an issue. With a low moan of frustration, she forced her legs to keep walking, stumbling on the rough footing every other step.

How long has it been dark? she wondered, cursing herself for the millionth time for not wearing a watch. Hours had passed, surely? Now that she was cold, the heat of the day seemed blissful in comparison and she wished for sunrise with such intensity that she almost started to cry again.

To distract herself, she started thinking about Harry. And Ky. She imagined them all together in Harry's big bed, laughing, drinking huge glasses of ice water—no, lemonade. No, hot chocolate. Beth shook her head. Stop. Enough with the sweet, thirst-quenching, delicious drinks, she ordered her brain.

They would all be naked. Harry would pull her against him, teasing her breasts against the flat planes of his chest, and Ky would press against her back, his erect cock tucked into the crevice of her ass, and she would be so warm...

Her head tipped forward, her eyes closing, and she tripped again, barely managing to catch her footing before she ended up facedown on the ground. She was falling asleep on her feet, she realized, amazed that it was even possible. *Maybe if I just sit down for a moment*, she thought longingly, swaying where she stood. A rough shiver shook her and she rubbed her arms. She pulled them under her tank top but the thin knit didn't provide much protection.

Keep walking, her brain ordered and her feet grudgingly obeyed, although she was stumbling almost every step now. Her legs felt weighted and Beth had to concentrate on each step, right foot, left, right again, trudging forward until she realized that she was actually warmer. Her shivering had even stopped.

Her toe caught and she went down, hard. She lay still for several moments, the side of her face resting against the ground, too exhausted to get up. With an extreme effort, Beth managed to roll onto her back. The stars were beautiful, bright pinpricks that left a trail when she turned her head.

She actually felt hot now and her skin prickled beneath her jeans. She wanted to strip off her clothes and lay naked under the stars and blue-white moon but she was too tired. Her eyes drifted shut, closing out the night sky.

"Beth."

She opened her eyes drowsily, smiling a little. "Harry," she said, frowning when his name came out slurred. "Ky," she tried, still sounding drunk. She heard her name again and lifted her head. Something nagged at her, interrupted her peaceful rest, as if she had forgotten an important appointment.

"Beth!"

The voice had a hoarse, frantic edge and she had a moment of pity for the person yelling—he sounded so worried. She knew she should call out, let him know it was okay, but her mouth was disconnected from her brain and words didn't seem to work anymore. Anxiety seeped through her lassitude and she managed to push herself into a sitting position. The moonlit landscape rocked, making her dizzy.

A man was running toward her and she knew she should be scared, should leap to her feet and sprint away, but her body had followed her mouth's lead and refused to move. Beth could only stare as he got closer, morphing into Harry in front of her.

He snatched her up, squeezing her against the incredible, painful heat of him. Her skin burned and she struggled, fighting his hold, the warmth waking her up enough to remember her panic—not the reason for it, but just the idea that she should be running, had to leave, had to escape.

"It's okay, it's okay, it's okay," he was repeating over and over, his hand pressing her head against his chest. Suddenly Ky was there too, and they were both clutching her against their hard bodies, wrapping her in enormous jackets, their voices blending together in an unintelligible babble.

Beth let the words run over her. The small, still-functioning portion of her brain realized that, since Harry and Ky were with her, it was finally safe to sleep. With a sigh of utter relief, she let her eyes close.

When Beth woke up, they were still with her. The three of them were squeezed into the backseat of a strange vehicle, Ky and Harry on either side of her. She seemed to have acquired several layers of clothing, along with a thin blanket made of some metallic material. The driver's face was briefly illuminated by a passing car and Beth decided that she definitely did not know him.

"I'm Beth," she announced, her voice a rough croak. Both men next to her jumped.

The driver glanced in the rearview mirror and one side of his mouth twitched. "Hammer," he grunted.

Beth nodded. "As in shark, not MC."

The driver snorted. "You got it."

Harry and Ky both began fussing, asking her how she felt, feeling her forehead, tucking the shiny blanket more tightly around her until she felt like a corndog. An overheated corndog.

"I'm hot," she complained, trying to work her arms free.

Harry shook his head, keeping a tight grip on the blanket. "That's what happens with hypothermia," he told her.

Beth considered that for a moment but shook her head. "No, I'm sweating. I think I'm really hot. How many coats did you guys put on me? Do you have water?"

Ky held an opened bottle to her mouth, tipping it up as Beth drank. She tasted the sweet flavor of a sports drink and then went mindless with absolute bliss. When the liquid filled her mouth, she couldn't swallow fast enough, desperate to pull mouthfuls down her throat. She groaned with disappointment when Ky took the drink away.

"Not too much," he warned. "Or you'll puke all over Hammer's backseat."

"Please don't," Hammer said mildly.

Although she eyed the bottle with longing, Beth nodded and sat back. "Where are we?" she asked, looking out the window into the darkness.

"West of Denver," Harry answered.

"Oh."

The interior of the SUV was silent for several seconds.

"What the fuck, Barbie!" Ky burst out, drawing Beth's startled gaze. "How can you be so calm?"

She stared at him.

"You got into his van!" Ky's words got louder and louder until he was shouting. "A stranger! In his van!" His livid face was inches from hers as he twisted a fist into her blanket. Even through all the layers, Beth could feel him shaking.

"Enough!" Now Harry was shouting too, gripping Ky's shoulder as if to hold him off. "That's enough!"

Ky's face crumpled, his mask of anger dissolving in front of Beth's eyes. "Fuck, Beth." His voice was just a broken rasp now and he slumped into her, burying his face against her chest. Beth managed to free one of her arms from the blanket's hold and wrapped it around Ky's back.

Looking up at Harry, at his unshaven, tautly drawn cheeks and sunken eyes, Beth felt her own body begin to shiver, harder and harder, until she was vibrating and her teeth chattered.

"Sorry," was all she could manage to get out.

Harry shook his head, kept shaking it, his jaw locked so tightly that Beth could see the muscles in his face quivering, even in the dim light. With a bitten-out curse, he wrapped his hand around her skull and pulled her face into his neck. His scent surrounded her, familiar and loved, and it was there, with her two men twisted desperately against her, that she finally started to cry.

Chapter Fourteen

ᔈᔩ

"I have to go."

Harry scowled at her. "You don't have to."

Beth imitated him, crossing her arms over her chest and giving him her fiercest look. "Yes, I do."

"You can stay here."

"If I miss one more day, I'll be fired." Her voice lost its tough edge and ended close to a wail.

"So?" Harry wasn't budging from his spot in front of the door.

"So? What about, oh, I don't know—money? Health insurance? 401K?"

"You could work for me," Harry offered. "That would be fun—we'd be together all day."

Beth winced. "Yeah—that's not going to happen. Come on, Cap'n—I'm going to be late. I've already said you can drive me there, pick me up, call as much as you want—I just really need to go now."

"You could paint?" Harry gave it one last effort.

Grabbing his arm and turning him around so he faced the door, Beth told him, "I will. At night. After work. Now let's go."

"She's really going?" Ky asked, leaning against the wall where he'd been listening silently to their argument.

Harry raised an eyebrow at Beth.

"Yes," she said firmly. "I'm really going to work."

With a short nod, Ky left the room.

"I'm going to call you a lot," Harry warned and Beth grinned at him.

"Good," she said, drawing a grudging smile from him.

It had been two weeks since they had pulled her, hypothermic and dehydrated, out of the mountains. Harry and Ky had not let her out of their sight since, even though Ed had been denied bail. Searchers had found four bodies in the rock pile at the base of the cliff, as well as hair from his victims tucked into a hiding space in the cabin wall, and he was now the subject of local, state *and* federal investigations. Beth had told her story so many times that she could recite it without thinking, which is what she was trying very hard to do—not think.

The media had not released her name, although they made her out to be a heroine. Beth was embarrassed by that, especially when she found out that she had gone in the completely wrong direction that first night after she escaped. The next day, she had looped around and headed the other way, almost crossing her original panicked path. The last night, she had just wandered in wavy circles. Although she was mortified by her lack of orienteering skills, they were ultimately what saved her life. Ky and Harry had picked up her eastbound trail and found her in a little over seven hours.

She was worried about returning to work—the questions and stares from her co-workers, not having Harry and Ky within sight, just being out in public—but it was time. As she sat in the SUV's passenger seat next to Harry, Beth was suddenly very glad that he was driving her. She would probably never be able to ride the bus again.

"Ky's not okay," she told Harry as he maneuvered through the rush-hour traffic.

He took one hand off the wheel to scrub it over his head. "Yeah," he sighed.

"He's like, I don't know, a ghost. Always there, but not really. So quiet and…" Beth trailed off. "I just wish he would insult me or something."

Harry barked out a laugh. "I know what you mean. I've tried to talk with him but…" He shrugged. "I'll give it another shot tonight."

He pulled up to her building. "I'll walk you in," he said, reaching for the release button on his seat belt, but Beth caught his hand.

"No," she told him firmly, leaning across to kiss his mouth and stop his protests. "Love you. See you at five?"

His mouth was drawn into a stubborn line but, after a short hesitation, he nodded. Catching the back of her head, he pulled her into a long, sweet, hot kiss. When she finally pulled back, Beth was panting.

"Now I don't want to go," she complained but when his eyes lit up, she shook her head, laughing. "But I have to— bye!"

She swung out of the SUV and slammed the door, trotting up the stairs to the main entrance. When she turned to give him a final wave, Beth saw him watching her, his face serious, his worry obvious even from a distance.

"Fucking Ed," she muttered, suddenly furious that he had caused such turmoil in their lives. Forcing a smile for Harry, she gave him a jaunty wave. With a deep breath, she pulled open the door and stepped inside.

After work, Harry was waiting for her in the exact same place he had been when he'd dropped her off, making her think for an illogical second that he hadn't left, but had been watching the Anchor Paper building all day, guarding the door. She knew it wasn't true, that it was a silly idea, but it made her feel oddly warm and safe.

When they got home, Beth climbed the stairs to the loft slowly, watching out of the corner of her eye as Harry maneuvered the stairs. Ever since his long jog through the mountains, his knee had been swollen and sore. His knuckles had been raw and bruised as well, but Beth hadn't asked about that.

He noticed her watching his slow progress and flushed. "Hurry up," he growled. "You're slowing me down."

Beth just shook her head at him. "Going to get over yourself and have a doctor look at that?" she asked.

Harry scowled. "It's fine — or as fine as it'll ever be."

"Whatever, tough guy." She rolled her eyes and stomped up the rest of the stairs.

"I'm still faster than you," he teased, pressing one hand against the wall and holding the railing with the other so he could hurdle the remaining four steps. Harry landed behind her on his good leg and snaked his arms around her waist as she unlocked the door, making her shriek and laugh. They tumbled into the loft, wrestling playfully as Harry swung the door closed behind them.

"You're late."

Ky's accusation cut off their laughter and they both looked at him.

"Sorry, Ky," Beth began, "I asked Harry to drive through the bank —"

Before she could finish, Ky pivoted around and stalked through the living room. Beth and Harry watched, startled, as his stiff back disappeared into the guest room.

With a heavy sigh, Harry leaned against the door and rubbed the side of his swollen knee.

"What is that all about?" Beth asked. "Just because we're five minutes late?"

"Shit, I don't know," Harry said heavily, rubbing a hand across his face. He pushed himself off the door, giving Beth a kiss on the head and a final squeeze. "I'll talk to him," he said, heading toward the guest room.

He found Ky tossing clothes into his duffel.

"What's going on?" Harry asked, leaning his shoulder against the doorframe, playing casual while his stomach twisted.

"What's it look like?" Ky muttered, not looking up as he mashed a handful of socks into his bag.

"It looks like you're leaving." Harry crossed his arms across his chest, as if to physically keep himself from flying apart.

"Two points for you." Ky crossed the room with an armful of t-shirts.

Pushing himself off the doorjamb, Harry got to the bed first, blocking Ky's access to the duffel by sitting on it. "I can't stop you from leaving," he said, "but at least tell me why you're taking off like this."

Ky still wouldn't meet his eyes. Instead, he stared at the wall over Harry's head for a long moment. Finally, Ky let the t-shirts in his arms drop to the floor and sank down next to Harry. He flopped back to lie crossways on the bed.

He was quiet for so long, just staring at the textured ceiling, that Harry figured he wasn't going to talk. Pulling the lumpy bag out from under his rear and tossing it to the floor, Harry tried to think of what to say, those magical words that would make Ky stay. Harry's mind remained hopelessly blank. He sank back to lie next to Ky.

Beth found them like that, bodies parallel as they frowned at the ceiling. She saw the duffel bag on the floor and her breath stalled. Stretching out on her stomach between them, she twisted around so she could lay her head on Ky's chest, be lifted by the rise and fall of his rib cage and hear the slow, steady *lub-dub* of his heart. She felt his fingers stroking her hair, pushing the strands off her cheek and over her ear and Beth stilled, afraid that he would take his hand away if she moved.

"You leaving us, Pokey?" she asked quietly, unable to bear not knowing any longer. Harry's hand found hers and their fingers intertwined.

"Can't stay," Ky told her. With her ear on his chest, Beth could hear the hollow ring of his voice twice — inside and out.

"Why not?" Harry turned his face so he could see Ky's profile. The question hung in the air, unanswered, for a long time.

"When I look at people, I imagine what they would look like dead," Ky finally said. "It's one thing to see strangers that way but something totally different when it's people who...matter."

At the flat statement, Harry turned onto his side, reaching his free hand over Beth to rest his palm on the other man's stomach, feeling the muscles under his t-shirt jump at the touch. Harry stayed silent, waiting.

Ky finally looked at him and what was in his eyes made Harry want to cry. *A twenty-three-year-old shouldn't have seen things, done things, to make him look like that,* he thought, sick to his stomach. No one should. Harry felt helpless, only able to move his thumb against Ky's middle in a small, useless gesture of comfort.

"It was bad enough with just you," Ky told him, his voice ragged and rough. "With you...you know what's out there, you know how to take care of yourself. But Beth? She's a fucking baby."

Beth made an attempt to rear her head off his chest but Ky's hand kept it down. "I'm almost a whole year older than you, thank you very much." Her muffled voice was indignant. "I can take care of myself too." Both of the men ignored her.

"I don't know what to tell you, man," Harry told him. "It *is* hard — I'm scared every time she's out of my sight. I try to protect her but..." He shrugged. "I can't lock her up."

"Why not?" Ky asked, a corner of his mouth tucking up at Beth's muffled, "Hey!"

Harry grinned. "Caring sucks." Sobering, he held Ky's gaze. "It's hard to love someone—you think I don't worry about your cranky ass all the time?"

Clenching his jaw, Ky looked away. "I can't stay," he repeated.

Beth finally managed to push his hand away so she could pop her head up. "You want to leave people who love you because you worry about them?" she asked. "How nuts is that, Ky?"

"You don't get it, Barbie," he told her, shaking his head. "Don't you realize all the things that could happen to you? Things like—oh, I don't know—being kidnapped? Barely escaping the asshole to wander around the wilderness until you almost die?"

"But *you* were the reason I got away," Beth protested. "You taught me how to break his hold. And that was just one lesson—just think what a bad-ass I'd be if you stick around and show me a few more things."

Looking grim, Ky promised, "I'll show you how to break someone's shoulder."

"Really?" Beth's eyes lit with a bloodthirsty gleam.

Harry groaned. "Pokey, what did I tell you about creating a monster?"

"So you're staying?" Beth asked, bouncing a little in excitement, making the bed quake under all of them. "If I promise to be very careful and be suspicious of everybody and learn how to break the shoulder of anyone who even looks at me funny, will you stay?"

Ky hesitated. "You guys don't need a third wheel hanging around," he muttered.

"Sure we do," Beth contradicted him. "We're more of a tricycle, really."

"Right." Ky didn't sound convinced. Beth turned to Harry with a wide-eyed, "go on" look, tipping her head toward Ky, who had resumed glaring at the ceiling.

Harry's stomach clenched. His words had disappeared again. Not since high school had he been so scared of a rebuff.

Ah, fuck it, he thought, *just do it.* Harry leaned in toward Ky, his hand coming up to cup the other man's startled face. They were just a bare inch apart when Ky jerked back a little.

"Don't do it unless you mean it," he warned Harry, his voice rough. "I couldn't stand —"

Harry cut him off by bringing his mouth down on Ky's. It started out tentative, both men feeling their way. Harry was shocked by the softness of Ky's mouth, such a contrast to the rough cheek against his palm. He pushed a little further, tasting the edge of Ky's teeth with his tongue.

With a groan, Ky wrapped one hand around the back of Harry's head to pull him in hard. The kiss lost its last shreds of hesitancy, need flaming to life between them. They were almost rough with each other, eating at each other's mouths as if they were starving. Ky made a noise, almost a purr, and nipped Harry's lower lip, making him growl and press harder into the open-mouthed kiss. A small squeak from Beth pulled the men apart, glassy-eyed and panting. She was watching them, breathing hard, her pupils dilated and her mouth slightly open, just enough to show a white line of teeth. Ky's hand was still on her head, clenched on a handful of tangled curls.

"Jesus, I'm sorry," Ky said, releasing her hair. As realization set in, he glanced at a hot-eyed Harry and back to Beth. "I'm really sorry," he repeated but this time with a different meaning.

"I'm not," she said, her voice husky. She cleared her throat and tried again. "Whose idea do you think this was?"

"Seriously?" Ky asked, glancing back at Harry, who nodded. Ky's face closed.

"Don't get me wrong," Harry explained, guessing at the reason for Ky's withdrawal. "I want this. Never have before — with a guy, I mean — but you've always made me hard."

After a suspicious look, Ky must have believed him, because he smiled. Harry caught his breath.

"God, Pokey, you're just too pretty to be let out in public," Beth told him in an awestruck tone, echoing Harry's thoughts. "You've probably caused traffic accidents just by walking down the sidewalk."

The compliment made Ky flush and scowl in embarrassment.

"Do you two…" Beth started again. "I mean, do you want me to leave?" Although she asked them both, her eyes were on Ky.

"Do you *want* to leave?" Ky asked.

"God no!" she replied, so fervently that both of the men laughed.

"Then stay." He pulled her up his chest so she was draped over him. Harry slid closer to the stacked pair, smoothing his hand down Beth's back before working his fingers beneath the soft cotton of Ky's underwear until his fingertips could touch the smooth, feverish skin of his trapped cock. Ky's hips jerked under his touch.

Ky ignored Beth's hesitation and pulled her head down to capture her mouth. Her kiss was as incredible as he'd imagined — better, in fact. It was long and wet and deep and when her tongue touched his, he could feel it all the way down to his toes. Beth held his head with both hands, lightly scratching at his scalp through the thick stubble. She straddled his stomach, grinding her crotch against his ribbed muscles.

He tried to deepen the kiss but she pulled back.

"Do you really want to do this?" she asked him.

Despite her serious expression, Ky laughed, pulling one of her hands behind her, pressing her fingers against his crotch so she could feel his straining erection. "What do you think?" he teased.

"I meant, do you really want to do this with *me*?" she clarified, although she kept her hand on his denim-covered cock, trapping Harry's hand beneath the material.

"Yes." Ky pulled her head toward him again but she dodged his mouth.

"But you're gay!" she persisted. "How could you want me? I'm a girl!"

Scowling in irritation, Ky rolled his eyes at Harry. "Does she always talk this much?" Harry nodded, grinning.

Ky turned back to Beth. "Okay, listen," he clipped out, short of breath and sweating from the teasing brushes of Harry's fingertips on his cock, as well as Beth's yielding curves notching into the hollows of his body. It had been too long since he'd had sex and, since he had moved in with Harry and Beth, Ky felt like he was hard and ready twenty-four hours a day. "I want to fuck you. If that makes me not gay, then I guess I'm not gay."

He lifted his head to kiss her but she pulled back to ask, "But you want Harry too, right?"

With a groan, Ky let his head fall back against the bed and closed his eyes. "The two of you are going to drive me insane," he muttered. "Yes, I do want to fuck Harry. I've wanted to fuck Harry for years. I've been living in the same apartment with both of you, sleeping with you, listening to the noises you make when you're screwing in the bathroom or the kitchen or the fucking broom closet or wherever, and my balls are the bluest of any balls in the history of the world. I've said I want you both and you both said you want me. By the noises you make, you obviously want each other..." Opening his eyes to glare at Beth and Harry, he snarled, "Can we just get down to it?"

"Quit your yapping, Pokey, and kiss me," Beth commanded, a smile lurking in the corners of her mouth. With a growl, he yanked her down and did just that. All of his tentative exploring was gone, replaced by driving need. Ky took over her mouth, holding her face in both hands as he invaded her mouth with his tongue, then pulled back to nip sharply at her lips.

The sharp command of his kiss melted Beth into his chest. She felt Harry's free hand on her jeans-covered ass, kneading and massaging until her skin was buzzing. Beth was desperate — desperate to be naked, desperate for the men's hands on her bare flesh, desperate for two hard cocks to fill her completely.

Harry's fingers slid out of Ky's jeans at the same time his other hand left Beth's ass. They both groaned at the loss but were unwilling to relinquish their kiss to complain in actual words. Ky switched the angle of his head and pressed into her mouth again, his fists closing in her hair.

Beth felt Harry's hands return, this time at her waist. He circled them beneath her to work her button and zipper open, tugging her jeans down over her hips and down her thighs. Straightening her legs so that he could remove the pants completely, Beth had to cling to Ky's wide forearms so that Harry didn't yank her across the room along with the jeans.

After a quick slip of his hands over her cotton-covered ass, Harry began to remove Ky's jeans as well. Beth heard the burr of his zipper going down, felt the tugs vibrating through Ky's body beneath her lightly covered crotch. Ky pulled his head back a fraction, closing his eyes against the pleasurable friction. Beth heard him make that sexy purring sound again and shivered as a current of heat traveled from her chest to her pussy, dampening her panties.

Ky must have felt it even through his t-shirt, because he opened his eyes and gritted, "You're wet."

Incapable of speech, Beth could just nod, her breath spurting from her in little pants.

"Let me feel."

The command liquefied her. She tugged up his t-shirt, leaving his stomach bare, and ground her pussy against him, rubbing herself against his skin with only a damp wisp of fabric separating them.

He shivered, grunting, "More." His fingers slid beneath her panties, drawing a mew from her as he barely brushed against her swollen pussy lips. Pushing her upper body upright as she straddled him, Beth tilted her hips toward him, wanting. Instead of obeying her silent demand for another touch, Ky tugged at her panties, growling impatiently at their constraints. With a savage yank, he snapped the narrow, delicate bands that ran over her hips and tossed the torn scrap of fabric away.

Between the two of them, I'm not going to have any underwear left, Beth thought half-hysterically and then stopped thinking as Ky circled his fingertips in the curly hair that framed her pussy.

Kneeling behind her and straddling Ky's bare hips, Harry caught the bottom hem of her shirt and pulled it over her head as she raised her arms obediently. As he unhooked her bra, her heavy breasts bounced free and were quickly captured by Harry's calloused palms as he cupped them from behind.

He was naked, Beth realized, feeling the light scratch of his chest hair against her shoulder blades and the burn of his erection against the hollow of her lower back. Ky's fingers were getting braver, investigating every fold and hollow between her legs—the line where her leg met her hip, the folds of her pussy, the crevice that tucked between the cheeks of her bottom. Spreading her knees wider, begging for more attention from his curious fingers, Beth leaned back against Harry when her trembling thighs threatened to give out.

Breathing hard, Harry pulled at her straining nipples, his eyes fixed on the movement of Ky's hand. He sucked in a rasping breath when Ky abruptly thrust two fingers into Beth's pussy, drew them out, shiny with her moisture, and plunged them back in. She arched into the invasion, crying out with relief as he penetrated her again.

Ky groaned. "So tight and wet." His eyes were molten gold as he looked at Harry. "Can I fuck her?" he asked, his eager shiver vibrating against Harry's knees.

Harry's cock jumped at the question, at the implication that he was in charge, that he could tell them what to do and they would do it. Anything. It was almost too much and he gritted his teeth against an overwhelming wave of desire.

"No," he snapped and Beth's face turned to him, her bottom lip caught in her teeth. Her look of wide-eyed trepidation blasted him with another surge of lust. He stood up next to the bed, towering over them as he commanded, "Take off your shirt."

Ky hurried to obey, pushing himself to a seated position as Beth slid backward along his thighs so he could sit up. She reached up to help pull his shirt over his head. Watching the two of them scrambling to do his bidding, Harry clenched his fists as a drop of pre-cum gathered on the tip of his rigid erection. Sweat beaded over his brows and across his lip as he fought for self-control. He squeezed his eyes closed, opening them to find Beth and Ky both looking at him, waiting for instructions.

"Suck him," he rasped. Beth knelt between Ky's legs, her back to Harry, bending forward until her lips were just inches from the head of Ky's thick cock. Her knees were braced wide, exposing her glossy, wet pussy and the dusky, puckered entrance to her ass. The sight was too much, and only by digging his fingers into the muscles of his own thighs was Harry able to keep from exploding.

Beth was tormenting Ky, brushing against his bobbing erection with the lightest touches of her cheeks and lips and chin.

"I love how you smell," she murmured, breathing him in. "So...primal."

Her words made Harry's eyes almost roll back in his head. Ky must have had the same wild surge of lust, since he grabbed her head, trying to force her to take him into her mouth. Beth dodged his attempts to thrust his desperate cock toward her lips.

"She's teasing," Ky accused.

"You sound just like a little kid on a car trip," Beth giggled.

Her smile disappeared when Harry's hand smacked against her ass cheek. She pulled in a tight breath, her stomach dissolving in want as the heat radiated from her bottom to her soaking-wet pussy.

"Tattletale," she breathed, the word barely more than a hungry moan. The air from her words brushed against the tip of Ky's cock, making him groan and thrust his hips upward. Harry spanked her again, on the other cheek this time. Driven to the edge of what she could bear, Beth swallowed the heavy length of Ky's cock.

"Fuck," he hissed as the suctioning heat of her mouth closed around him. His back arched and his fingers tightened in Beth's hair, pulling her down, trying to make her take more of him. She choked a little as he bumped the back of her throat and Harry wrapped his fingers around Ky's wrists.

"Careful," Harry warned and Ky nodded tightly, lightening his grip. She rewarded him by relaxing her throat, swallowing another inch of him. Her fingers wrapped around the base of his cock and she began to move, sliding her lips upward until only the head remained in her mouth. Her tongue found his slit, probing it, before sliding down the back of his erection as she swallowed him whole.

Harry released Ky's wrists. The sight of Ky's dark cock, wet and gleaming, disappearing and reemerging from the pink circle of Beth's eager lips must have been more than Harry could stand. Sinking his fingers into the flesh of her hips, he buried his cock into the tight, wet passage of her pussy. Beth closed her eyes at the incredible friction. Her inner walls clung to him as he pulled out and paused, leaving her hungry and frantic to be filled again.

"Do you want to fuck her now?" he asked and Ky nodded, easing Beth's mouth free of his cock.

213

"Condoms?" Harry asked.

"In there," Ky rasped, jerking his head at his partially packed bag. Crouching down, Harry dug through the duffel, tossing the clothes onto the floor as he searched. When he finally found the box and tore it open, Beth thought she would cry from sheer relief. She tried to take the condom from Harry but he shook his head, moving to sheathe Ky's erection himself.

"No." Ky's hand shot out and caught Harry's wrist. "Touch me and it's over." Harry relinquished the condom and they both watched, fascinated, as Ky rolled it on.

Catching Beth under the arms, Ky pulled her up to straddle his hips. His erection burned against her. Lifting herself up until the head of his cock was just touching her pussy lips, heat against heat, Beth looked over her shoulder at Harry.

"May I?" she asked, watching his taut face. He almost flinched at her question, his eyes burning the electric blue of the hottest fire as he visibly gathered himself enough to nod tightly. With a small sound of relief, Beth lowered her hips, impaling herself on Ky's rock-hard erection. His head and neck curled back against the bed as she surrounded him with her suctioning heat, so tight that the pleasure flirted with pain.

Beth began to raise herself, to release his desperate cock from its welcome prison, only to bury him inside her again. Ky grasped her hips, stopping the movement.

"Please," he gasped. "Please." Beth didn't know if he was begging for cessation or continuation.

"Please what?" she panted.

"I don't know." He gave a small, choked laugh. "All I know is that if you move an inch, I'm going to fucking explode into tiny pieces."

"Oh." Beth hesitated. *Exploding doesn't sound so bad to me,* she thought, shifting a little and making Ky groan. She wanted to move, to break Ky's control, but Harry's touch on her back made her go still.

With a firm hand between her shoulder blades, Harry pressed Beth's upper body down until her nipples were burning holes into Ky's chest. She felt the wet tip of Harry's erection asking for entrance into her ass and her blood coursed through her veins at breakneck speed.

Here it was—the daydream that was the cause of more wet panties than she could count was about to become reality.

"Okay?" Harry rasped, not sure what he would do if she said no. He wanted this, *needed* it, felt like he would die if he couldn't bury himself in her ass, to feel the friction of Ky's cock moving inside her, to share the explosive moment of climax with both of his lovers.

"Please," she begged, and, with a groan made up of relief and lust and overwhelming love, Harry pressed into her, slowly, carefully, until he and Ky filled her entirely. Harry began to move, desperately realizing that he was at the end of his tether. He heard Ky's shout of release as the slide of Harry's cock, barely separated from his, drove him over the edge into ecstasy.

Harry pumped into her ass, feeling her muscles tighten as she reached her own climax, her scream coinciding with the squeezing clamp around his cock. He exploded into her, the hot, sweet pleasure multiplied a thousand times by the knowledge that the three of them were together, all feeling the same elated bliss.

In the sweaty, boneless aftermath, as they lay tangled together in peaceful languor, Beth asked, "So does this mean you're staying?"

Harry was too spent to even laugh but heard Ky groan, "For fuck's sake, Barbie. Yes, I'm staying. But only if you shut up and let me sleep."

Smiling, Beth didn't say another word.

215

Chapter Fifteen

ᔕᓂ

Harry woke to Beth's mouth on him, trailing teasing nibbles across his jaw and up to his temple, curling her tongue in the curve of his ear and making him shiver. Ky's hand rested heavily against his belly, and Harry nearly jumped out of his skin when full, soft lips brushed his ribs. The feeling of two mouths on him at one time was amazing, almost overwhelming, especially since one of the mouths belonged to beautiful Ky, who for so many years had kept him conflicted and horny and wondering.

As Beth tugged his earlobe into her mouth with a gentle suction, Ky ran his roughened palm along the underside of Harry's stiff, swollen cock. He teased it with a light pressure, a touch that was barely there, but that still drew Harry's balls tight and high. When Ky finally grasped his shaft, Harry nearly came from just his firm grip, rougher than Beth's. The difference between the two hands, hard and soft, magnified Harry's arousal, until he had to clench his teeth to prevent his eruption.

Ky swallowed his cock at the same time that Beth's teeth closed on his nipple, as if they had rehearsed. Harry's hips wrenched upward and his hand caught the back of Ky's closely shorn head, holding him still as Harry drove his pulsing cock deeper into the other man's throat. Plunging in and out of the irresistible suction, Harry felt his control fraying, the dual mouths—one eagerly slurping at his cock and the other pulling at his nipple—working at him until need and love and raw desire twisted together, dragging his release from the deepest part of him, shooting pulse after pulse of semen into Ky's welcoming mouth. His climax seemed to last forever, until his body shuddered a final time, replete with exhaustion and wonder.

Harry felt stripped, naked and vulnerable. He kept his eyes closed as his breathing slowed and his heartbeat quieted, no longer filling his head with its urgent pound. Beth soothed his chest with gentle strokes as Ky suckled his easing cock, as if neither wanted to move away from him. Opening his eyes, Harry looked at them both, met Beth's questioning gaze and Ky's wary one. Ky's mouth stilled, pulling away as he watched Harry, looking unsure about whether he was going to get a kiss or a kick in the teeth.

Curling one arm around Beth, Harry tucked her tight against him. With his other hand, he reached down and cradled the back of Ky's skull. Ky's eyes grew glossy. He dipped his head down and hid his face against the seam where Harry's thigh and groin met. Harry felt the soft prickle of Ky's couple-day scruff and massaged the head he still cupped. The vulnerable skull bones, the tight tendons of his neck, the delicate curve of the back of his ear—all were exposed by Ky's military buzz cut.

Swallowing, Harry held his two lovers against him, overwhelmed for a moment by a panicked responsibility. These two people—these *babies*, all of twenty-three and -four years old—were his now. His to protect, to keep safe. It had been almost inevitable, he realized, pulling Beth and Ky even closer. When he saw Ky across the gym, his belongings in hand and his longing and desperation covered by a thin sheen of pride, Harry knew that Ky was going to stay. And Beth...Harry couldn't imagine life without Beth. It was like playing with his nephew's Legos—he and Beth and Ky fit together—perfectly matched pieces.

Harry locked the front door of the cleared-out gym just after eight. Closing on Saturday nights was a treat—not like the weekdays, when he had to boot out the stragglers who were trying to squeeze in a few more reps at eleven-fifteen. He

217

took the steps to the loft two at a time, letting himself in to find Ky and Beth lounging at the kitchen island.

"Whatcha doing?" he asked idly, giving Beth and then Ky a one-armed hug and a kiss on the temple.

"Frito football," Beth told him, flicking a chip through the open-topped square that Ky had made with his thumbs and index fingers. "Score!" she crowed, shooting her fists over her head.

Shaking his head, Harry picked up the Frito football and ate it. "You two are sad. It's Saturday night—why don't we go out instead?"

"Really?" Beth asked. "Yay! We haven't gone out in forever."

"Okay," Ky shrugged.

The same thought occurred to both Beth and Ky at the same time. They eyed each other for a second before bolting from their stools and sprinting to the bathroom.

"Dibs on the shower," Beth called.

"Don't think so," Ky rejoined. They reached the doorway at the same time and both tried to squeeze in, jostling against each other.

"I called it!" Beth protested.

"Too bad. I'm bigger, so I get my way."

Beth elbowed him in the stomach and used the leverage to shove herself through in front of him with a victorious "Woo!"

"Foul!" Ky accused, following her in.

Harry rolled his eyes as he leaned against the island, eating another corn chip.

"Babies," he grumbled, albeit cheerfully. "Like a freakin' daycare in here." It had been almost a week since they had merged into a—what? Couple didn't really work. A triplet? Whatever it was called, Harry was shocked by how well it was working. They had fallen into an easy intimacy, as if the three of them had always been together. He heard Beth's laughing shriek, quickly cut off. His ears perked up at the silence, as did his cock. Popping one last Frito into his mouth, Harry pushed away from the island to make his way to the bathroom, stripping off his clothes as he went.

The open shower door framed Ky and Beth, both still half-dressed under the spray of water—Beth in her bra and panties and Ky in his jeans. Beth's back was against the smooth wall, her wrists crossed above her head, pinned there by one of Ky's hands. The contrast between his broad, brown hand and her pale wrists, so delicate and trapped, dried Harry's mouth and made him swallow.

Ky's other hand was tracing the rivulets of water down the top slopes of her breasts, dodging around her instantly peaked nipples thrusting against the sheer pink fabric of her wet bra. Beth's mesmerized gaze followed the path of his fingers.

"When you change sides, you really do it with a vengeance," she told him breathlessly.

"I didn't switch," Ky corrected her absently, following the trickles of water down her belly now. "I'm just...batting for both teams."

"Teams?" Beth's voice was throaty now, as distracted as Ky's. His fingers slid against her stomach and lower, under the edge of her panties and though the curls beneath. She gasped as his middle finger pushed into her pussy, parting the tight walls with penetrating force. Her body clutched him, trying to draw him deeper.

"It's not even that." Ky answered the question that Beth had already forgotten she'd asked. "That makes it sound like I'm up for screwing anything that walks and I'm not really interested in anyone except you and Harry."

She blinked, suddenly realizing something. "You're a romantic," she told him, a grin spreading across her face. The accusation brought an immediate scowl to Ky's face.

"What?"

Still grinning, she crowed, "You only want to have sex with people you're in love with. You're a closet romantic!"

"No, I'm not." He sounded as disgusted as if she had accused him of eating bugs.

"Okay, you're not," she said in an overly placating tone.

"I'm not."

She smirked at him silently.

Ky started to say something but must have realized that he had a more powerful weapon than words. As his amber eyes watched her with half-lowered lids, he twisted his finger inside her slippery depths. Beth couldn't hold back a moan and Ky, looking unbearably smug, gave a small grin as his eyes warmed to gold at the sound.

Apparently no longer able to stand just watching, Harry stepped into the shower, pressing Ky against Beth's front, smooshing her against the wall. Abruptly pulling his teasing finger free, Ky caught himself with both hands flat against the wall. Although she was still tingling with arousal, Beth gave a breathless laugh as she was flattened between hard tile and harder male.

"Okay, no. Until we get a bigger shower," she paused to give Ky a futile shove, "there will be no threesome shower time." She wiggled around until she could squeeze out sideways. "Seriously, guys, it's like a fricking clown car in here. Ky, your jeans are still on. Okay, that's it." She gave Harry a shove. "Out!" Pivoting around Ky, she maneuvered behind him and heaved.

"But—"

"Hey!"

The two men spluttered and protested but stepped out of the shower. Beth pulled the door closed with a bang, stripping off her nearly transparent bra and underwear and tossing them out over the door with a satisfied smile. *I knew I could get the shower first*, she thought smugly.

"No problem." Harry's voice held a self-satisfied note that made Beth glance through the wavy glass suspiciously. "We'll be just fine without you." Pressing Ky against the wall, Harry flattened his palms on either side of Ky's head and leaned in.

Fascinated, Beth pushed the shower door open so that she had a clear view as Harry took Ky's mouth, kissing him hard enough to press his head back against the wall. After a startled moment, Ky responded frantically, wrapping his fingers around the back of Harry's skull, pressing their bodies together from thigh to chest, twisting his head to plunge his tongue deep into Harry's mouth.

Enthralled by the two masculine bodies locked together in a desperate, almost violent embrace, Beth watched, the water pounding unheeded on her skin. Wetting her lips with her tongue, she slid one hand between her legs to brush her clit, teasing the already excited nub of flesh.

What had started as a playful jab at Beth after she'd kicked them out of the shower turned into an uncontrollable conflagration of need. It wasn't just the buildup of tension since Ky had moved in with them, but the months of frustrated longing from two years before, from working and fighting together, weeks upon weeks of furtive glances, of hiding their feelings with rough, masculine bravado, burying concern and lust and obsessive thoughts so deeply that no one in their unit suspected anything except friendship. All of this pressed-back desire now exploded into flames. They ground their mouths, their bellies, their cocks together, clashing teeth and tongues in a raw kiss, Ky's wet jeans the only barrier between them.

Just watching was enough to send Beth over the edge of orgasm with only a few strokes of her hand. She grabbed the side of the shower door to steady her shaky knees, uncaring that water streamed onto the floor. The moment between the two men seemed intensely private but she still yearned to join in, to be a part of the wild mating in front of her.

Ky's fingers dug deep furrows in Harry's round, tight buttocks. The contrast between the dark skin of Ky's hands and the lighter tone of Harry's ass shortened her breath. She felt her nipples, already erect, tighten to aching points. Harry was fighting the wet denim, shoving the stubborn fabric down Ky's thighs. Unable to stay back any longer, Beth turned off the shower and stepped out.

She was mesmerized by the movement of Harry's back muscles, the flex and hollow under his skin. Beth explored the contours with her palms and felt Harry shiver in reaction. She loved how she could make such a powerful man tremble under her touch.

Growling, Harry jerked away despite Ky's protesting groan and grasping hands, abruptly turning Beth around so that she faced the sink. The quick movement made her gasp. Bending over at the waist, she grasped the edge of the counter, the cool tiles slippery beneath her wet hands. She caught a glimpse of their reflection in the mirror—the three of them, naked and wild eyed—and couldn't stop staring.

It was Ky who stepped behind her, bending his knees and plowing into her in one merciless stroke, his face tight with concentration. Beth felt like the breath had been knocked out of her at his entry, as if his cock had taken all the available space in her body, with no room left for air. Her eyes were locked on the reflection of Ky's face, on the fierce intent in the tight line of his mouth. She watched as he began to thrust, amazed at how watching the movement at the same time she was feeling his cock plunge, retreat and plunge again intensified the wrenching pleasure.

When Harry entered Ky, pressing inexorably into the other man's ass, Beth felt it in her own body, as if she was the one caught by the slow slide of his cock. She watched Ky climax in the mirror, saw his expression melt into ravaged bliss, felt the guttural groan that vibrated through her. Viewing Ky's ecstasy was enough to topple her into her own orgasm. Her body convulsed around Ky's cock, helpless to do anything except absorb the impact of Harry's thrusts through the man behind her.

As her legs quavered beneath her, threatening to drop her onto the bathroom floor, Beth's drifting thoughts pondered how strange it was that having another person between them just made her that much closer to Harry. How strange and how wonderful, she mused blissfully, letting Ky's powerful arms support her as she melted back against him.

Hands on her hips, Beth gave both men an exasperated look. "And they say that women hog the bathroom."

Harry looked over his shoulder at her and grinned through a faceful of shaving cream. "Says the woman who just used the mirror for *hours*."

"It was ten minutes—fifteen tops—and you guys hardly have any hair to worry about! Or makeup. In fact, what exactly are you doing in here?"

"Okay, out." Ky unceremoniously lifted her and placed her outside the bathroom before slamming the door in her face.

"Fine," she yelled through the closed door. "I didn't want to hang out with you guys anyway!" She huffed at the unrepentant laughter coming from inside the bathroom.

Might as well get dressed, she figured, heading for the bedroom. As she stood in front of the open closet, Beth realized that she was smiling. Despite her fake pout at being banished from guy time in the bathroom, happiness burbled inside her. *The three of us are good together,* she thought, her eyes dreamy as she stared, sightless, at the line of clothes.

Shaking her head but unable to lose her dopey grin, Beth rifled through her clothes, excited by the prospect of the evening ahead. It had been a long time since she'd had a night out—it was too easy to fall into the safe, easy, domestic routine of takeout and sex with Harry and now Ky. She realized that she was staring at the clothes again, her smile positively fatuous.

"Focus," Beth told herself firmly. She had serious business to attend to—figuring out what to wear. After the kidnapping, she'd only returned to her apartment once. Both Harry *and* Ky had insisted on coming with her, even though she'd just picked up the remainder of her things—those that hadn't already found their way from her place into Harry's closet.

She wasn't sure why she even kept her apartment. Maybe because six weeks seemed like an awfully short lead-up for moving in with a man—or *men*, she corrected herself. Sure it was quick, but it just felt *right*. She definitely did not want to stay alone, sleep alone. Beth shivered.

Even sandwiched between Harry and Ky in the big bed, she needed a light on at night. She hated the darkness now. The guys didn't seem to mind. In fact, although they would never admit it, the small glow of the nightlight that broke the darkness was probably a comfort to them too.

Beth made a face. Especially since all three of them were having nightmares now.

By the time Harry and Ky had finished their mysterious male preparations in the bathroom and joined her, most of her clothes were strewn around the room.

"Did the closet throw up?" Ky asked, glancing around.

Ignoring the sarcastic question, Beth did a twirl, quite pleased with her final choice—a short, flippy, black and white skirt topped by a dark red tank with skinny, criss-crossing straps. The heels on her delicate sandals were high enough to guarantee that she would be falling over at least once during the night. She ended her turn with her back toward them, giving her audience of two a flirty look over her shoulder. "So, what do you think?"

"You'll do," Ky said at his most casually dismissive but Beth just pressed back a smile. She had seen a flare in his eyes when he had gotten his first glimpse of her blonde curls cascading over the bare triangles of skin exposed by the skinny straps of her top.

"Yeah, you will," Harry growled, catching her around the waist and nuzzling the crook of her neck, making her giggle. "Don't know if we can let you out of the house like that."

Beth rolled her eyes. "Puh-lease," she scoffed. "If it were up to you, I wouldn't leave the house ever, even if I had a nun's habit on."

"There's an idea," suggested Ky, his eyes smoldering again as he watched them.

"I wonder where we could get one," Harry pondered. "Do you think you'd be struck down by lightning or something if you wore it and weren't a nun?"

"After the things I do with the two of you? Probably." Beth turned to give him a quick peck on the chin and then slipped out of reach as he tried to pull her in for a real kiss. She knew if she let him, Harry could have her stripped of makeup—and clothes, for that matter—in ten seconds flat. She had been promised a night out and she was going to get it, even if it used every drop of willpower she possessed not to be lured back to bed with her two smoking-hot men.

"Get dressed, slowpokes—I'm going to put on some get-my-party-on music." On her way out of the bedroom, she let her hand trail across Ky's arm. His eyes held a promise of retribution in the near future. Beth shivered in lovely anticipation.

Humming to herself, she plugged her MP3 player into the speakers and turned the volume up, glad that there were no close neighbors to be annoyed. She scrolled through the songs until she saw one that made her grin.

"Perfect," she murmured. "Nothing like Aqua to get things started."

"What the hell are you playing?" Ky walked into the living room, scowling at the bouncy music pounding from the speakers. Beth could only stare. In scrubby sweats and his worn Army t-shirt, Ky was beautiful, but dressed to go out, he was…breathtaking. She stared at him, realizing that his khakis and black short-sleeved shirt would just be ho-hum on any other man but the magic was in the way Ky's sleeves stretched over his upper arms and how the color emphasized the sooty smudge of his eyelashes. It took a few moments of staring and drooling before his question registered.

"A little '90s Euro-trash pop." She tilted her head, thinking. "Actually, I'm not sure if they're European but that has a better ring to it than U.S.-trash pop, don't you think?"

"Are you kidding?" he asked, appalled. "What else do you have on that thing?"

"Hey!" she protested as he wrestled the MP3 player away from her. "This is my song!"

Ky glanced at the screen and grinned. "'Barbie Girl'? Yeah, that is perfect." He scrolled through the songs, ignoring her attempts to grab the player. "Here's *my* song."

When Robbie Williams' "Dickhead" began playing, Beth laughed. "That's fabulous."

Ky just grinned, still checking out her music. "Ludacris, Aerosmith, Buju Banton and Yo-Yo Ma?"

"So I'm eclectic. What music do you listen to, hater?"

"Eclectic? More like a schizophrenic crackhead," he mocked her, dodging her punch to his arm. "My music is like a normal person's," he told her with enormous condescension. "Okay, this one's okay," he allowed, selecting a song.

"Finally," Beth sighed, rolling her eyes. Although she pretended to be annoyed, seeing Ky acting like his normal, sarcastic—and, yes, dickhead-like—self warmed her heart.

At the first beats of the hip-hop jam, she grinned. "I *love* this one," she cried and it was Ky's turn to roll his eyes.

"Well, I hope you like it—it was on your MP3 player, brain trust," he scoffed. Beth just ignored him and grabbed his hand.

"You can't *not* dance to this song," she told him, pulling Ky away from the speakers. He surprised her by following willingly and then shocked her even more by actually dancing.

"Look at you!" she said, impressed, but he shrugged away the compliment. They danced goofily, unself-consciously throwing in cheesy spins. Beth was pretty sure that they were do-si-doing at one point. They were both breathless with laughter when the song ended and they both turned to see Harry in the doorway, watching them.

Beth swallowed hard. *God, these two clean up well*, she thought, staring at Harry. His blue shirt highlighted his eyes, shading them to the exact color of a postcard sky.

"Holy moly, he's hot," she murmured, not really realizing that she had said it out loud.

"Yeah," Ky agreed, also staring.

"Want to jump him?" she asked.

"Fuck yeah."

They both pounced and Harry, laughing at their antics and flushed with pleasure, caught them against him. "All right, who just grabbed my ass?" he accused, not sounding too put out about it.

"Me," Ky and Beth said in stereo, making Harry laugh again.

"Great—it's bad enough trying to keep the hoards away from Beth and now I have to beat them away from you too?" He caught Ky in a playful headlock. "How many minutes do you think we'll be at the club before I get kicked out for punching someone who looked at one of you?"

"You?" Beth demanded. "Women are going to be swarming all over the pair of you and everyone knows that they're more vicious. I'm going to get home tonight with all my hair pulled out and a spike heel imbedded in my forehead."

"We could just stay home and go to bed," Ky suggested hopefully.

"No." Beth shook her head. "We are going out. These shoes are not happy staying in." She held up a foot, displaying a strappy sandal. "They need the nightlife. They need the music."

"God knows they don't get any decent music just hanging out with you," Ky muttered, grinning when Beth smacked his arm.

"Okay then." Harry braced himself. "Let's take those shoes on the town and see who punches someone first."

"My money's on Beth," Ky said.

Harry nodded. "Mine too."

Looking at her two beautiful men, Beth gave a fatalistic sigh. "Probably."

They were riding the light rail train to LoDo, Denver's lower downtown area, when Ky dug a small box out of his pocket and tossed it into Beth's lap.

"Here," he grunted as she looked up in surprise, fumbling the box but managing not to drop it.

"What's this?" she asked, glancing from the tiny box to Ky's averted face. She looked at Harry in question.

"Open it," he suggested, grinning in a way that told Beth he knew perfectly well what was inside.

"It's not one of those snakes that pop out at you, is it?" she asked suspiciously. "I've always hated things like that. Like Jack-in-the-Boxes—how creepy are they? Freakin' clowns jumping out at you with those scary grins painted on their faces—how is that a toy? More like a way to terrify some poor little kid—"

"Are you going to open it or not?" Ky was glaring at her.

"Just making sure nothing is going to shoot out at me," she defended herself, holding back a grin.

"Fine, give it back," he snapped, reaching for the box. Beth clutched it in her fist and held it out of reach.

"Okay, okay!" she laughed. "I'll open it!" Lifting the lid, her giggles stopped immediately. Nestled inside was a tiny platinum pair of boxing gloves. She touched the pendant gently with one finger and then carefully lifted the necklace from its box.

"Oh!" was all she could say. The gloves had tiny gold laces and an ice-blue sapphire set in each of the palms. Her eyes prickled and she waved her hand, fanning her face like a beauty contestant in an unsuccessful attempt not to cry. "Oh," she said again. "It's so…"

"Is that good or bad?" Ky asked Harry uncertainly.

"Good, I think." Harry didn't sound too sure either.

"Yes!" Beth was laughing and snuffling back her tears at the same time. "It's good. It's wonderful. It's perfect!" Glancing up at Ky, she almost missed the sweet, sincere smile that touched his mouth for a fleeting moment before it disappeared, morphing back into his habitual scowl. "Did you both pick this out?" she asked, looking back and forth between the two men.

Harry shook his head. "That was all Pokey," he told her. "He showed it to me, but that was all."

"Well, I love it." Beth clutched it against her chest, rubbing at her damp face with her other hand. "Thank you, Ky," she told him sincerely and he shrugged, looking away in embarrassment. Beth fastened it around her neck, loving the gentle bump of it against her breastbone.

They arrived at their stop and Beth nearly took a header onto the street as she got off the train.

"Okay, you need to stop looking at your necklace and concentrate on walking," Harry ordered, catching her arm before she could hit the pavement.

229

"Hmmm?" Beth murmured, turning the pendant so that the stones caught the glow from a streetlight. "I love the sapphires."

Harry rolled his eyes at Ky, who smirked. "Harry thought I should have gone with diamonds."

"I'm a traditionalist," Harry shrugged. "The blue things are pretty too."

Beth caught Ky's gaze. She knew precisely why he had insisted on the sapphires—they were the exact color of Harry's eyes when he was excited. At her knowing look, Ky ducked his head.

"Come on, you guys," he said gruffly. "Do we want to go somewhere or not?"

Chapter Sixteen

&

They decided to start the evening with beer and pool and then work up to dancing. Beth glanced down at herself and then shrugged. At least she would look good while playing pool. Maybe flashing a little cleavage while she took her shot would distract the guys and keep them from noticing that she was a dismal pool player.

"Okay, now the five ball in the corner pocket—you have a straight shot," Harry coached her. She lined up her cue and slid it across her thumb, closing her eyes as stick met ball. At Harry's triumphant shout, she popped her eyes open, astounded that it had actually gone in. She must have reached that fragile place where she had drank just enough beer and was having just enough luck to be good at pool, she figured, pretending as if she wasn't completely shocked to be playing well.

Doing a little victory dance, she sang, "Go me, it's my birthday. Go me, it's my birthday."

Ky snorted. Ignoring his nonverbal critique of her singing, she bent over the table to line up her next shot when she heard someone calling her name. Standing back up, she scanned the crowd and saw Sheri heading her way.

"Sheri!" Beth called over the noise, waving at her friend.

Sheri reached her and gave her a hug. "You look fabulous," she said, pulling back a little so she could eye Beth up and down approvingly. "Not just hot—*super* hot!" She glanced up at Harry. "Things are going well, I see," she said to Beth under her breath.

Beth did the introductions, stepping back so Harry could shake Sheri's hand and smile his heart-blowing grin. Beth could almost see Sheri's knees turn to jelly. For Ky's turn, he didn't move from the pillar he was leaning against but just gave a small flip of his hand as a wave. Sheri looked back and forth between the two men and then grabbed Beth's hand.

"Excuse us, gentlemen," Sheri announced, hauling Beth away. "Need to visit the girls' room — be back in a flash."

She towed Beth toward the bathroom, ignoring Beth's questioning, "I do?"

Once inside the bustling, tiled room, Sheri whirled on Beth. "Okay, what's the story? Your one hottie has multiplied into two and they're both looking at you like you're chocolate-mousse pie and they're starving for a bite — are you cheating on Harry?" she demanded, not letting Beth squeeze a word in.

Beth blushed and hesitated, unsure how to explain the crazy situation she found herself in. Sheri would be the first person to hear about the three of them outside of their little triangle. "Umm...well, define 'cheat'."

Sheri stared at her, mouth gaping. "Are you seriously sleeping with both of them, you lucky little slut?" she gasped.

Bright red, Beth gave a helpless shrug. "You make it sound so dirty," she complained.

"It *is* dirty!" Sheri yelped. "You going at it with two gorgeous guys? I can't believe that *you* of all people...what if one of them finds out?"

Looking at her friend quizzically, Beth explained, "Of course they know. They're both right there."

Sheri was struck silent for a good ten seconds before screeching, "*What*?!"

The rush of red color under Beth's skin returned as she babbled, "You know, *us*. The three of us. Together while we're...well, together."

Staring dumbstruck at an apprehensive Beth, Sheri finally began to smile, a slow, awed smile that spread across her face. "That. Is. Awesome!" She leapt at Beth, who flinched, catching her in an enthusiastic hug. "Having both of those guys — I still can't believe you managed it but however you did, you totally deserve every hot and sweaty moment!"

"Thanks," Beth said with a little laugh, "I think. You really don't think it's insane?"

"Of course it's insane—totally and completely nuts," Sheri told her, giving her shoulders a shake. "But it's every woman's dream, so enjoy every second!" Lowering her voice, she asked, "So what's it like? Do they get jealous of each other? Do *you* get jealous? Is it both of them, umm, *servicing* you, or do they get into it with each other?" Sheri's eyes bulged at the thought. "How hot is *that*?"

"I don't know," Beth answered awkwardly, not really having everything straight in her own mind yet. "It just works." She shook her head with a laugh. "I'm not telling you all the details."

"But I'm dying to hear!" wailed Sheri. "We have to go to lunch so you can spill everything."

"I'll go to lunch with you, but nothing's being spilled— well, except for my lunch, probably," Beth admitted wryly. Food did tend to end up on her lap.

"Fine," pouted Sheri but she couldn't hold back her amazed grin. "I just can't believe it." Glancing toward the bathroom door, she sighed, "I should probably get back to my date."

"You're on a date?" Beth asked. "Poor guy—he probably thinks you bailed on him."

"Eh." Sheri shrugged. "He's okay—nothing to compare with you in a threesome, though!"

"Go!" Beth gave her friend a shove toward the door. "I promise I'll have lunch with you soon."

"Fine—but I'd better be getting at least a few of the details," Sheri threatened over her shoulder as she reluctantly left the bathroom.

Taking a deep breath, Beth checked her makeup and straightened her top. Actually, telling Sheri about her two men hadn't been as traumatic as she had expected. In fact, it had been almost, well…fun. With a quick smile at her reflection, Beth hurried out to rejoin her guys.

They were both standing outside the women's bathroom door.

"We lost," Harry admitted, throwing an arm over her shoulders.

"I can't leave you for a minute," Beth sighed with fake resignation.

"A minute?" Ky scoffed. "You were in there forever."

"Sheri had some…questions," she admitted. Both men looked at her in surprise.

"You told her about us?" Ky questioned.

Beth nodded. "Was that okay?" she asked uncertainly, trying to read his expression.

"Yeah," he said after a thoughtful pause. "Sure. It…I don't know, it makes it more real or something."

"Like we're in a legitimate relationship," Harry agreed and then grinned. "We'll be meeting the parents next."

Ky winced a little at that. "God forbid," he muttered.

Laughing, Harry threw his other arm around Ky in a sideways hug. "Okay, maybe not yet. Now who's up for the club?"

Beth sipped her drink, eyeing the dance floor from her vantage point on a balcony overlooking the crowd. The club was packed, a mass of people obscuring the floor as they danced to the pounding bass beat that vibrated inside Beth's rib cage. She saw Harry and Ky scanning the crowd—looking for her, she figured.

When she had slipped away to the bathroom, she knew that she wouldn't have long before her self-appointed bodyguards came looking. *Not that I mind*, she thought, smiling to herself as she waved, catching Ky's eye. He nudged

Harry and pointed, and both men motioned for her to join them. She nodded and carefully picked her way down the stairs, wary of her slightly tipsy state and her tall, tall shoes.

"Hey, baby." A man with the half-lidded eyes of complete drunkenness swayed in front of her. She nodded coolly, dodging around him, a flash of uneasy memory chilling her stomach.

"Hey!" he repeated but she was already deep into the crowd, moving quickly to the safety of her two men. After setting her empty glass on a nearby table, she fought through a mass of hopefuls, both male and female, that had gathered around Harry and Ky.

"Quite the fan club," she yelled in Harry's ear. He turned and latched onto her arm, tugging her between him and Ky. They danced to the heavy beat, grinding and sliding against each other, an isolated threesome in the teeming crowd. A few strangers tried to slip in, to move into their small circle, but were deflected by a glare from Ky or a head shake from Harry.

Beth pressed back against Harry, rotating against him as she mirrored Ky's movements, following his hips, his shoulders, his head with hers. Both men were natural dancers, that liquid, easy motion of their bodies matching the music effortlessly. As Beth watched a drop of sweat track down the flat plane of Ky's cheek, she felt incredibly happy, incredibly lucky.

Flattening her hands against the sides of Ky's face, feeling the slick chocolate skin under her palms, she couldn't help kissing him. She had to taste him, claim him, to show all the watching, longing dancers surrounding them that he was hers — that they both were hers. She felt Harry's lips on her neck, the barest graze of his teeth, and she reached a hand up to cup the back of his head, holding him against her. The two men trapped her between their hips, pressing their erections against her, front and back. The club disappeared, the crowd, the noise, until the pounding beat felt like it emerged from the three of them, the echoing, heavy pulse of their bodies, the actual sound of their desperate need.

Ky was the first to pull back. "Let's go," he rasped. When Beth just stared at him, dazed, Harry's mouth still on her neck, Ky grabbed her with one hand and Harry with the other and dragged them out of the club. The cold night air hit them in a sobering blast but Beth's blood still ran hot and fast as Harry flagged a cab.

The ride home was torture for Beth, sandwiched between the two men, heat radiating from all sides. Each bump in the road jostled her against them and sent jagged shocks of pleasure across her skin. She could feel her panties clinging wetly against her folds and even that inanimate contact made her clit swell and throb.

Shifting on the seat, she couldn't hold back a quiet moan. Harry's hand settled onto her leg, right above her knee. Ky's hand copied his, wrapping around her other thigh. Beth couldn't breathe. She was going to come, right in this cab, and she was frantic enough to not care that the driver would hear her screams of release.

She panted in excitement as the two hands climbed her thighs, disappearing under her short skirt and meeting at her panties. Harry's finger found its way under the silky fabric first, pushing steadily into her soaking, grasping depths. The interior of the cab spun around her as Ky tucked the crotch of her panties to the side and caught her clit between his finger and thumb, the gentle pinch sending her off the seat. As she came back down, Harry's finger slid more deeply into her and Beth bit her lip hard enough to hurt.

With an abrupt jerk, the taxi stopped in front of the gym. Beth didn't know whether to be relieved or cry as both hands left her wet and empty. They piled out, all three jostling against each other as they all tried to pay the driver, eventually giving up and thrusting too much cash at the happy cabbie before rushing for the door to the gym.

Ky and Beth pressed against Harry as he fumbled with his keys. The moment the door swung open they tumbled in, barely having the presence of mind to lock the deadbolt behind them before they were stripping off clothes, their own and each other's, until they were all naked in the dark shadows of the empty gym except for Beth's strappy heels and her new pendant.

Wanting some revenge for their torture in the cab, Beth dropped to her knees between the two men, wrapping her lips around Harry's turgid erection, sucking him deep into her mouth. Air hissed between his teeth as his hips involuntarily jerked toward her, driving his cock farther into her mouth until it bumped the back of her throat.

Ky pulled Harry's head toward his own, taking his mouth with a ravenous hunger. Beth pulled back, turning so that she could swallow Ky's cock. Before Harry could groan from the loss, her hand wrapped around his slick erection, pumping up the thick length in rhythm with the bobs of her head as she drew on Ky. The men's kiss intensified, their mouths grinding against each other, lips and tongues battling as Beth switched again, her fist closing around Ky's shaft as her mouth pulled at Harry's cock with slippery, squeezing, mind-blowing pressure.

His face drawn tight, eyes narrowed, Ky pulled free of Beth's gripping hand and Harry's hungry mouth. With restrained urgency, he pressed Harry down until he was on his hands and knees on the mat-lined floor. Harry tensed as Ky's cock, slippery from Beth's mouth, brushed against the hard cheek of his ass.

"Fuck," Ky groaned. "Lube's upstairs."

"Wait!" Beth scrambled up and darted over to the front desk. When she opened the top drawer, Harry realized what she was doing. If he hadn't been so desperately aroused, he would have laughed. He really needed to thank Dominic.

Harry looked over his shoulder and caught Ky's startled expression as Beth handed over the lube and a condom.

"I'm not even going to ask," Ky muttered, hurrying to put on the condom.

Beth explained anyway. "Dominic's the lube fairy."

He paused at that and then shook his head. "Now I *really* don't want to know."

Harry didn't even smile at the exchange. He was too focused on the way Ky's hands, slippery with lube, massaged the taut muscles of Harry's ass, how every squeeze of the hard fingers sent a jolting pulse of pleasure straight to his cock. A fingertip brushed Harry's anus and his muscles clenched at the sensation. He was taken off-guard by the overwhelming rush of need that the small touch evoked.

"May I?" Beth's raspy question brought Harry's head around. At Ky's short nod, she squeezed lube into her palm. The sight of her fingers curling around Ky's erection, the way his head tipped back at the slippery slide of her hands—it stopped Harry's breath. He stared, transfixed, unable to even blink.

Ky closed his fingers around Beth's wrists. "Enough," he gritted out. She released him obediently as Ky turned his focus back to Harry. Beth must have seen the flash of nervousness that passed over Harry's face because she crouched in front of him, cupping his cheeks in her hands. She kissed him gently, thoroughly, and he leaned into her, deepening the pressure. Beth's tongue slid into his mouth as Ky worked the head of his erection into the tight entrance. Once the tip of his cock was buried in the squeezing clamp of Harry's muscles, Ky paused, panting.

Harry felt the hesitation and pushed back, impaling himself further on Ky's burning shaft, wanting to take it all, to feel the entire length of Ky's cock filling him, heating him from within. The small movement ripped apart Ky's last shred of self-control and he slammed into Harry. The single thrust was too much—a hoarse cry tore from Ky's throat as he exploded into Harry's tight, hot depths.

As Ky slid free, Harry caught his breath, sitting back on his heels.

"Okay?" Ky asked, his voice rough.

"Yeah." He actually was, Harry realized. "Except for this," he grunted with a pained smile, gesturing at his lap.

"For me?" Beth asked. Her tongue peeked out, touching her upper lip at the sight of his engorged cock.

"Be my guest." He accepted her offer, his voice raspy.

She pushed Harry to a sitting position and straddled him, sinking slowly until the head of his cock brushed against her hot, slick crease, nudging between her labia.

"No more torture, Beth, please," Harry groaned, unable to take another second of delay.

At his words, Beth dropped to his lap, driving him through her like a burning spike, buried so deeply that he bumped her cervix. Ky knelt behind her, his hands cupping her breasts, his fingers plucking at the rigid points of her nipples.

"Fuck," Harry grunted as her inner muscles gripped his length. She lifted up, holding herself above him. Unable to stand the teasing another second, Harry grabbed her hips and yanked her back down. Ky pinched the tips of her breasts and her body tightened around Harry's erection. He felt the tremors of her orgasm begin as her head dropped back against Ky.

Harry took over, lifting and lowering her body in jerky movements, his control shattered by the pulsing spasms of her pussy around his cock. Shuddering, he pulled her tightly to him, locking her onto his lap. The tendons in his neck pulled tight as he exploded, pulsing into her in unending jolts of incredible pleasure. Toppling backward, he pulled Beth and Ky over with him and they collapsed into a boneless heap.

Harry was sliding into sleep, Beth limp and unconscious on top of him, when he heard Ky's short laugh.

Opening one eye, Harry grunted, "What?"

"Nothing. It's just…us. The three of us, on the gym floor — it's just all so fucking incredible."

"Yeah." Harry, holding a sleeping Beth securely against his chest, rolled to his side to kiss Ky, a gentle brush of his lips. "Pretty fucking incredible."

Chapter Seventeen

ஐ

It was late morning when Beth woke up but both men were still sprawled across the bed, sound asleep and snoring. She grimaced cheerfully at the noise. This arrangement could have its downside, after all—snores in stereo. They had stumbled upstairs around four that morning, stiff and sore from the gym floor.

Carefully extricating herself from the sleeping bodies, she slipped out of bed and headed for the shower, humming cheerfully. Everything had turned out so much better than she'd even imagined it could—so far, at least. She decided to make an attempt at breakfast—ever since Ky had moved in, they actually had groceries in the fridge.

Beth unearthed a waffle iron, obviously never used since it was still in its original box—a gift from Harry's mother or sister, she assumed. There were even fresh strawberries, she discovered. Having Ky around had its advantages, Beth decided, and then smiled, remembering the previous night.

Several advantages, she amended mentally.

She started the waffle batter enthusiastically, managing to spatter her short dress in the first few minutes. Ignoring the mess, she threw some sausages in a pan to cook and began pouring the batter into the iron.

A knock on the apartment door made Beth jump and she glanced down at herself. The dress was short and she hadn't bothered to put any underwear on but, as long as she didn't attempt any cartwheels, she was decent. After wiping her hands on a dishtowel, she hurried to the door and pulled it open.

A stocky black man stood there and Beth knew immediately who he was, even though Ky's features were sharper, his eyes lighter and narrower.

"Is Malachi here?" Ky's father asked, discomfort seeping out from beneath his stoic expression.

Beth shook herself from her surprised freeze and stepped back from the doorway, holding the door wide. "Of course. Come in."

"Don't you want to know who I am before you invite me in?" he asked, eyebrows raised.

"You're Ky's dad."

He gave an awkward nod and stepped inside. "Malcolm West. Most people don't see any resemblance between us."

Shrugging, Beth led the way to the kitchen. "You have the same...hmmm...*confident* attitude."

Mr. West gave a bark of laughter at her diplomatic phrasing and Beth smiled over her shoulder at the sound. "You laugh like him too."

In the kitchen, she gestured toward a chair. *I need to warn the guys*, she thought. They were more than likely going to wander into the kitchen naked and holding hands. His dad knew he was gay but it was one thing to know it and a whole other thing to see him and his lover exposed in more ways than one.

"I'll be right back," she told Malcolm and hurried down the hall. When she stuck her head into their room, she saw Ky sitting on the edge of the bed, watching Harry pull on a pair of sweatpants with narrow, molten-gold eyes. Both the men glanced up at her when she slipped inside, pulling the door closed behind her.

"Your dad's here," she told Ky in a low voice. "I just thought you'd want a heads-up."

Ky's shocked expression quickly settled into a scowl. "You didn't let him in, did you?"

"Of course I did. He's in the kitchen."

His glower deepened. "Well, you can just tell him to leave. I don't want to talk to him."

Hands on her hips, Beth gave him glare for glare. "That's just too bad. He came all this way to see you—the least you can do is walk the twenty steps into the kitchen and be polite. So wipe that sulky look off your face and go talk to your dad before I have to kick your ass." With that, she left the room, closing the door behind her firmly, restraining the urge to slam it.

Pasting on a smile, Beth returned to the kitchen. Malcolm had taken over the waffles.

"He doesn't want to see me." It was a statement, not a question, but Beth quickly shook her head.

"He'll be out," she said confidently. *If he isn't,* she thought grimly, *I'll go in there and drag him out by his ear.*

Malcolm forked a crispy brown waffle onto the top of a stack building up on a plate. "I'm a little confused...are you his girlfriend?"

Oh boy. This could get complicated, she thought. "I think I'll leave it to Ky to explain." As she sidestepped the question, Beth pulled some plates from the cupboard. Malcolm gave her a curious look.

"You're his friend—the one who was kidnapped."

Beth winced. "That's me. Thank you for your help, by the way. If you hadn't told them about the cabin, they never would have found me in time."

He cocked his head. "What did happen?"

"Ky didn't tell you?" Beth asked in surprise.

Malcolm shook his head. "He called, said you were found and that you should be okay—you were at the emergency room at the time—and then hung up."

Rolling her eyes, Beth stabbed some waffles and loaded them onto her plate. Malcolm had rescued the sausages too, and she balanced a few links against her waffle stack. "He's a surly bastard."

Ky's dad snorted.

"Well, the short version is that I managed to get away from the cabin—using a maneuver that Ky taught me, by the way—but ended up walking in circles, slowly freezing to death. Or dying of thirst—I'm not sure which would have come first."

"Hypothermia."

Beth gave herself a little shake. "Anyway, they did find me in time. Apparently, I'm really easy to track."

"And the asshole who grabbed you?"

Her hand was shaking, so she put down the plate before she dropped it. "He's locked up," she said shortly and then changed the subject. Talking about Ed meant thinking about him, and she just wasn't ready for that yet. "I'm sorry—I'm being rude. Are you hungry?"

"Eh." He held up a hand and waggled it back and forth. "Not really."

"Nervous stomach?" she asked sympathetically. She didn't blame him—Ky wasn't the easiest person to talk to in a non-estranged situation. Malcolm just shrugged, closing the waffle iron with more care than was warranted.

"Ky's lucky, you know." Beth knew she was babbling but couldn't stop herself. "To have a dad who stuck around. Especially since, and I'm just guessing here, but he doesn't seem like he would have been the easiest kid to raise."

Malcolm gave another one of the short laughs that reminded Beth of Ky. "Not the easiest, no."

Beth took a bite of waffle as she tried to think of something to say. Ky could move a little faster, she grumbled mentally.

"So what do you do?" Malcolm asked into the heavy silence. Beth, grateful for the conversation starter, swallowed her mouthful of waffles so she could answer his question.

"I'm a receptionist at a paper company—nothing too fancy. I was fresh out of school with a degree in art, so I was lucky to get something that didn't involve me asking, 'Do you want fries with that?' It's only been six months, so it's still tolerable."

"Right out of school? So you must be right around Ky's age—twenty-three?"

"Twenty-four, actually. I have almost a whole year on him, which I like to rub in his face, although Harry calls us both babies—"

"Harry?" A sharp note of interest caught in Malcolm's voice. "Captain Harry Morris?"

Beth looked at him curiously. "That'd be the Cap'n. Do you know him?"

Shaking his head, Malcolm shifted another waffle onto the growing stack. "Just from Malachi's letters and emails. Captain Morris' name popped up a lot, so I thought, after Ky told me—" He broke off and stared at the counter, the muscles pulling along his jaw.

Feeling that it was her turn to save the conversation from crashing and burning in Awkward Town, Beth seized on the first conversational topic that came to mind. "This is Harry's gym, actually. That's how I met him..." She trailed off when she noticed Malcolm's attention was fixed on the doorway. Glancing over, Beth saw why—Ky was propped against the wall, his moody expression still in place.

"Malachi," his father said quietly. Ky nodded shortly and Beth took another bite of waffle, not sure whether she should take her food elsewhere or try to cram it down as quickly as possible so she could leave the kitchen. With a sigh, she put down her fork. It seemed that the fates were determined that she wasn't going to eat anytime soon. She should market her life as a weight-loss regimen. Lots of sex and awkward reunions made for a pretty effective diet.

Leaving her plate with a last longing glance, she headed for the hallway, not able to resist giving Ky's arm an encouraging squeeze as she passed. Surprisingly, Ky didn't pull away.

Harry was reading, sprawled out on his stomach across the bed. Stretching out beside him, Beth craned her neck to press a quick, syrup-sticky kiss on the side of his mouth. Harry touched the spot with his tongue.

"Is that food I taste?" he growled playfully, abandoning his book to roll Beth onto her back.

"One bite of waffles," she told him mournfully. "Okay, maybe it was two. How long do you think they're going to take before they work out the whole father-son dealie-bob?"

"It could take awhile," Harry said, his grave tone contradicted by the teasing glint in his eyes. "Hours, even."

Beth groaned, flopping her arms out to her sides. "We could starve. Why don't you keep a box of Twinkies stashed in your room somewhere?"

"Because that's disgusting." Harry looked at her in horror. "I refuse to eat anything that could outlive me—and stay soft. You didn't keep a box of Twinkies in your bedroom at your apartment, did you?"

"Of course not. But I don't have dramatic father-son scenes in my kitchen either. Hence, there is no need for said box of yummy snacks."

"Hence?" Grinning at her, Harry covered her outspread hands with his, pinning her to the bed. "Are you turning into a lawyer on me?"

"Nope," Beth said lightly, ignoring the warm rush to her pussy at even his most playful restraint. "Hence is pretty much the extent of my legal knowledge. Well, that, and not to steal things. Or kill people. Or covet your neighbor's wife—oh wait—I've gone from laws to Ten Commandments."

Nipping her smiling lower lip, Harry's face suddenly turned serious. "Are you really okay with all of this?"

"Really and truly," Beth assured him. "How about you? I mean, was last night..."

"It was good," he admitted. "I wanted it. Been wanting it for a long time, actually. So watching was...?"

"Hot." No reason to beat around the bush, she figured. "Watching the two of you in the bathroom last night — whew. I hardly had to touch myself before I came."

His eyes dilated at her words, almost losing the blue irises to the black of his pupils. "Fuck," he swore roughly, his hands tightening on hers. Beth swallowed at his intense stare, the way his skin drew tight across his cheekbones. "Do you know how hard that gets — "

Ky threw open the bedroom door. "Knock it off, you two — the waffles are getting cold," he tossed at them and headed back to the kitchen.

With a groan, Harry turned back to Beth and raised an eyebrow.

"Waffles, Cap'n," she said wistfully. "With fresh strawberries."

"Okay, okay," he grumbled, rolling off her. "Your stomach wins this time."

Beth grinned, twisting to give his sulking mouth a quick kiss. "Waffles," she reminded him and his irrepressible smile returned.

"Fresh strawberries?" he asked.

"If Ky doesn't eat them all."

Harry sat up. "Then what are you waiting for, woman? We have to hurry!"

Laughing, they ran to the kitchen, sliding to an awkward halt when they saw Ky and his dad poking at the waffles on their plates.

"Hello." Harry was the first to recover. He stepped toward Malcolm, offering a hand. "I'm Harry Morris."

"I figured as much," Malcolm said dryly, shaking Harry's hand after an almost unnoticeable hesitation. "Malcolm West."

"I figured as much," Harry said with a good-natured smile. "I wanted to thank you for all your help when Beth was missing—you're the reason we were able to find her in time." His smile dropped away as his eyes took on the haunted cast they always had when he thought about the kidnapping.

"Glad I could help," Malcolm said with a self-conscious frown.

Awkward silence fell over the kitchen until Harry spoke again. "Staying in town long?"

After a quick glance at an expressionless Ky, Malcolm shrugged. "Not too sure yet."

"We should all go out to dinner tonight," Beth suggested impulsively, then threw a quick glance at Ky. She was relieved to see that he just shrugged—the exact shrug that Malcolm had given just a second before. There was two of Ky, Beth marveled. That was a little scary.

"I don't want to intrude on your plans," Malcolm began stiffly but Harry waved off his reservations.

"We don't have any plans," he told the older man. "We're usually homebodies."

Malcolm looked at the three of them, his expression curious but guarded. "What exactly is your relationship?" he asked Harry.

"He's my boyfriend," Ky said before Harry could even open his mouth, Ky's challenging stare fixed on his father's face.

Without any change of expression, Malcolm nodded slowly, absorbing that bit of information. "So where do you fit in?" he finally asked Beth.

"I—" Breaking off, she looked helplessly at the men. It was one thing to tell Sheri about their threesome but a whole other thing to tell Ky's dad.

"She's my girlfriend," Ky answered with a pugnacious scowl.

Malcolm's forehead creased. He was obviously baffled. "I don't understand," he said, looking from one person to another. "So the three of you..." He trailed off, looking shocked as comprehension hit him.

"We're together. All of us," Ky confirmed, watching his father warily. A kaleidoscope of emotions passed over the older man's face. "Still want to have dinner?" Ky asked, his challenging tone disguising a core of sincerity.

Malcolm was silent for several moments. Beth was pretty sure that they all held their breath until he spoke again, his eyes on his son's face. "Sure. Dinner sounds...interesting."

"Great!" Beth and Harry chorused, relieved, then looked at each other and laughed. They both looked over at Ky, who was trying to hold onto his unreadable expression. Despite his best efforts, his eyes flashed gold with relief.

"Great," he echoed, obviously shooting for sarcasm, but his quick, sincerely pleased grin took the bite out of his words.

Malcolm, still looking a bit shell-shocked, got up to leave. Resting a tentative hand on Ky's shoulder, he said, "See you tonight then, son." With an awkward nod to Harry and Beth, he left.

They eyed each other in silence for a few moments before Beth said, "Wow." She plopped down on a stool at the island.

"I was just joking about the whole 'meet the parents' thing, you know," Harry said. His straight-faced delivery was broken by a grin when Ky punched his arm in retaliation. "Seriously, Ky, that's great—I'm glad that you and your dad are making up."

Ky shrugged as usual but he did look, if not relaxed, at least less belligerent. "What's with you?" he asked Beth, who was staring blankly into space, food ignored.

"Hmmm?" she murmured absently, before snapping back into the moment. "Sorry, I was thinking about tonight."

"Uh-oh," Ky grumbled. "What are you plotting now?" His sigh was heavy and martyred.

"No 'plotting', as you call it," she defended herself. "Just what to wear. I want your dad to…I mean, I don't want him to think that…" She trailed off, flustered.

"What?" Ky asked, moving in behind her. "That you're a wild woman with two men in your bed?" He teasingly nipped the side of her neck, missing her embarrassed flush. Harry caught it though, and his smile fell away.

"Stop," Beth commanded, keeping her voice light as she attempted to jab him with her elbow. Ky was too quick and her elbow just hit empty air. "I don't want him to think I'm a slut."

"What do you care?" Ky took the stool next to hers, adding flippantly, "He's not *your* dad."

Beth shrugged, trying to hide the flash of silly hurt that darted through her. She must not have been successful, since Harry went still and was watching her closely. Faking a careless smile, she pushed off her stool and headed for the bedroom.

"What's wrong?" Harry called after her.

"Nothing," she tossed back over her shoulder. "Be right back." Slipping into the bedroom, she quietly closed the door.

Chapter Eighteen

&

Harry reached over to smack his palm against the back of Ky's head.

"Ow!" Ky rubbed the injured spot, scowling. "What the hell was that?" he demanded.

"For hurting her feelings," Harry snapped.

Ky stared at him. "What'd I say?" he asked.

"I don't know—something. Just go fix it," Harry ordered. He turned his back on Ky and started tossing breakfast dishes into the sink with little regard for anything breakable.

Ky, wincing at the noise, watched Harry's stiff back for a few seconds before climbing off the stool and heading toward the bedroom. The door was closed but Ky didn't knock. He pushed it open in a spurt of righteous annoyance, feeling put-upon. *How am I supposed to guess what hurts her feelings?* he thought indignantly.

His irritation faded a little when he saw her small figure sitting cross-legged on the bed. She didn't look up at his entrance and he stood by the bed for a few moments, feeling awkward and churlish.

Beth's blonde curls hung along her cheeks, hiding her expression from him. She had been looking at something in her hand when he'd burst in on her, something that she had quickly tucked beneath her knee.

"What's that?" Ky asked gruffly, plopping down onto the bed next to her.

"Nothing. Go away." She turned her head so he still couldn't see her face.

"Come on, Beth—don't be mad." Scowling, he muttered almost too low for her to hear, "I'm sorry."

Surprise at hearing an actual apology from Ky brought her head up. "I'm not mad at you, Pokey," she eventually admitted. "I guess I'm just a little sensitive about the whole father thing. It was silly."

"Yeah, it was," Ky agreed, bumping her lightly with his shoulder. "You know I don't mean any of the shit I say. For fuck's sake, I love you, stupid."

Beth had to laugh at that. "Thanks," she told him dryly.

"Now let me see that," he ordered, reaching for the item she had tucked out of sight.

"Hey!" Beth protested, trying unsuccessfully to grab it before he did.

Ky triumphantly pulled a photo out from under her and held it up so he could see. "Huh," he grunted. "This your dad?"

"Yeah." Beth tucked her knees up under her chin. "I rescued that before it went into the shredder. My mom cut him out of all our pictures. Our family album has a lot of strangely shaped photos in it."

"I take it he didn't stick around?" Ky guessed, handing the picture back to her.

She shook her head. "I don't know why I even keep this. He obviously didn't care, so why should I?" Despite her words, her thumb slid carefully across the smiling face in the photograph.

Ky shrugged. "Dunno. I mean, no matter what shitty things they do, they're still your parents, you know? Can't really do anything about how you feel."

Beth gave him a quick glance. "Your mom…?"

"She lives in Japan. Went back there when I was two."

"Why didn't she—" Beth broke off when the extreme tactlessness of her question occurred to her too late.

252

Ky just raised an eyebrow at her, the corner of his mouth inching up at her discomfort. "Take me with her?" he finished.

"Well, yeah," she admitted, squirming.

"Same reason your dad didn't take you along—didn't want the responsibility. Or the reminder. Some lame-ass reason."

She nodded and they both sat in silence for a few moments.

"Seems like a parent should know what things will really fuck up their kids," Ky said conversationally.

"Yeah," she sighed. "And maybe not do those things?"

"Yeah," he agreed and then smiled at her, his rare, painfully sweet grin. *If he only knew what I would do for him when he smiles like that,* Beth thought.

"I'm still hungry," Ky announced. "Think we can have an hour of drama-free time to actually eat?"

"Sounds good," she said, slipping the partial photo into the bedside table drawer. "I'm all for a drama-free zone."

He rubbed his head. "Harry's pissed at me," he admitted a little sheepishly.

Beth grinned. "That's okay. The Cap'n is pretty hot when he's mad."

Ky thought about that. "Yeah," he agreed, his eyes heating to gold. "He really is." With that, he grabbed her hand and towed her back toward the kitchen.

Harry had to man the front desk that afternoon, so Beth settled into a corner with her sketch pad. She roughed out an outline of Ky as he sparred with Dominic in the ring, managing to capture his cocky, balanced stance but having a hard time with his face. *He's just too fricking gorgeous,* Beth grumped, grabbing her eraser for the fiftieth time. How was she supposed to draw something so beautiful?

She lost her model as the men climbed out of the ring but she was more relieved than anything. She needed a break anyway. Putting down her pad of paper, Beth stretched her arms over her head, deciding to harass Ky until he agreed to teach her how to break someone's shoulder. She wandered over to the two men.

"Check it out, you guys," Dominic stage whispered when Beth got within hearing distance. He jerked his thumb toward the front of the gym. Ky and Beth looked over to see a woman talking to Harry. The tall brunette looked familiar.

"Who is she?" Beth asked, standing on her tiptoes to get a better view.

"That's Cruella De Vil," Dominic told them with glee, rolling his eyes when they looked at him blankly. "His ex? Candice?"

"Oh!" That's why she looked familiar, Beth realized. "She threw a drink in his face!"

"That's the one," Dominic said. Stepping closer, he asked, "Do you think she's here trying to get him back?"

"If she tries, I'll rip her hair out," Beth growled, making Dominic snort with laughter.

"Bitch," muttered Ky. Beth glanced at him, offended, but realized that his gaze was on Candice.

"Total bitch," Dominic agreed, nodding wholeheartedly.

"Total fucking bitch," Beth hissed, feeling her fingers folding into fists. Dominic and Ky looked at her in surprise. "Look at her, with her perfect hair and her perfect face and her perfect size-two body…" She trailed off, her vindictive tone fading to a forlorn sigh. "Do you think she wants him back, Ky?"

Wrapping his arms around her from behind, Ky hugged her back into his chest and rested his chin on the top of her head. "Don't worry," he told her, his voice oddly kind. "You're twenty times hotter than she is."

"Thanks, Pokey," she sighed, resting her cheek against the hard curve of his arm. "I love you too, you know."

"Yeah." He dropped a kiss on her temple. "I know."

Dominic stared at them, his mouth hanging open. "Does Harry know about this?" he finally asked.

"Yeah, he does," Harry said from behind him. Dominic jumped. Beth looked toward the front of the gym where Harry had been talking to his ex just moments before and caught a glimpse of her sleek dark head as Candice stalked out the door.

"God, you're fast," Beth told Harry. "How's the girlfriend?" Although she was striving for nonchalance, her words came out less casual and more wildly jealous.

"You two are dumbasses," Harry told them. "Don't you know that you both have me completely whipped?" He kissed Beth, a quick, possessive press against her startled lips. Looking at Ky, Harry shook his head. "I'm in love with a pair of idiots." Then he kissed Ky, the same hard, claiming kiss that he had just given Beth.

"Whoa," Dominic breathed, his eyes huge. The gym members who had been working out within view of the scene stared in fascination but Harry ignored them.

"Come on," he said, throwing an arm over Beth's and Ky's shoulders and pulling them tightly into his sides.

"I've been thinking," he mused as they walked toward the back stairs, "that there's not much privacy living here. Maybe we should buy a house."

"A house?" Beth stared at him.

"Sure," he said. "We could get a dog."

"Yeah?" she asked, a smile starting at the idea. "I'd like a dog. Can I have a studio to paint in too?"

"Sure. And a deck for barbeques," Harry suggested, grinning.

"Can it be close to DU?" Ky asked, his usual diffident tone offset by his shy glance toward the other two. "I thought I might take some classes. Law enforcement or some shit like that."

Harry hauled him in for a hard kiss on the temple. "Definitely," he agreed.

"With a guest room," Ky added, meeting his eyes. "In case my dad wants to visit."

"At least three bedrooms. And a couple bathrooms so you two don't have to fight over the shower." Harry laughed. "Watch out—when we get a big house, everyone will be expecting us to host Christmas."

Ky and Beth looked at each other and smiled.

"Sounds good," Beth said.

"Yeah," Ky agreed. "It does."

Also by Katie Allen

Breaking the Silence
Chasing Her Tail
Private Dicks
Raw Footage
Seeing Blind

About the Author

Katie Allen grew up in the Midwest with a horde of sisters (five) and one beleaguered brother. After an enjoyable four years working on her creative writing/art degree, and two not-so-pleasant years struggling towards her MBA, Katie somehow ended up as a mechanical engineer in Denver, Colorado. When her job disappeared during the recession, it was the kick in the rear that she needed to head back to Minnesota and jump into writing full-time.

When she's not writing (many books are necessary to pay for her unfortunate equine addiction), Katie rides horses, reads (of course), does gymnastics and looks for new (and occasionally insane) ways to research her books (cop school, anyone?).

Katie welcomes comments from readers. You can find her website and email address on her author bio page at www.ellorascave.com.

Tell Us What You Think

We appreciate hearing reader opinions about our books. You can email us at Comments@EllorasCave.com.

Why an electronic book?

We live in the Information Age — an exciting time in the history of human civilization, in which technology rules supreme and continues to progress in leaps and bounds every minute of every day. For a multitude of reasons, more and more avid literary fans are opting to purchase e-books instead of paper books. The question from those not yet initiated into the world of electronic reading is simply: *Why?*

1. *Price.* An electronic title at Ellora's Cave Publishing and Cerridwen Press runs anywhere from 40% to 75% less than the cover price of the exact same title in paperback format. Why? Basic mathematics and cost. It is less expensive to publish an e-book (no paper and printing, no warehousing and shipping) than it is to publish a paperback, so the savings are passed along to the consumer.

2. *Space.* Running out of room in your house for your books? That is one worry you will never have with electronic books. For a low one-time cost, you can purchase a handheld device specifically designed for e-reading. Many e-readers have large, convenient screens for viewing. Better yet, hundreds of titles can be stored within your new library — on a single microchip. There are a variety of e-readers from different manufacturers. You can also read e-books on your PC or laptop computer. (Please note that Ellora's Cave does not endorse any specific brands.

You can check our websites at www.ellorascave.com or www.cerridwenpress.com for information we make available to new consumers.)

3. *Mobility.* Because your new e-library consists of only a microchip within a small, easily transportable e-reader, your entire cache of books can be taken with you wherever you go.

4. *Personal Viewing Preferences.* Are the words you are currently reading too small? Too large? Too... ANNOYING? Paperback books cannot be modified according to personal preferences, but e-books can.

5. *Instant Gratification.* Is it the middle of the night and all the bookstores near you are closed? Are you tired of waiting days, sometimes weeks, for bookstores to ship the novels you bought? Ellora's Cave Publishing sells instantaneous downloads twenty-four hours a day, seven days a week, every day of the year. Our webstore is never closed. Our e-book delivery system is 100% automated, meaning your order is filled as soon as you pay for it.

Those are a few of the top reasons why electronic books are replacing paperbacks for many avid readers.

As always, Ellora's Cave and Cerridwen Press welcome your questions and comments. We invite you to email us at Comments@ellorascave.com or write to us directly at Ellora's Cave Publishing Inc., 1056 Home Avenue, Akron, OH 44310-3502.

erridwen, the Celtic Goddess of wisdom, was the muse who brought inspiration to story-tellers and those in the creative arts. Cerridwen Press encompasses the best and most innovative stories in all genres of today's fiction. Visit our site and discover the newest titles by talented authors who still get inspired - much like the ancient storytellers did, once upon a time.

Cerridwen Press

www.cerridwenpress.com

Discover for yourself why readers can't get enough
of the multiple award-winning publisher

Ellora's Cave.

Whether you prefer e-books or paperbacks,

be sure to visit EC on the web at
www.ellorascave.com

for an erotic reading experience that will leave you
breathless.

Made in the USA
Lexington, KY
30 May 2010